ALSO BY JEFFREY EUGENIDES

The Marriage Plot
My Mistress's Sparrow Is Dead (editor)
Middlesex
The Virgin Suicides

FRESH COMPLAINT

FRESH COMPLAINT

STORIES

JEFFREY EUGENIDES

FARRAR, STRAUS AND GIROUX NEW YORK

Farrar, Straus and Giroux
18 West 18th Street, New York 10011

Printed in the United States of America
First edition, 2017

Library of Congress Cataloging-in-Publication Data
Names: Eugenides, Jeffrey, author.
Title: Fresh complaint : stories / Jeffrey Eugenides.
Description: First edition. | New York : Farrar, Straus and Giroux, 2017.
Identifiers: LCCN 2017007576 | ISBN 9780374203061 (hardcover) |
    ISBN 9780374717384 (ebook)
Classification: LCC PS3555.U4 A6 2017 | DDC 813/.54—dc23
LC record available at https://lccn.loc.gov/2017007576

Open Market edition ISBN: 978-0-374-90307-7

Designed by Jonathan D. Lippincott

Our books may be purchased in bulk for promotional, educational, or
business use. Please contact your local bookseller or the Macmillan Corporate
and Premium Sales Department at 1-800-221-7945, extension 5442, or by
e-mail at MacmillanSpecialMarkets@macmillan.com.

www.fsgbooks.com
www.twitter.com/fsgbooks • www.facebook.com/fsgbooks

1   3   5   7   9   10   8   6   4   2

*In memory of my mother, Wanda Eugenides (1926–2017),
and of my nephew, Brenner Eugenides (1985–2012)*

Contents

COMPLAINERS

Coming up the drive in the rental car, Cathy sees the sign and has to laugh. "Wyndham Falls. Gracious Retirement Living."

Not exactly how Della has described it.

The building comes into view next. The main entrance looks nice enough. It's big and glassy, with white benches outside and an air of medical orderliness. But the garden apartments set back on the property are small and shabby. Tiny porches, like animal pens. The sense, outside the curtained windows and weather-beaten doors, of lonely lives within.

When she gets out of the car, the air feels ten degrees warmer than it did outside the airport that morning, in Detroit. The January sky is a nearly cloudless blue. No sign of the blizzard Clark's been warning her about, trying to persuade her to stay home and take care of him. "Why don't you go next week?" he said. "She'll keep."

Cathy's halfway to the front entrance when she remembers Della's present and doubles back to the car to get it. Taking it out of her suitcase, she's pleased once again by her gift-wrapping job. The paper is a thick, pulpy, unbleached kind that counterfeits birch bark. (She had to go to three different stationery stores to find something she liked.) Instead of sticking on a gaudy bow Cathy clipped sprigs from her Christmas tree—which they were about to put at the curb—and fashioned a garland. Now the present looks handmade and organic, like an offering in a Native American ceremony, something given not to a person but to the earth.

What's inside is completely unoriginal. It's what Cathy always gives Della: a book.

But it's more than that this time. A kind of medicine.

Ever since moving down to Connecticut Della has complained that she can't read anymore. "I just don't seem to be able to stick with a book lately," is how she puts it on the phone. She doesn't say why. They both know why.

One afternoon last August, during Cathy's yearly visit to Contoocook, where Della was still living at the time, Della mentioned that her doctor had been sending her for tests. It was just after five, the sun falling behind the pine trees. To get away from the paint fumes they were having their margaritas on the screened-in porch.

"What kind of tests?"

"All kinds of stupid tests," Della said, making a face. "For instance, this therapist she's been sending me to— she *calls* herself a therapist but she doesn't look more than twenty-five—she'll make me draw hands on clocks. Like I'm back in kindergarten. Or she'll show me a bunch of pictures and tell me to remember them. But then she'll start talking about other things, see. Trying to distract me. Then later on she'll ask what was in the pictures."

Cathy looked at Della's face in the shadowy light. At eighty-eight Della is still a lively, pretty woman, her white hair cut in a simple style that reminds Cathy of a powdered wig. She talks to herself sometimes, or stares into space, but no more than anyone who spends so much time alone.

"How did you do?"

"Not too swell."

The day before, driving back from the hardware store, in nearby Concord, Della had fretted about the shade of paint they chose. Was it bright enough? Maybe they should take it back. It didn't look as cheerful as it had on the paint sample in the store. Oh, what a waste of money! Finally, Cathy said, "Della, you're getting anxious again."

That was all it took. Della's expression eased as if sprinkled with fairy dust. "I know I am," she said. "You have to tell me when I get like that."

On the porch, Cathy sipped her drink and said, "I wouldn't worry about it, Della. Tests like that would make anybody nervous."

A few days later Cathy went back to Detroit. She didn't hear any more about the tests. Then, in September, Della called to say that Dr. Sutton had arranged a house call and had asked Bennett, Della's oldest son, to be in attendance. "If she wants Bennett to drive on up here," Della said, "it's probably bad news."

The day of the meeting—a Monday—Cathy waited for Della to call. When she finally did, her voice sounded excited, almost giddy. Cathy assumed the doctor had granted her a clean bill of health. But Della didn't mention the test results. Instead, in a mood of almost delirious happiness, she said, "Dr. Sutton couldn't get over how cute we've got my house looking! I told her what a wreck it was when I moved in, and how you and I have a project every time you visit, and she couldn't believe it. She thought it was just darling!"

Maybe Della couldn't face the news, or had already forgotten it. Either way, Cathy felt afraid for her.

It was left for Bennett to get on and tell her the medical details. These he delivered in a dry, matter-of-fact tone. Bennett works for an insurance company, in Hartford, calculating the probabilities of illness and death on a daily basis, and this was maybe the reason. "The doctor says my mom can't drive anymore. Or use the stove. She's going to put her on some medicine, supposed to stabilize her. For a while. But, basically, the upshot is she can't live on her own."

"I was just out there last month and your mom seemed fine," Cathy said. "She just gets anxious, that's all."

There was a pause before Bennett said, "Yeah, well. Anxiety's part of the whole deal."

What could Cathy do from her position? She was not only out in the Midwest but a kind of oddity or interloper in Della's life. Cathy and Della have known each other for forty years. They met when they both worked at the College of Nursing. Cathy was thirty at the time, recently divorced. She'd moved back in with her parents so that her mother could look after Mike and John while she was at work. Della was in her fifties, a suburban mother who lived in a fancy house near the lake. She'd gone back to work not because she was desperate for money—like Cathy—but because she had nothing to do. Her two oldest boys had already left home. The youngest, Robbie, was in high school.

Normally they wouldn't have come in contact at the college. Cathy worked downstairs, in the bursar's office, while Della was the executive secretary to the dean. But one day in the cafeteria Cathy overheard Della talking about Weight Watchers, raving about how easy the program was to stick to, how you didn't have to starve.

Cathy had just begun to date again. Another way of putting it was she was sleeping around. In the wake of her divorce she'd been seized by a desperation to make up for lost time. She was as reckless as a teenager, doing it with men she barely knew, in the backseats of cars, or on the floors of carpeted vans, while parked on city streets outside houses where good Christian families lay peacefully sleeping. In addition to the sporadic pleasures she took from these men, Cathy was seeking some kind of self-correction, as if the men's butting and thrusting might knock some sense into her, enough to keep her from marrying anyone like her ex-husband ever again.

Coming home after midnight from one of these encounters, Cathy took a shower. After getting out, she stood before the bathroom mirror, appraising herself with the same objective eye she later brought to renovating houses. What could be fixed? What camouflaged? What did you have to live with and ignore?

She started going to Weight Watchers. Della drove her to the meetings. Small and pert, with frosted hair, large glasses with translucent pinkish frames, and a shiny rayon blouse, Della sat on a pillow to see over the wheel of her Cadillac. She wore corny pins in the shape of bumblebees or dachshunds, and drenched herself in perfume. It was some department-store brand, floral and cloying, engineered to mask a woman's natural smell rather than accentuate it like the body oils Cathy dabbed on her pressure points. She pictured Della spritzing perfume from an atomizer and then prancing around in the mist.

After they'd both lost a few pounds, they splurged, once a week, on drinks and dinner. Della brought her calorie counter in her purse to make sure they didn't go too wild. That was how they discovered margaritas. "Hey, you know what's lo-cal?" Della said. "Tequila. Only eighty-five calories an ounce." They tried not to think about the sugar in the mix.

Della was only five years younger than Cathy's mom. They shared many opinions about sex and marriage, but it was easier to listen to these outdated edicts coming from the mouth of someone who didn't presume ownership over your body. Also, the ways Della differed from Cathy's mother made it clear that her mom wasn't the moral arbiter she'd always been in Cathy's head, but just a personality.

It turned out that Cathy and Della had a lot in common. They both liked crafts: decoupage, basket weaving, antiquing—whatever. And they loved to read. They lent library books to each other and after a while took out the same books so they could read and discuss them simultaneously. They didn't consider themselves intellectuals but they knew good writing from bad. Most of all, they liked a good story. They remembered the plots of books more often than their titles or authors.

Cathy avoided going to Della's house, in Grosse Pointe. She didn't want to subject herself to the shag carpeting or pastel drapes, or run into Della's Republican husband. She never invited Della over to her parents' house, either. It was better if they met on neutral ground, where no one could remind them of their incongruity.

One night, two years after they met, Cathy took Della to a party some women friends were having. One of them had attended a talk by Krishnamurti, and everyone sat on the floor, on throw pillows, listening to her report. A joint started going around.

Uh-oh, Cathy thought, when it reached Della. But to her surprise Della inhaled, and passed the joint on.

"Well, if that doesn't beat all," Della said, afterward. "Now you got me smoking pot."

"Sorry," Cathy said, laughing. "But—did you get a buzz?"

"No, I did not. And I'm glad I didn't. If Dick knew I was smoking marijuana, he'd hit the roof."

She was smiling, though. Happy to have a secret.

They had others. A few years after Cathy married Clark, she got fed up and moved out. Checked into a motel, on Eight

Mile. "If Clark calls, don't tell him where I am," she told Della.
And Della didn't. She just brought Cathy food every night
for a week and listened to her rail until she got it out of her
system. Enough, at least, to reconcile.

"A present? For me?"

Della, still full of girlish excitement, gazes wide-eyed at
the package Cathy holds out to her. She is sitting in a blue
armchair by the window, the only chair, in fact, in the small,
cluttered studio apartment. Cathy is perched awkwardly on
the nearby daybed. The room is dim because the venetian
blinds are down.

"It's a surprise," Cathy says, forcing a smile.

She'd been under the impression, from Bennett, that
Wyndham Falls was an assisted-living facility. The website
makes mention of "emergency services" and "visiting angels."
But from the brochure Cathy picked up in the lobby, on
her way in, she sees that Wyndham advertises itself as a
"55+ retirement community." In addition to the many elderly
tenants who negotiate the corridors behind aluminum walk-
ers, there are younger war veterans, with beards, vests, and
caps, scooting around in electric wheelchairs. There's no
nursing staff. It's cheaper than assisted living and the benefits
are minimal: prepared meals in the dining room, linen service once a week. That's it.

As for Della, she appears unchanged from the last time
Cathy saw her, in August. In preparation for the visit she has
put on a clean denim jumper and a yellow top, and applied
lipstick and makeup in the right places and amounts. The only
difference is that Della uses a walker herself now. A week after
she moved in, she slipped and hit her head on the pavement
outside the entrance. Knocked out cold. When she came to, a

big, handsome paramedic with blue eyes was staring down at her. Della gazed up at him and asked, "Did I die and go to heaven?"

At the hospital, they gave Della an MRI to check for bleeding in the brain. Then a young doctor came in to examine her for other injuries. "So there I am," Della told Cathy over the phone. "Eighty-eight years old and this young doctor is checking over every inch of me. And I mean every inch. I told him, 'I don't know how much they're paying you, but it isn't enough.'"

These displays of humor confirm what Cathy has felt all along, that a lot of Della's mental confusion is emotional in origin. Doctors love to hand out diagnoses and pills without paying attention to the human person right in front of them.

As for Della, she has never named her diagnosis. Instead she calls it "my malady," or "this thing I've got." One time she said, "I can never remember the name for what it is I have. It's that thing you get when you're old. That thing you most don't want to have. That's what I've got."

Another time she said, "It's not Alzheimer's but the next one down."

Cathy isn't surprised that Della represses the terminology. *Dementia* isn't a nice word. It sounds violent, invasive, like having a demon scooping out pieces of your brain, which, in fact, is just what it is.

Now she looks at Della's walker in the corner, a hideous magenta contraption with a black leatherette seat. Boxes protrude from under the daybed. There are dishes piled in the sink of the tiny efficiency kitchen. Nothing drastic. But Della has always kept the tidiest of houses, and the disarray is troubling.

Cathy's glad she brought the present.

"Aren't you going to open it?" she asks.

Della looks down at the gift as though it has just materialized in her hands. "Oh, right." She turns the package over. Examines its underside. Her smile is uncertain. It's as though she knows that smiling is required at this moment but isn't sure why.

"Look at this gift-wrapping!" she says, finally. "It's just precious. I'm going to be careful not to tear it. Maybe I can reuse it."

"You can tear it. I don't mind."

"No, no," Della insists. "I want to save this nice paper."

Her old spotted hands work at the wrapping paper until it comes unstuck. The book falls into her lap.

No recognition.

That doesn't mean anything, necessarily. The publishers have put out a new edition. The original cover, with the illustration of the two women sitting cross-legged in a wigwam, has been replaced by a color photograph of snowcapped mountains, and jazzier type.

A second later, Della exclaims, "Oh, hey! Our favorite!"

"Not only that," Cathy says, pointing at the cover. "Look. 'Twentieth-Anniversary Edition! Two Million Sold!' Can you believe it?"

"Well, we always knew it was a good book."

"We sure did. People should listen to us." In a softer voice Cathy says, "I thought it might get you back to reading, Della. Since you know it so well."

"Hey, right. Sort of prime the pump. The last book you sent me, that *Room*? I've been reading that for two months now and haven't gotten further than twenty pages."

"That book's a little intense."

"It's all about someone stuck in a room! Hits a little close to home!"

Cathy laughs. But Della isn't entirely joking and this gives Cathy an opportunity. Sliding off the daybed, she gesticulates at the walls, groaning, "Couldn't Bennett and Robbie get you a better place than this?"

"They probably could," Della says. "But they *say* they can't. Robbie's got alimony and child support. And as far as Bennett goes, that Joanne probably doesn't want him spending any money on me. She never liked me."

Cathy sticks her head in the bathroom. It's not as bad as she expects, nothing dirty or embarrassing. But the rubberized shower curtain looks like something in an asylum. That's something they can fix right away.

"I've got an idea." Cathy turns back to Della. "Did you bring your family photos?"

"I sure did. I told Bennett I wasn't going anywhere without my photo albums. As it is, he made me leave all my good furniture behind, so the house will sell. But do you know what? So far not a single person has even come through."

If Cathy is listening, she doesn't show it. She goes to the window and yanks up the blinds. "We can start by brightening things up a little in here. Get some pictures on the walls. Make this place look like somewhere you live."

"That would be good. If this place wasn't so pitiful-looking, I think I might feel better about being here. It's almost like being—incarcerated." Della shakes her head. "Some of the people in this place are sort of on the edge, too."

"They're edgy, huh?"

"*Real* edgy," Della says, laughing. "You have to be careful who you sit next to at lunch."

After Cathy leaves, Della watches the parking lot from her chair. Clouds are massing in the distance. Cathy said the storm won't get here until Monday, after she's gone, but Della, feeling apprehensive, reaches for the remote.

She points it at the TV and presses the button. Nothing

happens. "This new TV Bennett got me isn't worth a toot," she says, as though Cathy, or someone, is still there to listen. "You have to turn on the TV and then this other box underneath. But even when I manage to get the darn TV on, I can never find any of my good shows."

She has put down the remote just as Cathy emerges from the building, on the way to her car. Della follows her progress with perplexed fascination. Part of why she discouraged Cathy from coming out now wasn't about the weather. It's that Della isn't sure she's up to this visit. Since her fall and the hospital stay, she hasn't felt too good. Sort of punky. Going around with Cathy, getting caught up in a whirlwind of activity, might be more than she can handle.

On the other hand, it would be nice to brighten up her apartment. Looking at the drab walls, Della tries to imagine them teeming with beloved, meaningful faces.

And then a period ensues where nothing seems to happen, nothing in the present, anyway. These interludes descend on Della more and more often lately. She'll be looking for her address book, or making herself coffee, when suddenly she'll be yanked back into the presence of people and objects she hasn't thought about for years. These memories unsettle her not because they bring up unpleasant things (though they often do) but because their vividness so surpasses her day-to-day life that they make it feel as faded as an old blouse put through the wash too many times. One memory that keeps coming back lately is of that coal bin she had to sleep in as a child. This was after they moved up to Detroit from Paducah, and after her father ran off. Della, her mom, and her brother were living in a boardinghouse. Her mom and Glenn got regular rooms, in the upstairs, but Della had to sleep in the basement. You couldn't even get to her room from inside the house. You had to go out to the backyard and lift doors that led down to the cellar. The landlady had whitewashed the room and put in a bed and some pillows made from flour sacks. But that didn't fool Della. The door was made of metal, and there weren't any windows. It was black as pitch down there. Oh, did I ever hate going down into that coal bin every night! It was like walking right down into a crypt!

But I never complained. Just did what I was told.

Della's little house, in Contoocook, was the only place that was ever hers alone. Of course, at her age, it was getting to be a headache. Making it up her hill in the winter, or finding someone to shovel the snow off her roof so it didn't cave in and bury her alive. Maybe Dr. Sutton, Bennett, and Robbie are right. Maybe she's better off in this place.

When she looks out the window again Cathy's car is nowhere to be seen. So Della picks up the book Cathy brought her. The blue mountains on the cover still baffle her. But the title's the same: *Two Old Women: An Alaska Legend of Betrayal, Courage and Survival*. She opens the book and flips through it, stopping every so often to admire the drawings.

Then she goes back to page one. Focuses her eyes on the words and tracks them across the page. One sentence. Two. Then a whole paragraph. Since her last reading, she's forgotten enough of the book that the story seems new again, yet familiar. Welcoming. But it's mostly the act itself that brings relief, the self-forgetfulness, the diving and plunging into other lives.

Like so many books Della has read over the years, *Two Old Women* came recommended by Cathy. After she left the College of Nursing, Cathy went to work at a bookstore. She was remarried by then and had moved with Clark into an old farmhouse that she spent the next ten years fixing up.

Della memorized Cathy's schedule and stopped in during her shifts, especially on Thursday evenings when customers were few and Cathy had time to talk.

That was the reason Della chose a Thursday to tell Cathy her news.

"Go on, I'm listening," Cathy said. She was pushing a cart of books around the store, restocking, while Della sat in an armchair in the poetry section. Cathy had offered to make tea but Della said, "I'd just as soon have a beer." Cathy had found one in the office refrigerator, left over from a book signing. It was after seven on an April night and the store was empty.

Della started telling Cathy how strangely her husband had been acting. She said she didn't know what had got into him. "For instance, a few weeks ago, Dick gets out of bed in the middle of the night. Next thing I know, I heard his car backing down the drive. I thought to myself, 'Well, maybe this is it. Maybe he's had enough and that's the last I'll see of him.'"

"But he came back," Cathy said, placing a book on a shelf.

"Yeah. About an hour later. I came downstairs and there he was. He was down on his knees, on the carpet, and he's got all these road maps spread out all over."

When Della asked her husband what on earth he was doing, Dick said that he was scouting for investment opportunities in Florida. Beachfront properties in undervalued areas that were reachable by direct flights from major cities. "I told him, 'We've got enough money already. You can just retire and we'll be fine. Why do you want to go and take a risk like that now?' And do you know what he said to me? He said, '*Retirement* isn't in my vocabulary.'"

Cathy disappeared into the self-help section. Della was too engrossed in telling her story to get up and follow. She hung her head dejectedly, staring at the floor. Her tone was full of wonder and outrage at the ideas men latched on to, especially as they got older. They were like fits of insanity, except that the husbands experienced these derangements as bolts of insight. "I just had an idea!" Dick was always saying. They could be doing anything, having dinner, going to a movie, when inspiration struck and he stopped dead in his tracks to announce, "Hey, I just had a thought." Then he stood motionless, a finger to his chin, calculating, scheming.

His latest idea involved a resort near the Everglades. In the Polaroid he showed Della, the resort appeared as a charming but dilapidated hunting lodge surrounded by live oaks. What was different this time was that Dick had already acted on his idea. Without telling Della, he'd taken a mortgage on the place and used a chunk of their retirement savings as a down payment.

"We are now the proud owners of our own resort in the Florida Everglades!" he announced.

As much as it pained Della to tell Cathy this, it gave her pleasure as well. She held her beer bottle in both hands. The bookstore was quiet, the sky dark outside, the surrounding shops all closed for the night. It felt like they owned the place.

"So now we're stuck with this doggone old resort," Della said. "Dick wants to convert it into condos. To do that, he says he has to move down to Florida. And as usual he wants to drag me with him."

Cathy re-emerged with the cart. Della expected to find a look of sympathy on her face but instead Cathy's mouth was tight.

"So you're moving?" she said coldly.

"I have to. He's making me."

"Nobody's making you."

This was spoken in Cathy's recently acquired know-it-all tone. As if she'd read the entire self-help section and could now dispense psychological insight and marital advice.

"What do you mean, no one's making me? Dick is."

"What about your job?"

"I'll have to quit. I don't want to, I like working. But—"

"But you'll give in as usual."

This remark seemed not just unkind but unjust. What

did Cathy expect Della to do? Divorce her husband after forty years of marriage? Get her own apartment and start dating strange men, the way Cathy was doing when they first met?

"You want to quit your job and go off to Florida, fine," Cathy said. "But I *have* a job. And if you don't mind, I've got some things to do before closing up."

They had never had a fight before. In the following weeks, every time Della considered calling Cathy she found that she was too angry to do so. Who was Cathy to tell her how to run her marriage? She and Clark were at each other's throats half the time.

A month later, just as Della was packing up the last boxes for the movers, Cathy appeared at her house.

"Are you mad at me?" Cathy said when Della opened the door.

"Well, you *do* sometimes think you know everything."

That was maybe too mean, because Cathy burst out crying. She hunched forward and wailed in a pitiful voice, "I'm going to miss you, Della!"

Tears were streaming down her face. She opened her arms as if for a hug. Della didn't approve of the first of these responses and she was hesitant about the second. "Now quit that," she said. "You're liable to start me crying, too."

Cathy's blubbering only got worse.

Alarmed, Della said, "We can still talk on the phone, Cathy. And write letters. And visit. You can come stay in our 'resort.' It's probably full of snakes and alligators but you're welcome."

Cathy didn't laugh. Through her tears, she said, "Dick won't want me to visit. He hates me."

"He doesn't hate you."

"Well, I hate him! He treats you like crap, Della. I'm sorry but that's the truth. And now he's making you quit your job and go down to Florida? To do what?"

"That's enough of that," Della said.

"OK! OK! I'm just so *frustrated*!"

Nevertheless, Cathy was calming down. After a moment, she said, "I brought you something." She opened her purse. "This came into the store the other day. From a little publisher out in Alaska. We didn't order it but I started reading it and I couldn't put it down. I don't want to give the story away, but, well—it just seems really appropriate! You'll see when you read it." She was looking into Della's eyes. "Sometimes books come into your life for a reason, Della. It's really strange."

Della never knew what to do when Cathy got mystical on her. She sometimes claimed the moon affected her moods, and she invested coincidences with special meanings. On that day, Della thanked Cathy for the book and managed not to cry when they finally did hug goodbye.

The book had a drawing on the cover. Two Indians sitting in a tepee. Cathy was into all that kind of stuff, too, lately, stories about Native Americans or slave uprisings in Haiti, stories with ghosts or magical occurrences. Della liked some better than others.

She packed the book in a box of odds and ends that hadn't been taped shut yet.

And then what happened to it? She shipped the box down to Florida with all the others. It turned out there wasn't room for all their belongings in their one-bedroom at the hunting lodge, so they had to put them in storage. The resort went bust a year later. Soon Dick made Della move to Miami, and then to Daytona, and finally up to Hilton Head as he tried to make a go of other ventures. Only after he died, while Della was going through the bankruptcy, was she forced to open up the storage facility and sell off their furniture. Going through the boxes she'd shipped to Florida almost a decade before, she cut open the box of odds and ends and *Two Old Women* fell out.

The book is a retelling of an old Athabascan legend, which the author, Velma Wallis, heard growing up as a child. A legend handed down "from mothers to daughters" that told the story of the two old women of the title, Ch'idzigyaak and Sa', who are left behind by their tribe during a time of famine.

Left behind to die, in other words. As was the custom.

Except the two old women don't die. Out in the woods, they get to talking. Didn't they used to know how to hunt and fish and forage for food? Couldn't they do that again? And so that's what they do, they relearn everything they knew as younger people, they hunt for prey and they go ice-fishing, and at one point they hide out from cannibals who pass through the territory. All kinds of stuff.

One drawing in the book showed the two women trekking across the Alaskan tundra. In hooded parkas and sealskin boots, they drag sleds behind them, the woman in front slightly less stooped than the other. The caption read: *Our tribes have gone in search of food, in the land our grandfathers told us about, far over the mountains. But we have been judged unfit to follow them, because we walk with sticks, and are slow.*

Certain passages stood out, like one with Ch'idzigyaak speaking:

"I know that you are sure of our survival. You are younger." *She could not help but smile bitterly at her remark, for just yesterday they both had been judged too old to live with the young.*

"It's just like the two of us," Della said, when she finally read the book and called Cathy. "One's younger than the other, but they're both in the same fix."

It started out as a joke. It was amusing to compare their

own situations, in suburban Detroit and rural New Hampshire, with the existential plight of the old Inuit women. But the correspondences felt real, too. Della moved to Contoocook to be closer to Robbie but, two years later, Robbie moved to New York, leaving her stranded in the woods. Cathy's bookstore closed. She started a pie-baking business out of her home. Clark retired and spent all day in front of the TV, entranced by pretty weather ladies on the news. Buxom, in snug, brightly colored dresses, they undulated before the weather maps, as though mimicking the storm fronts. All four of Cathy's sons had left Detroit. They lived far away, on the other side of the mountains.

There was one illustration in the book that Della and Cathy particularly liked. It showed Ch'idzigyaak in the act of throwing a hatchet, while Sa' looked on. The caption read, *Perhaps if we see a squirrel, we can kill it with our hatchets, as we did when we were young.*

That became their motto. Whenever one of them was feeling downhearted, or needed to deal with a problem, the other would call and say, "It's hatchet time."

Take charge, they meant. Don't mope.

That was another quality they shared with the Inuit women. The tribe didn't leave Ch'idzigyaak and Sa' behind only because they were old. It was also because they were complainers. Always moaning about their aches and pains.

Husbands were often of the opinion that wives complained too much. But that was a complaint in itself. A way men had of shutting women up. Still, Della and Cathy knew that some of their unhappiness was their own fault. They let things fester, got into black moods, sulked. Even if their husbands asked what was wrong, they wouldn't say. Their victimization felt too pleasurable. Relief would require no longer being themselves.

What was it about complaining that felt so good? You

and your fellow sufferer emerging from a thorough session as if from a spa bath, refreshed and tingling?

Over the years Della and Cathy have forgotten about *Two Old Women* for long stretches. Then one of them will reread it, regain her enthusiasm, and get the other to reread it, too. The book isn't in the same category as the detective stories and mysteries they consume. It's closer to a manual for living. The book *inspires* them. They won't stand to hear it maligned by their snobby sons. But now there's no need to defend it. Two million copies sold! Anniversary editions! Proof enough of their sound judgment.

When Cathy arrives at Wyndham Falls the next morning, she can feel snow in the air. The temperature has dropped and there's that stillness, no wind, all the birds in hiding.

She used to love such ominous quiet, as a girl, in Michigan. It promised school cancellations, time at home with her mother, the building of snow forts on the lawn. Even now, at seventy, big storms excite her. But her expectation now has a dark wish at its center, a desire for self-annihilation, almost, or cleansing. Sometimes, thinking about climate change, the world ending in cataclysms, Cathy says to herself, "Oh, just get it over with. We deserve it. Wipe the slate clean and start over."

Della is dressed and ready to go. Cathy tells her she looks nice but can't refrain from adding, "You have to tell the hairdresser not to use crème rinse, Della. Your hair's too fine. Crème rinse flattens it down."

"*You* try telling that lady anything," Della says, as she pushes her walker down the hall. "She doesn't listen."

"Then get Bennett to take you to a salon."

"Oh, sure. Fat chance."

As they come outside, Cathy makes a note to e-mail

Bennett. He might not understand how a little thing like that—getting her hair done—can lift a woman's spirits.

It's slow going with Della's walker. She has to navigate along the sidewalk and down the curb to the parking lot. At the car, Cathy helps her into the passenger seat and then takes the walker around to put it in the trunk. It takes a while to figure out how to collapse it and flip up the seat.

A minute later, they're on their way. Della leans forward in her seat, alertly scanning the road and giving Cathy directions.

"You know your way around already," Cathy says approvingly.

"Yeah," Della says. "Maybe those pills are working."

Cathy would prefer to get the frames somewhere nice, a Pottery Barn or Crate & Barrel, but Della directs her to a Goodwill in a nearby strip mall. In the parking lot, Cathy performs the same operation in reverse, unfolding the walker and bringing it around so that Della can hoist herself to her feet. Once she gets going, she moves at a good clip.

By the time they get inside the store, it's like old times. They move through the shiny-floored, fluorescently lit space as eagle-eyed as if on a scavenger hunt. Seeing a section of glassware, Della says, "Hey, I need some good new drinking glasses," and they divert their operation.

The picture frames are way in the back of the store. Halfway there, the linoleum gives way to bare concrete. "I have to be careful about the floor in here," Della says. "It's sort of lippity."

Cathy takes her arm. When they reach the aisle, she says, "Just stay here, Della. Let me look."

As usual with secondhand merchandise, the problem is finding a matching set.

Nothing's organized. Cathy flips through frame after frame, all of different sizes and styles. After a minute, she finds a set of matching simple black wooden frames. She's pulling them out when she hears a sound behind her. Not a cry, exactly. Just an intake of breath. She turns to see Della with a look of surprise on her face. She has reached out to take a look at something—Cathy doesn't know what—and let her hand slip off the handle of her walker.

Once, years ago, when Della and Dick had the sailboat, Della almost drowned. The boat was moored at the time and Della slipped trying to climb aboard, sinking down into the murky green water of the marina. "I never learned to swim, you know," she told Cathy. "But I wasn't scared. It was sort of peaceful down there. Somehow I managed to claw my way to the surface. Dick was hollering for the dock boy and finally he came and grabbed hold of me."

Della's face looks the way Cathy imagined it then, under the water. Mildly astonished. Serene. As though forces beyond her control have taken charge and there's no sense resisting.

This time, wonderment fails to save her. Della falls sideways, into the shelving. The metal edge shaves the skin off her arm with a rasping sound like a meat slicer. Della's temple strikes the shelf next. Cathy shouts. Glass shatters.

They keep Della at the hospital overnight. Perform an MRI to check for bleeding in the brain, X-ray her hip, apply a damp chamois bandage over her abraded arm, which will have to stay on for a week before they remove it to see if the skin will heal or not. At her age, it's fifty-fifty.

All this is related to them by a Dr. Mehta, a young woman of such absurd glamour that she might play a doctor in a medical drama on TV. Two strands of pearls twine around her fluted throat. Her gray knit dress falls loosely over a curvaceous figure. Her only defect is her spindly calves, but she camouflages these with a pair of daring diamond-patterned stockings, and gray high heels that match her dress exactly. Dr. Mehta represents something Cathy isn't quite prepared for, a younger generation of women surpassing her own not only in professional achievement but in the formerly retrograde department of self-beautification. Dr. Mehta has an engagement ring, too, with a sizeable diamond. Marrying some other doctor, probably, combining fat salaries.

"What if the skin doesn't heal?" Cathy asks.

"Then she'll have to keep the bandage on."

"Forever?"

"Let's just wait and see how it looks in a week," Dr. Mehta says.

All this has taken hours. It's seven in the evening. Aside from the arm bandage, Della has the beginning of a black eye.

At eight thirty, the decision is made to keep Della overnight for observation.

"You mean I can't go home?" Della asks Dr. Mehta. She sounds forlorn.

"Not yet. We need to keep an eye on you."

Cathy elects to stay in the room with Della through the night. The lime-green couch converts into a bed. The nurse promises to bring her a sheet and blanket.

Cathy is in the cafeteria, soothing herself with chocolate pudding, when Della's sons appear.

Years ago, her son Mike got Cathy to watch a sci-fi movie about assassins who return to Earth from the future. It was the usual mayhem and preposterousness, but Mike, who was in college at the time, claimed that the movie's acrobatic fight scenes were infused with profound philosophical meaning. *Cartesian* was the word he used.

Cathy didn't get it. Nevertheless, it's of that movie she

thinks, now, as Bennett and Robbie enter the room. Their pale, unsmiling faces and dark suits make them look inconspicuous and ominous at once, like agents of a universal conspiracy.

Targeting her.

"It was all my fault," Cathy says as they reach her table. "I wasn't watching her."

"Don't blame yourself," Bennett says.

This seems a mark of kindness, until he adds, "She's old. She falls. It's just part of the whole deal."

"It's a result of the ataxia," Robbie says.

Cathy isn't interested in what *ataxia* means. Another diagnosis. "She was doing fine right up until she fell," she says. "We were having a good time. Then I turned my back for a second and—wham."

"That's all it takes," Bennett said. "It's impossible to prevent it."

"The medicine she's taking, the Aricept?" Robbie says. "It's not much more than a palliative treatment. The benefits, if any, taper off after a year or two."

"Your mom's eighty-eight. Two years might be enough."

The implication of this hangs in the air until Bennett says, "Except she keeps falling. And ending up in the hospital."

"We're going to have to move her," Robbie says in a slightly louder, strained tone. "Wyndham's not safe for her. She needs more supervision."

Robbie and Bennett are not Cathy's children. They're older, and not as attractive. She feels no connection to them, no maternal warmth or love. And yet they remind her of her sons in ways she'd rather not think about.

Neither of them has offered to have Della come live with him. Robbie travels too much, he says. Bennett's house has too many stairs. But it isn't their selfishness that bothers Cathy the most. It's how they stand before her now, infused—bloated—with rationality. They want to get this problem solved quickly and decisively, with minimum effort. By taking emotion out of the equation they've convinced themselves that they're acting prudently, even though their wish to settle the situation arises from nothing *but* emotions—fear, mainly, but also guilt, and irritation.

And who is Cathy to them? Their mom's old friend. The one who worked in the bookstore. The one who got her stoned.

Cathy turns away to look across the cafeteria, filling up now with medical staff coming in on their dinner break. She feels tired.

"OK," she says. "But don't tell her now. Let's wait."

The machines click and whir through the night. Every so often an alarm sounds on the monitors, waking Cathy up. Each time a nurse appears, never the same one, and presses a button to silence it. The alarm means nothing, apparently.

It's freezing in the room. The ventilation system blows straight down on her. The blanket she's been given is as thin as paper toweling.

A friend of Cathy's in Detroit, a woman who has seen a therapist regularly for the past thirty years, recently passed on advice the therapist had given her. Pay no attention to the terrors that visit you in the night. The psyche is at its lowest ebb then, unable to defend itself. The desolation that envelops you feels like truth, but isn't. It's just mental fatigue masquerading as insight.

Cathy reminds herself of this as she lies sleepless on the slab of mattress. Her impotence in helping Della has filled her mind with nihilistic thoughts. Cold, clear recognitions, lacerating in their strictness. She has never known who Clark is. Theirs is a marriage devoid of intimacy. If Mike, John, Chris, and Palmer weren't her children, they would be people of whom she disapproves. She has spent her life catering to people who disappear, like the bookstore she used to work in.

Sleep finally comes. When Cathy wakes the next morning, feeling stiff, she is relieved to see that the therapist was right. The sun is up and the universe isn't so bleak. Yet some darkness must remain. Because she's made her decision. The idea of it burns inside her. It's neither nice nor kind. Such a novel feeling that she doesn't know what to call it.

Cathy is sitting next to Della's bed when Della opens her eyes. She doesn't tell her about the nursing home. She only says, "Good morning, Della. Hey, guess what time it is?"

Della blinks, still groggy from sleep. And Cathy answers, "It's hatchet time."

It begins snowing as they cross the Massachusetts state line. They're about two hours from Contoocook, the GPS a beacon in the sudden loss of visibility.

Clark will see this on the Weather Channel. He'll call or text her, concerned about her flight being canceled.

Poor guy has no idea.

Now that they're in the car, with the wipers and the defroster going, it appears that Della doesn't quite grasp the situation. She keeps asking Cathy the same questions.

"So how will we get in the house?"

"You said Gertie has a key."

"Oh, right. I forgot. So we can get the key from Gertie and get into the house. It'll be cold as the dickens in there. We were keeping it at about fifty to save on oil. Just warm enough to keep the pipes from freezing."

"We'll warm it up when we get there."

"And then I'm going to stay there?"

"We both will. Until we get things sorted out. We can get one of those home health aides. And Meals on Wheels."

"That sounds expensive."

"Not always. We'll look into it."

Repeating this information helps Cathy to believe in it. Tomorrow, she'll call Clark and tell him that she's going to stay with Della for a month, maybe more, maybe less. He won't like it, but he'll cope. She'll make it up to him somehow.

Bennett and Robbie present a greater problem. Already she has three messages from Bennett and one from Robbie on her phone, plus voice mails asking where she and Della are.

It was easier than Cathy expected to sneak Della out of the hospital. Her IV had been taken out, luckily. Cathy just walked her down the hall, as though for exercise, then headed for the elevator. All the way to the car she kept expecting an alarm to sound, security guards to come running. But nothing happened.

The snow is sticking to trees but not the highway yet. Cathy exits the slow lane when traffic gets light. She exceeds the speed limit, eager to get where they're going before nightfall.

"Bennett and Robbie aren't going to like this," Della says, looking out at the churning snow. "They think I'm too stupid to live on my own now. Which I probably am."

"You won't be alone," Cathy says. "I'll stay with you until we get things sorted out."

"I don't know if dementia is the kind of thing you *can* sort out."

Just like that: the malady named and identified. Cathy looks at Della to see if she's aware of this change, but her expression is merely resigned.

By the time they reach Contoocook, the snow is deep

enough that they fear they won't make it up the drive. Cathy takes the slope at a good speed and, after a slight skid, powers to the top. Della cheers. Their return has begun on a note of triumph.

"We'll have to get groceries in the morning," Cathy says. "It's snowing too hard to go now."

The following morning, however, snow is still coming down. It continues throughout the day, while Cathy's voice mail fills with more calls from Robbie and Bennett. She doesn't dare answer them.

Once, early in her friendship with Della, Cathy forgot to leave dinner in the fridge for Clark to heat up. When she came home later that night, he got on her right away. "What is it with the two of you?" Clark said. "Christ. Like a couple of lezzies."

It wasn't that. Not an overflow of forbidden desire. Just a way of compensating for areas of life that produced less contentment than advertised. Marriage, certainly. Motherhood more often than they liked to admit.

There's a ladies' group Cathy has read about in the newspapers, a kind of late-life women's movement. The members, middle-aged and older, dress up to the nines and wear elaborate, brightly colored hats—pink or purple, she can't remember which. The group is known for these hats, in which its members swoop down on restaurants and fill entire sections. No men allowed. The women dress up for one another, to hell with everyone else. Cathy thinks this sounds like fun. When she's asked Della about it, Della says, "I'm not dressing up and putting on some stupid hat just to have dinner with a bunch of people I probably don't even want to talk to. Besides, I don't have any good clothes anymore."

Cathy might do it alone. After she gets Della settled. When she's back in Detroit.

In the freezer, Cathy finds some bagels, which she defrosts in the microwave. There are also frozen dinners, and coffee. They can drink it black.

Her face is still pretty banged up but otherwise Della feels fine. She is happy to be out of the hospital. It was impossible to sleep in that place, with all the noise and commotion, people coming in to check on you all the time or to wheel you down for some test.

Either that or no one came to help you at all, even if you buzzed and buzzed.

Heading off into a snowstorm seemed crazy, but it was lucky they left when they did. If they'd waited another day, they would never have made it to Contoocook. Her hill was slippery by the time they arrived. Snow covered the walk and back steps. But then they were inside the house and the heat was on and it felt cozy with the snow falling at every window, like confetti.

On TV the weather people are in a state, reporting on the blizzard. Boston and Providence are shut down. Sea waves have swept ashore and frozen solid, encasing houses in ice.

They are snowed in for a week. The drifts rise halfway up the back door. Even if they could get to the car, there's no way to get down the drive. Cathy has had to call the rental agency and extend her lease, which Della feels bad about. She has offered to pay but Cathy won't let her.

On their third day as shut-ins, Cathy jumps up from the couch and says, "The tequila! Don't we still have some of that?" In the cupboard above the stove she finds a bottle of tequila and another, half full, of margarita mix.

"Now we can survive for sure," Cathy says, brandishing the bottle. They both laugh.

Every evening around six, just before they turn on Brian Williams, they make frozen margaritas in the blender. Della wonders if drinking alcohol is a good idea with her malady. On the other hand, who's going to tell on her?

"Not me," Cathy says. "I'm your enabler."

Some days it snows again, which makes Della jumble up the time. She'll think that the blizzard is still going on and that she's just returned from the hospital.

One day she looks at her calendar and sees it is February. A month has gone by. In the bathroom mirror her black eye is gone, just a smear of yellow at the corner remains.

Every day Della reads a little of her book. It seems to her that she is performing this task more or less competently. Her eyes move over the words, which in turn sound in her head, and give rise to pictures. The story is as engrossing and swift as she remembers. Sometimes she can't tell if she is re-reading the book or just remembering passages from having read them so often. But she decides the difference doesn't matter much.

"Now we really *are* like those two old women," Della says one day to Cathy.

"I'm still the younger one, though. Don't forget that."

"Right. You're *young* old and I'm just plain *old* old."

They don't need to hunt or forage for food. Della's neighbor Gertie, who was a minister's wife, treks up from her house to bring them bread, milk, and eggs from the Market Basket. Lyle, who lives behind Della, crosses the snowy yard to bring other supplies. The power stays on. That's the main thing.

At some point Lyle, who has a side job plowing people out during the winter, gets around to plowing Della's drive, and after that Cathy takes the rental car to get groceries.

People start coming to the house. A male physical therapist who makes Della do balance exercises and is very strict

with her. A visiting nurse who takes her vitals. A girl from the
area who cooks simple meals on nights when Della doesn't
use the microwave.

Cathy is gone by that point. Bennett is there instead. He
comes up on the weekends and stays through Sunday night,
getting up early to drive to work on Monday morning. A few
months later, when Della gets bronchitis and wakes up unable
to breathe, and is again taken to the hospital by EMS, it is
Robbie who comes up, from New York, to stay for a week
until she's feeling better.

Sometimes Robbie brings his girlfriend, a Canadian gal
from Montreal who breeds dogs for a living. Della doesn't ask
much about this woman, though she is friendly to her face.
Robbie's private life isn't her concern anymore. She won't be
around long enough for it to matter.

She picks up *Two Old Women* from time to time to read
a little more, but she never seems to get through the whole
thing. That doesn't matter either. She knows how the book
ends. The two old women survive through the harsh winter,
and when their tribe comes back, still all starving, the two
women teach them what they've learned. And from that time
on those particular Indians never leave their old people behind
anymore.

A lot of the time Della is alone in the house. The people
who come to help her have left for the day, or it's their day
off, and Bennett is busy. It's winter again. Two years have
passed. She's almost ninety. She doesn't seem to be getting
any stupider, or only a little bit. Not enough to notice.

One day, it snows again. Stopping at the window, Della
is possessed by an urge to go outside and move into it. As
far as her old feet will take her. She wouldn't even need her
walker. Wouldn't need anything. Looking at the snow, blowing around beyond the window glass, Della has the feeling
that she's peering into her own brain. Her thoughts are like

that now, constantly circulating, moving from one place to another, just a whole big whiteout inside her head. Going out in the snow, disappearing into it, wouldn't be anything new to her. It would be like the outside meeting the inside. The two of them merging. Everything white. Just walk on out. Keep going. Maybe she'd meet someone out there, maybe she wouldn't. A friend.

2017

AIR MAIL

Through the bamboo Mitchell watched the German woman, his fellow invalid, making another trip to the outhouse. She came out onto the porch of her hut, holding a hand over her eyes—it was murderously sunny out—while her other, somnambulistic hand searched for the beach towel hanging over the railing. Finding it, she draped the towel loosely, only just extenuatingly, over her otherwise unclothed body, and staggered out into the sun. She came right by Mitchell's hut. Through the slats her skin looked a sickly, chicken-soup color. She was wearing only one flip-flop. Every few steps she had to stop and lift her bare foot out of the blazing sand. Then she rested, flamingo style, breathing hard. She looked as if she might collapse. But she didn't. She made it across the sand to the edge of the scrubby jungle. When she reached the outhouse, she opened the door and peered into the darkness. Then she consigned herself to it.

Mitchell dropped his head back to the floor. He was lying on a straw mat, with a plaid L.L.Bean bathing suit for a pillow. It was cool in the hut and he didn't want to get up himself. Unfortunately, his stomach was erupting. All night his insides had been quiet, but that morning Larry had persuaded him to eat an egg, and now the amoebas had something to feed on. "I told you I didn't want an egg," he said now, and only then remembered that Larry wasn't there. Larry was off down the beach, partying with the Australians.

So as not to get angry, Mitchell closed his eyes and took a series of deep breaths. After only a few, the ringing started up. He listened, breathing in and out, trying to pay attention to nothing else. When the ringing got even louder, he rose on one elbow and searched for the letter he was writing to his parents. The most recent letter. He found it tucked into Ephesians, in his pocket New Testament. The front of the aerogram was already covered with handwriting. Without bothering to reread what he'd written, he grabbed the ballpoint pen—wedged at the ready in the bamboo—and began:

Do you remember my old English teacher, Mr. Dudar? When I was in tenth grade, he came down with cancer of the esophagus. It turned out he was a Christian Scientist, which we never knew. He refused to have chemotherapy even. And guess what happened? Absolute and total remission.

The tin door of the outhouse rattled shut and the German woman emerged into the sun again. Her towel had a wet stain. Mitchell put down his letter and crawled to the door of his hut. As soon as he stuck out his head, he could feel the heat. The sky was the filtered blue of a souvenir postcard, the ocean one shade darker. The white sand was like a tanning reflector. He squinted at the silhouette hobbling toward him.

"How are you feeling?"

The German woman didn't answer until she reached a stripe of shade between the huts. She lifted her foot and scowled at it. "When I go, it is just brown water."

"It'll go away. Just keep fasting."

"I am fasting three days now."

"You have to starve the amoebas out."

"*Ja*, but I think the amoebas are maybe starving me out."

Except for the towel she was still naked, but naked like a sick person. Mitchell didn't feel anything. She waved and started walking away.

When she was gone, he crawled back into his hut and lay on the mat again. He picked up the pen and wrote, *Mohandas K. Gandhi used to sleep with his grandnieces, one on either side, to test his vow of chastity—i.e., saints are always fanatics.*

He laid his head on the bathing suit and closed his eyes. In a moment, the ringing started again.

It was interrupted some time later by the floor shaking. The bamboo bounced under Mitchell's head and he sat up. In the doorway, his traveling companion's face hung like a harvest moon. Larry was wearing a Burmese lungi and an Indian silk scarf. His chest, hairier than you expected on a little guy, was bare, and sunburned as pink as his face. His scarf had metallic gold and silver threads and was thrown dramatically over one shoulder. He was smoking a bidi, half bent over, looking at Mitchell.

"Diarrhea update," he said.

"I'm fine."

"You're fine?"

"I'm OK."

Larry seemed disappointed. The pinkish, sunburned skin on his forehead wrinkled. He held up a small glass bottle. "I brought you some pills. For the shits."

"Pills plug you up," Mitchell said. "Then the amoebas stay in you."

"Gwendolyn gave them to me. You should try them. Fasting would have worked by now. It's been what? Almost a week?"

"Fasting doesn't include being force-fed eggs."

"One egg," said Larry, waving this away.

"I was all right before I ate that egg. Now my stomach hurts."

"I thought you said you were fine."

"I am fine," said Mitchell, and his stomach erupted. He felt a series of pops in his lower abdomen, followed by an easing, as of liquid being siphoned off; then from his bowels came the familiar insistent pressure. He turned his head away, closing his eyes, and began to breathe deeply again.

Larry took a few more drags on the bidi and said, "You don't look so good to me."

"You," said Mitchell, still with his eyes closed, "are stoned."

"You betcha" was Larry's response. "Which reminds me. We ran out of papers." He stepped over Mitchell, and the array of aerograms, finished and unfinished, and the tiny New Testament, into his—that is, Larry's—half of the hut. He crouched and began searching through his bag. Larry's bag was made of a rainbow-colored burlap. So far, it had never passed through customs without being exhaustively searched. It was the kind of bag that announced, "I am carrying drugs." Larry found his chillum, removed the stone bowl, and knocked out the ashes.

"Don't do that on the floor."

"Relax. They fall right through." He rubbed his fingers back and forth. "See? All tidy."

He put the chillum to his mouth to make sure that it was drawing. As he did so he looked sideways at Mitchell. "Do you think you'll be able to travel soon?"

"I think so."

"Because we should probably be getting back to Bangkok. I mean, eventually. I'm up for Bali. You up?"

"As soon as I'm up," said Mitchell.

Larry nodded, once, as though satisfied. He removed the chillum from his mouth and reinserted the bidi. He stood, hunching over beneath the roof, and stared at the floor.

"The mail boat comes tomorrow."

"What?"

"The mail boat. For your letters." Larry pushed a few around with his foot. "You want me to mail them for you? You have to go down to the beach."

"I can do it. I'll be up tomorrow."

Larry raised one eyebrow but said nothing. Then he started for the door. "I'll leave these pills in case you change your mind."

As soon as he was gone, Mitchell got up. There was no putting it off any longer. He retied his lungi and stepped out on the porch, covering his eyes. He kicked around for his flip-flops. Beyond, he was aware of the beach and the shuffling waves. He came down the steps and started walking. He didn't look up. He saw only his feet and the sand rolling past. The German woman's footprints were still visible, along with pieces of litter, shredded packages of Nescafé or balled-up paper napkins that blew from the cook tent. He could smell fish grilling. It didn't make him hungry.

The outhouse was a shack of corrugated tin. Outside sat a rusted oil drum of water and a small plastic bucket. Mitchell filled the bucket and took it inside. Before closing the door, while there was still light to see, he positioned his feet on the platform to either side of the hole. Then he closed the door and everything became dark. He undid his lungi and pulled it up, hanging the fabric around his neck. Using Asian toilets had made him limber: he could squat for ten minutes without strain. As for the smell, he hardly noticed it anymore. He held the door closed so that no one would barge in on him.

The sheer volume of liquid that rushed out of him still

surprised him, but it always came as a relief. He imagined the amoebas being swept away in the flood, swirling down the drain of himself and out of his body. The dysentery had made him intimate with his insides; he had a clear sense of his stomach, of his colon; he felt the smooth muscular piping that constituted him. The combustion began high in his intestines. Then it worked its way along, like an egg swallowed by a snake, expanding, stretching the tissue, until, with a series of shudders, it dropped, and he exploded into water.

He'd been sick not for a week but for thirteen days. He hadn't said anything to Larry at first. One morning in a guesthouse in Bangkok, Mitchell had awoken with a queasy stomach. Once up and out of his mosquito netting, though, he'd felt better. Then that night after dinner, there'd come a series of taps, like fingers drumming on the inside of his abdomen. The next morning the diarrhea started. That was no big deal. He'd had it before in India, but it had gone away after a few days. This didn't. Instead, it got worse, sending him to the bathroom a few times after every meal. Soon he started to feel fatigued. He got dizzy when he stood up. His stomach burned after eating. But he kept on traveling. He didn't think it was anything serious. From Bangkok, he and Larry took a bus to the coast, where they boarded a ferry to the island. The boat puttered into the small cove, shutting off its engine in the shallow water. They had to wade to shore. Just that—jumping in—had confirmed something. The sloshing of the sea mimicked the sloshing in Mitchell's gut. As soon as they got settled, Mitchell had begun to fast. For a week now he'd consumed nothing but black tea, leaving the hut only for the outhouse. Coming out one day, he'd run into the German woman and had persuaded her to start fasting, too. Otherwise, he lay on his mat, thinking and writing letters home.

Greetings from paradise. Larry and I are currently staying on a tropical island in the Gulf of Siam (check the world atlas). We have our own hut right on the beach, for which we pay the princely sum of five dollars per night. This island hasn't been discovered yet so there's almost nobody here. He went on, describing the island (or as much as he could glimpse through the bamboo), but soon returned to more important preoccupations. *Eastern religion teaches that all matter is illusory. That includes everything, our house, every one of Dad's suits, even Mom's plant hangers—all maya, according to the Buddha. That category also includes, of course, the body. One of the reasons I decided to take this grand tour was that our frame of reference back in Detroit seemed a little cramped. And there are a few things I've come to believe in. And to test. One of which is that we can control our bodies with our minds. They have monks in Tibet who can mentally regulate their physiologies. They play a game called "melting snowballs." They put a snowball in one hand and then meditate, sending all their internal heat to that hand. The one who melts the snowball fastest wins.*

From time to time, he stopped writing to sit with his eyes closed, as though waiting for inspiration. And that was exactly how he'd been sitting two months earlier—eyes closed, spine straight, head lifted, nose somehow alert—when the ringing started. It had happened in a pale green Indian hotel room in Mahabalipuram. Mitchell had been sitting on his bed, in the half-lotus position. His inflexible left, Western knee stuck way up in the air. Larry was off exploring the streets. Mitchell was all alone. He hadn't even been waiting for anything to happen. He was just sitting there, trying to meditate, his mind wandering to all sorts of things. For instance, he was thinking about his old girlfriend, Christine Woodhouse, and her amazing red pubic hair, which he'd never get to see again. He was thinking about food. He was hoping they had something in this town besides *idli sambar*. Every so often he'd become aware of how much his mind was wandering, and then he'd try to direct it back to his breathing. Then, sometime in the middle of all this, when he least expected it, when he'd stopped even trying or waiting for anything to happen (which was exactly when all the mystics *said* it would happen), Mitchell's ears had begun to ring. Very softly. It wasn't an unfamiliar ringing. In fact, he recognized it. He could remember standing in the front yard one day as a little kid and suddenly hearing this ringing in his ears, and asking his older brothers, "Do you hear that ringing?" They said they didn't but knew what he was talking about. In the pale green hotel room, after almost twenty years, Mitchell heard it again. He thought maybe this ringing was what they meant by the Cosmic Om. Or the music of the spheres. He kept trying to hear it after that. Wherever he went, he listened for the ringing, and after a while he got pretty good at hearing it. He heard it in the middle of Sudder Street in Calcutta, with cabs honking and street urchins shouting for baksheesh. He heard it on the train up to Chiang Mai. It was the sound of the universal energy, of all the atoms linking up to create the colors before his eyes. It had been right there the whole time. All he had to do was wake up and listen to it.

He wrote home, at first tentatively, then with growing confidence, about what was happening to him. *The energy flow of the universe is capable of being apperceived. We are, each of us, finely tuned radios. We just have to blow the dust off our tubes.* He sent his parents a few letters each week. He sent letters to his brothers, too. And to his friends. Whatever he was thinking, he wrote down. He didn't consider people's reactions. He was seized by a need to analyze his intuitions, to describe what he saw and felt. *Dear Mom and Dad, I watched a woman being cremated this afternoon. You can tell if it's a woman by the color of the shroud. Hers was red. It burned off first. Then her skin did. While I was watching, her intestines filled up with hot gas, like a great big balloon. They got bigger and bigger until they finally popped.*

Then all this fluid came out. I tried to find something similar on a
postcard for you but no such luck.

   Or else: *Dear Petie, Does it ever occur to you that this world of*
earwax remover and embarrassing jock itch might not be the whole
megillah? Sometimes it looks that way to me. Blake believed in angelic
recitation. And who knows? His poems back him up. Sometimes at
night, though, when the moon gets that very pale thing going, I swear
I feel a flutter of wings against the three-day growth on my cheeks.

   Mitchell had called home only once, from Calcutta. The
connection had been bad. It was the first time Mitchell and
his parents had experienced the transatlantic delay. His father
answered. Mitchell said hello, hearing nothing until his last
syllable, the *o*, echoed in his ears. After that, the static changed
registers, and his father's voice came through. Traveling over
half the globe, it lost some of its characteristic force. "Now
listen, your mother and I want you to get on a plane and get
yourself back home."

   "I just got to India."

   "You've been gone six months. That's long enough. We
don't care what it costs. Use that credit card we gave you and
buy yourself a ticket back home."

   "I'll be home in two months or so."

   "What the hell are you doing over there?" his father
shouted, as best he could, against the satellite. "What is this
about dead bodies in the Ganges? You're liable to come down
with some disease."

   "No, I won't. I feel fine."

   "Well, your mother doesn't feel fine. She's worried half
to death."

   "Dad, this is the best part of the trip so far. Europe was
great and everything, but it's still the West."

   "And what's wrong with the West?"

   "Nothing. Only it's more exciting to get away from your
own culture."

"Speak to your mother," his father said.

And then his mother's voice, almost a whimper, had come over the line. "Mitchell, are you OK?"

"I'm fine."

"We're worried about you."

"Don't worry. I'm *fine*."

"You don't sound right in your letters. What's going on with you?"

Mitchell wondered if he could tell her. But there was no way to say it. You couldn't say, I've found the truth. People didn't like that.

"You sound like one of those Hare Krishnas."

"I haven't joined up yet, Mom. So far, all I've done is shave my head."

"You shaved your head, Mitchell!"

"No," he told her; though in fact it was true: he had shaved his head.

Then his father was back on the line. His voice was strictly business now, a gutter voice Mitchell hadn't heard before. "Listen, stop cocking around over there in India and get your butt back home. Six months is enough traveling. We gave you that credit card for emergencies and we want you . . ." Just then, a divine stroke, the line had gone dead. Mitchell had been left holding the receiver, with a queue of Bengalis waiting behind him. He'd decided to let them have their turns. He hung up the receiver, thinking that he shouldn't call home again. They couldn't possibly understand what he was going through or what this marvelous place had taught him. He'd tone down his letters, too. From now on, he'd stick to scenery.

But, of course, he hadn't. No more than five days had passed before he was writing home again, describing the incorruptible body of Saint Francis Xavier and how it had been carried through the streets of Goa for four hundred years until

an overzealous pilgrim had bitten off the saint's finger. Mitchell couldn't help himself. Everything he saw—the fantastical
banyan trees, the painted cows—made him start writing, and
after he described the sights, he talked about their effect on
him, and from the colors of the visible world he moved
straightaway into the darkness and ringing of the invisible.
When he got sick, he'd written home about that, too. *Dear
Mom and Dad, I think I have a touch of amoebic dysentery.* He'd
gone on to describe the symptoms, the remedies the other
travelers used. *Everybody gets it sooner or later. I'm just going to
fast and meditate until I get better. I've lost a little weight, but not
much. Soon as I'm better, Larry and I are off to Bali.*

He was right about one thing: sooner or later, everybody
did get it. Besides his German neighbor, two other travelers
on the island had been suffering from stomach complaints.
One, a Frenchman, laid low by a salad, had taken to his hut,
from which he'd groaned and called for help like a dying
emperor. But just yesterday Mitchell had seen him restored
to health, rising out of the shallow bay with a parrotfish impaled on the end of his spear gun. The other victim had been
a Swedish woman. Mitchell had last seen her being carried
out, limp and exhausted, to the ferry. The Thai boatmen had
pulled her aboard with the empty soda bottles and fuel con-
tainers. They were used to the sight of languishing foreigners.
As soon as they'd stowed the woman on deck, they'd started
smiling and waving. Then the boat had kicked into reverse,
taking the woman back to the clinic on the mainland.

If it came to that, Mitchell knew he could always be
evacuated. He didn't, however, expect it to come to that.
Once he'd gotten the egg out of his system, he felt better. The
pain in his stomach went away. Four or five times a day he
had Larry bring him black tea. He refused to give the amoebas
so much as a drop of milk to feed on. Contrary to what he
would've expected, his mental energy didn't diminish but

actually increased. *It's incredible how much energy is taken up with the act of digestion. Rather than being some weird penance, fasting is actually a very sane and scientific method of quieting the body, of turning the body off. And when the body turns off, the mind turns on. The Sanskrit for this is* moksa, *which means total liberation from the body.*

The strange thing was that here, in the hut, verifiably sick, Mitchell had never felt so good, so tranquil, or so brilliant in his life. He felt secure and watched over in a way he couldn't explain. He felt *happy.* This wasn't the case with the German woman. She looked worse and worse. She hardly spoke when they passed now. Her skin was paler, splotchier. After a while Mitchell stopped encouraging her to keep fasting. He lay on his back, with the bathing suit over his eyes now, and paid no attention to her trips to the outhouse. He listened instead to the sounds of the island, people swimming and shouting on the beach, somebody learning to play a wooden flute a few huts down. Waves lapped, and occasionally a dead palm leaf or coconut fell to the ground. At night, the wild dogs began howling in the jungle. When he went to the outhouse, Mitchell could hear them moving around outside, coming up and sniffing him, the flow of his waste, through the holes in the walls. Most people banged flashlights against the tin door to scare the dogs away. Mitchell didn't even bring a flashlight along. He stood listening to the dogs gather in the vegetation. With sharp muzzles they pushed stalks aside until their red eyes appeared in the moonlight. Mitchell faced them down, serenely. He spread out his arms, offering himself, and when they didn't attack, he turned and walked back to his hut.

One night as he was coming back, he heard an Australian voice say, "Here comes the patient now." He looked up to see Larry and an older woman sitting on the porch of the hut. Larry was rolling a joint on his *Let's Go: Asia.* The woman was smoking a cigarette and looking straight at Mitchell. "Hello, Mitchell, I'm Gwendolyn," she said. "I hear you've been sick."

"Somewhat."

"Larry says you haven't been taking the pills I sent over."

Mitchell didn't answer right away. He hadn't talked to another human being all day. Or for a couple of days. He had to get reacclimated. Solitude had sensitized him to the roughness of other people. Gwendolyn's loud whiskey baritone, for instance, seemed to rake right across his chest. She was wearing some kind of batik headdress that looked like a bandage. Lots of tribal jewelry, too, bones and shells, hanging around her neck and from her wrists. In the middle of all this was her pinched, oversunned face, with the red coil of the cigarette in the center blinking on and off. Larry was just a halo of blond hair in the moonlight.

"I had a terrible case of the trots myself," Gwendolyn continued. "Truly epic. In Irian Jaya. Those pills were a godsend."

Larry gave a finishing lick to the joint and lit it. He inhaled, looking up at Mitchell, then said in a smoke-tightened voice, "We're here to make you take your medicine."

"That's right. Fasting is all well and good, but after—what has it been?"

"Two weeks almost."

"After two weeks, it's time to stop." She looked stern, but then the joint came her way, and she said, "Oh, lovely." She took a hit, held it, smiled at both of them, and then launched into a fit of coughing. It went on for about thirty seconds. Finally she drank some beer, holding her hand over her chest. Then she resumed smoking her cigarette.

Mitchell was looking at a big stripe of moon on the ocean. Suddenly he said, "You just got divorced. Is why you're taking this trip."

Gwendolyn stiffened. "Almost right. Not divorced but separated. Is it that obvious?"

"You're a hairdresser," Mitchell said, still looking out to sea.

"You didn't tell me your friend was a clairvoyant, Larry."

"I must have told him. Did I tell you?"

Mitchell didn't answer.

"Well, Mr. Nostradamus, I have a prediction for you. If you don't take those pills right now, you are going to be hauled away on the ferry *one very sick boy*. You don't want that, do you?"

Mitchell looked into Gwendolyn's eyes for the first time. He was struck by the irony: she thought *he* was the sick one. Whereas it looked to him the other way around. Already she was lighting another cigarette. She was forty-three years old, getting stoned on an island off the coast of Thailand while wearing a piece of coral reef in each earlobe. Her unhappiness rose off her like a wind. It wasn't that he was clairvoyant. It was just obvious.

She looked away. "Larry, where are my pills now?"

"Inside the hut."

"Could you get them for me?"

Larry turned on his flashlight and bent through the doorway. The beam crossed the floor. "You still haven't mailed your letters."

"I forgot. Soon as I finish them, I feel like I've sent them already."

Larry reappeared with the bottle of pills and announced, "It's starting to smell in there." He handed the bottle to Gwendolyn.

"All right, you stubborn man, open up." She held out a pill.

"That's OK. Really. I'm fine."

"Take your medicine," Gwendolyn said.

"Come on, Mitch, you look like shit. Do it. Take a god-damn pill."

For a moment there was silence, as they stared at him. Mitchell wanted to explain his position, but it was pretty obvious that no amount of explanation would convince them that what he was doing made any sense. Everything he thought to say didn't quite cover it. Everything he thought to say cheapened how he felt. So he decided on the course of least resistance. He opened his mouth.

"Your tongue is bright yellow," Gwendolyn said. "I've never seen such a yellow except on a bird. Go on. Wash it down with a little beer." She handed him her bottle.

"Bravo. Now take these four times a day for a week. Larry, I'm leaving you in charge of seeing that he does it."

"I think I need to go to sleep now," Mitchell said.

"All right," said Gwendolyn. "We'll move the party down to my hut."

When they were gone, Mitchell crawled back inside and lay down. Without otherwise moving, he spat out the pill, which he'd kept under his tongue. It clattered against the bamboo, then fell through to the sand underneath. Just like Jack Nicholson in *Cuckoo's Nest*, he thought, smiling to him-self, but was too genuinely exhausted to write it down.

With the bathing suit over his eyes, the days were more per-fect, more obliterated. He slept in snatches, whenever he felt like it, and stopped paying attention to time. The rhythms of the island reached him: the sleep-thickened voices of people breakfasting on banana pancakes and coffee; later, shouts on the beach; and in the evening, the grill smoking, and the Chi-nese cook scraping her wok with a long metal spatula. Beer bottles popped open; the cook tent filled with voices; then the various small parties bloomed in neighboring huts. At some point Larry would come back, smelling of beer, smoke, and suntan lotion. Mitchell would pretend to be asleep. Sometimes he was awake all night while Larry slept. Through his back, he could feel the floor, then the island itself, then the circulation of the ocean. The moon became full and, on rising, lit up the hut. Mitchell got up and walked down to the silver edge of the water. He waded out and floated on his back, staring up at the moon and the stars. The bay was a warm bath; the island floated in it, too. He closed his eyes and concentrated on his breathing. After a while, he felt all sense of outside and inside disappearing. He wasn't breathing so much as *being* breathed. The state would last only a few seconds, then he'd come out, then he'd get it again.

His skin began to taste of salt. The wind carried it through the bamboo, coating him as he lay on his back, or blew over him as he made his way to the outhouse. While he squatted, he sucked the salt from his bare shoulders. It was his only food. Sometimes he had an urge to go into the cook tent and order an entire grilled fish or a stack of pancakes. But stabs of hunger were rare, and in their wake he felt only a deeper, more complete peace. The floods continued to rush out of him, with less violence now but rawly, as though from a wound. He opened the drum and filled the water bucket, washed himself with his left hand. A few times he fell asleep, crouching over the hole, and came awake only when someone knocked on the metal door.

He wrote more letters. *Did I ever tell you about the leper mother and son I saw in Bangalore? I was coming down this street and there they were, crouching by the curb. I was pretty used to seeing lepers by this point, but not ones like this. They were almost all the way gone. Their fingers weren't even stubs anymore. Their hands were just balls at the ends of their arms. And their faces were sliding off, as if they were made of wax and were melting. The mother's left eye was all filmy and gray and stared up at the sky. But when I gave her 50 paise she looked at me with her good eye and it was full of intelligence. She touched her arm-knobs together, to thank me. Right then my coin hit the cup, and her son, who couldn't see, said "Atcha." He smiled, I think, though it was hard to tell because of his disfigurement. But what happened right then was this: I saw that they were people, not beggars or unfortunates—just a mother and her kid. I could see them back before they got leprosy, back when they used to just go out for a walk. And then I had another revelation. I had a hunch that the kid was a nut for mango lassi. And this seemed a very profound revelation to me at the time. It was as big a revelation as I think I ever need or deserve. When my coin hit the cup and the boy said, "Atcha," I just knew that he was thinking about a nice cold mango lassi.* Mitchell put down his pen, remembering. Then he went outside to watch the sunset. He sat on the porch cross-legged. His left knee no longer stuck up. When he closed his eyes, the ringing began at once, louder, more intimate, more ravishing than ever.

So much seemed funny viewed from this distance. His worries about choosing a major. His refusal to leave his dorm room when afflicted with glaring facial pimples. Even the searing despair of the time he'd called Christine Woodhouse's room and she hadn't come in all night was sort of funny now. You could waste your life. He *had*, pretty much, until the day he'd boarded that airplane with Larry, inoculated against typhus and cholera, and had escaped. Only now, with no one watching, could Mitchell find out who he was. It was as though riding in all those buses, over all those bumps, had dislodged his old self bit by bit, so that it just rose up one day and vaporized into the Indian air. He didn't want to go back to the world of college and clove cigarettes. He was lying on his back, waiting for the moment when the body touched against enlightenment, or when nothing happened at all, which would be the same thing.

Meanwhile, next door, the German woman was on the move again. Mitchell heard her rustling around. She came down her steps, but instead of heading for the outhouse, she climbed the steps to Mitchell's hut. He removed the bathing suit from his eyes.

"I am going to the clinic. In the boat."

"I figured you might."

"I am going to get an injection. Stay one night. Then come back." She paused a moment. "You want to come with me? Get an injection?"

"No, thanks."

"Why not?"

"Because I'm better. I'm feeling a lot better."

"Come to the clinic. To be safe. We go together."

"I'm fine." He stood up, smiling, to indicate this. Out in the bay, the boat blew its horn.

Mitchell came out onto the porch to send her off. "I'll see you when you get back," he said. The German woman waded out to the boat and climbed aboard. She stood on deck, not waving, but looking in his direction. Mitchell watched her recede, growing smaller and smaller. When she disappeared at last, he realized that he'd been telling the truth: he *was* better.

His stomach was quiet. He put a hand over his belly, as though to register what was inside. His stomach felt hollowed out. And he wasn't dizzy anymore. He had to find a whole new aerogram, and in the light from the sunset he wrote, *On this day in I think November, I would like to announce that the gastrointestinal system of Mitchell B. Grammaticus has hereby been cured by purely spiritual means. I want especially to thank my greatest supporter, who stuck with me through it all, Mary Baker Eddy.*

The next solid shit I take is really for her. He was still writing when Larry came in.

"Wow. You're awake."

"I'm better."

"You are?"

"And guess what else?"

"What?"

Mitchell put down his pen and gave Larry a big smile. "I'm really hungry."

Everyone on the island had heard about Mitchell's Gandhian fast by this point. His arrival in the cook tent brought applause and cheers. Also gasps from some of the women, who couldn't bear to see how skinny he was. They got all maternal and made him sit down and felt his forehead for lingering fever. The tent was full of picnic tables, the counters stacked with pineapples and watermelons, beans, onions, potatoes, and lettuce. Long blue fish lay on chopping blocks. Coffee thermoses lined one wall, full of hot water or tea, and in the back was another room containing a crib and the Chinese cook's baby. Mitchell looked around at all the new faces. The dirt under the picnic table felt surprisingly cool against his bare feet.

The medical advice started up right away. Most people had fasted for a day or two during their Asian travels, after which they'd gone back to eating full meals. But Mitchell's fast had been so prolonged that one American traveler, a former medical student, said it was dangerous for Mitchell to eat too much too quickly. He advised having only liquids at first. The Chinese cook scoffed at this idea. After taking one look at Mitchell, she sent out a sea bass, a plate of fried rice, and an onion omelet. Most everyone else advocated pure gluttony, too. Mitchell struck a compromise. First he drank a glass of papaya juice. He waited a few minutes and then began, slowly, to eat the fried rice. After that, still feeling fine, he moved cautiously to the sea bass. After every few bites, the former medical student said, "OK, that's enough," but this was greeted by a chorus of other people saying, "Look at him. He's a skeleton. Go on, eat. Eat!"

It was nice to be around people again. Mitchell hadn't become quite as ascetic as he'd thought. He missed socializing. All the girls were wearing sarongs. They had truly accomplished suntans and fetching accents. They kept touching Mitchell, patting his ribs or encircling his wrists with their fingers. "I'd die for cheekbones like yours," one girl said. Then she made him eat some fried bananas.

Night fell. Somebody announced a party in hut number six. Before Mitchell knew what was happening, two Dutch girls were escorting him down the beach. They waited tables in Amsterdam five months of the year and spent the rest traveling. Apparently, Mitchell looked exactly like a Van Honthorst Christ in the Rijksmuseum. The Dutch girls found the resemblance both awe-inspiring and hilarious. Mitchell wondered if he'd made a mistake by staying in the hut so much. A kind of tribal life had sprouted up here on the island. No wonder Larry had been having such a good time. Everyone was so friendly. It wasn't even sexual so much as just warm and intimate. One of the Dutch girls had a nasty rash on her back. She turned around to show him.

The moon was rising over the bay, casting a long swath of light to shore. It lit up the trunks of palm trees and gave the sand a lunar phosphorescence. Everything had a bluish tint except for the orange, glowing huts. Mitchell felt the air rinsing his face and flowing through his legs as he walked behind Larry. There was a lightness inside him, a helium balloon around his heart. There was nothing a person needed beyond this beach.

He called out, "Hey, Larry."

"What?"

"We've gone everywhere, man."

"Not everywhere. Next stop Bali."

"Then home. After Bali, home. Before my parents have a nervous breakdown."

He stopped walking and held the Dutch girls back. He thought he heard the ringing—louder than ever—but then realized that it was just the music coming from hut number six. Right out front, people were sitting in a circle in the sand. They made room for Mitchell and the new arrivals.

"What do you say, doctor? Can we give him a beer?"

"Very funny," the medical student said. "I suggest one. No more."

In due course, the beer was passed along the fire brigade and into Mitchell's hands. Then the person to Mitchell's right put her hand on his knee. It was Gwendolyn. He hadn't recognized her in the darkness. She took a long drag on her cigarette. She turned her face away, to exhale primarily, but also with the suggestion of hurt feelings, and said, "You haven't thanked me."

"For what?"

"For the pills."

"Oh, right. That was really thoughtful of you."

She smiled for a few seconds and then started coughing. It was a smoker's cough, deep-seated and guttural. She tried to suppress it by leaning forward and covering her mouth, but the coughing only grew more violent, as if ripping holes in her lungs. When it finally subsided, Gwendolyn wiped her eyes. "Oh, I'm dying." She looked around the circle of people. Everyone was talking and laughing. "Nobody cares."

All this time Mitchell had been examining Gwendolyn closely. It seemed clear to him that if she didn't have cancer already, she was going to get it soon.

"Do you want to know how I knew you were separated?" he said.

"Well, I think I might."

"It's because of this glow you have. Women who get divorced or separated always have this glow. I've noticed it before. It's like they get younger."

"Really?"

"Yes, indeed," said Mitchell.

Gwendolyn smiled. "I am feeling rather restored."

Mitchell held out his beer and they clinked bottles.

"Cheers," she said.

"Cheers." He took a sip of beer. It tasted like the best beer he'd ever had. He felt ecstatically happy, suddenly. They weren't sitting around a campfire, but it felt like that, everyone glowing and centrally warmed. Mitchell squinted at the different faces in the circle and then looked out at the bay. He was thinking about his trip. He tried to remember all the places he and Larry had gone, the smelly pensions, the baroque cities, the hill stations. If he didn't think about any single place, he could sense them all, kaleidoscopically shifting around inside his head. He felt complete and satisfied. At some point the ringing had started up again; he was concentrating on that, too, so that at first he didn't notice the twinge in his intestines. Then, from far off, piercing his consciousness, came another twinge, still so delicate that he might have imagined it. In another moment it came again, more insistently. He felt a valve open inside him, and a trickle of hot liquid, like acid, begin burning its way toward the outside. He wasn't alarmed. He felt too good. He just stood up again and said, "I'm going down to the water a minute."

"I'll go with you," said Larry.

The moon was higher now. As they approached, it lit the bay up like a mirror. Away from the music, Mitchell could hear the wild dogs barking in the jungle. He led Larry straight down to the water's edge. Then, without pausing, he let his lungi drop and stepped out of it. He waded into the sea.

"Skinny-dip?"

Mitchell didn't answer.

"What's the water temp?"

"Cold," said Mitchell, though this wasn't true: the water was warm. It was just that he wanted to be alone in it. He waded out until the water was waist deep. Cupping both hands, he sprinkled water over his face. Then he dropped into the water and began to float on his back.

His ears plugged up. He heard water rushing, then the silence of the sea, then the ringing again. It was clearer than ever. It wasn't a ringing so much as a beacon penetrating his body.

He lifted his head and said, "Larry."

"What?"

"Thanks for taking care of me."

"No problem."

Now that he was in the water, he felt better again. He sensed the pull of the tide out in the bay, retreating with the night wind and the rising moon. A small hot stream came out of him, and he paddled away from it and continued to float. He stared up at the sky. He didn't have his pen or aerograms with him, so he began to dictate silently: *Dear Mom and Dad, The earth itself is all the evidence we need. Its rhythms, its perpetual regeneration, the rising and falling of the moon, the tide flowing in to land and out again to the sea, all this is a lesson for that very slow learner, the human race. The earth keeps repeating the drill, over and over, until we get it right.*

"Nobody would believe this place," Larry said on the beach. "It's a total fucking paradise."

The ringing grew louder. A minute passed, or a few minutes. Finally he heard Larry say, "Hey, Mitch, I'm going back to the party now. You OK?" He sounded far away.

Mitchell stretched out his arms, which allowed him to float a little higher in the water. He couldn't tell if Larry had gone or not. He was looking at the moon. He'd begun to notice something about the moon that he'd never noticed before. He could make out the wavelengths of the moonlight. He'd managed to slow his mind down enough to perceive that. The moonlight would speed up a second, growing brighter, then it would slow down, becoming dim. It *pulsed.* The moonlight was a kind of ringing itself. He lay undulating in the warm water, observing the correspondence of moonlight and ringing, how they increased together, diminished together. After a while, he began to be aware that he, too, was like that. His blood pulsed with the moonlight, with the ringing. Something was coming out of him, far away. He felt his insides emptying out. The sensation of water leaving him was no longer painful or explosive; it had become a steady flow of his essence into nature. In the next second, Mitchell felt as though he were dropping through the water, and then he had no sense of himself at all. He wasn't the one looking at the moon or hearing the ringing. And yet he was aware of them. For a moment, he thought he should send word to his parents, to tell them not to worry. He'd found the paradise beyond the island. He was trying to gather himself to dictate this last message, but soon he realized that there was nothing left of him to do it—nothing at all—no person left to hold a pen or to send word to the people he loved, who would never understand.

1996

BASTER

The recipe came in the mail:

Mix semen of three men.
Stir vigorously.
Fill turkey baster.
Recline.
Insert nozzle.
Squeeze.

INGREDIENTS:
1 pinch Stu Wadsworth
1 pinch Jim Freeson
1 pinch Wally Mars

There was no return address but Tomasina knew who had
sent it: Diane, her best friend and, recently, fertility special-
ist. Ever since Tomasina's latest catastrophic breakup, Diane
had been promoting what they referred to as Plan B. Plan A
they'd been working on for some time. It involved love and a
wedding. They'd been working on Plan A for a good eight
years. But in the final analysis—and this was Diane's whole

point—Plan A had proved much too idealistic. So now they were giving Plan B a look.

Plan B was more devious and inspired, less romantic, more solitary, sadder, but braver, too. It stipulated borrowing a man with decent teeth, body, and brains, free of the major diseases, who was willing to heat himself up with private fantasies (they didn't have to include Tomasina) in order to bring off the tiny sputter that was indispensable to the grand achievement of having a baby. Like twin Schwarzkopfs, the two friends noted how the battlefield had changed of late: the reduction in their artillery (they'd both just turned forty); the increasing guerrilla tactics of the enemy (men didn't even come out into the open anymore); and the complete dissolution of the code of honor. The last man who'd got Tomasina pregnant—not the boutique investment banker, the one before him, the Alexander Technique instructor—hadn't even gone through the motions of proposing marriage. His idea of honor had been to split the cost of the abortion. There was no sense denying it: the finest soldiers had quit the field, joining the peace of marriage. What was left was a ragtag gang of adulterers and losers, hit-and-run types, village-burners. Tomasina had to give up the idea of meeting someone she could spend her life with. Instead, she had to give birth to someone who would spend life with her.

But it wasn't until she received the recipe that Tomasina realized she was desperate enough to go ahead. She knew it before she'd even stopped laughing. She knew it when she found herself thinking, Stu Wadsworth I could maybe see. But Wally Mars?

Tomasina—I repeat, like a ticking clock—was forty. She had pretty much everything she wanted in life. She had a great job as an assistant producer of *CBS Evening News with Dan*

Rather. She had a terrific, adult-size apartment on Hudson Street. She had good looks, mostly intact. Her breasts weren't untouched by time, but they were holding their own. And she had new teeth. She had a set of gleaming new bonded teeth. They'd whistled at first, before she got used to them, but now they were fine. She had biceps. She had an IRA kicked up to $175,000. But she didn't have a baby. Not having a husband she could take. Not having a husband was, in some respects, preferable. But she wanted a baby.

"After thirty-five," the magazine said, "a woman begins to have trouble conceiving." Tomasina couldn't believe it. Just when she'd got her head on straight, her body started falling apart. Nature didn't give a damn about her maturity level. Nature wanted her to marry her college boyfriend. In fact, from a purely reproductive standpoint, nature would have preferred that she marry her *high school* boyfriend. While Tomasina had been going about her life, she hadn't noticed it: the eggs pitching themselves into oblivion, month by month. She saw it all now. While she canvassed for RIPIRG in college, her uterine walls had been thinning. While she got her journalism degree, her ovaries had cut estrogen production. And while she slept with as many men as she wanted, her fallopian tubes had begun to narrow, to clog. During her twenties. That extended period of American childhood. The time when, educated and employed, she could finally have some fun. Tomasina once had five orgasms with a cabdriver named Ignacio Veranes while parked on Gansevoort Street. He had a bent, European-style penis and smelled like machine oil. Tomasina was twenty-five at the time. She wouldn't do it again, but she was glad she'd done it then. So as not to have regrets. But in eliminating some regrets you create others. She'd only been in her twenties. She'd been playing around was all. But the twenties become the thirties, and a few failed relationships put you at thirty-five, when one day you pick up

Mirabella and read, "After thirty-five, a woman's fertility begins to decrease. With each year, the proportion of miscarriages and birth defects rises."

It had risen for five years now. Tomasina was forty years, one month, and fourteen days old. And panicked, and sometimes not panicked. Sometimes perfectly calm and accepting about the whole thing.

She thought about them, the little children she never had. They were lined at the windows of a ghostly school bus, faces pressed against the glass, huge-eyed, moist-lashed. They looked out, calling, "We understand. It wasn't the right time. We understand. We *do*."

The bus shuddered away, and she saw the driver. He raised one bony hand to the gearshift, turning to Tomasina as his face split open in a smile.

The magazine also said that miscarriages happened all the time, without a woman's even noticing. Tiny blastulas scraped against the womb's walls and, finding no purchase, hurtled downward through the plumbing, human and otherwise. Maybe they stayed alive in the toilet bowl for a few seconds, like goldfish. She didn't know. But with three abortions, one official miscarriage, and who knows how many unofficial ones, Tomasina's school bus was full. When she awoke at night, she saw it slowly pulling away from the curb, and she heard the noise of the children packed in their seats, that cry of children indistinguishable between laughter and scream.

Everyone knows that men objectify women. But none of our sizing up of breasts and legs can compare with the cold-blooded calculation of a woman in the market for semen. Tomasina was a little taken aback by it herself, and yet she couldn't help it: once she made her decision, she began to see men as walking spermatozoa. At parties, over glasses of Barolo (soon to be giving it up, she drank like a fish), Tomasina ex-amined the specimens who came out of the kitchen, or loi-tered in the hallways, or held forth from the armchairs. And sometimes, her eyes misting, she felt that she could discern the quality of each man's genetic material. Some semen auras glowed with charity; others were torn with enticing holes of savagery; still others flickered and dimmed with substandard voltage. Tomasina could ascertain health by a guy's smell or complexion. Once, to amuse Diane, she'd ordered every male party guest to stick out his tongue. The men had obliged, asking no questions. Men always oblige. Men *like* being objectified. They thought that their tongues were being in-spected for nimbleness, toward the prospect of oral abilities. "Open up and say ah," Tomasina kept commanding, all night long. And the tongues unfurled for display. Some had yellow spots or irritated taste buds, others were blue as spoiled beef. Some performed lewd acrobatics, flicking up and down or curling upward to reveal spikes depending from their under-sides like the armor of deep-sea fish. And then there were two or three that looked perfect, opalescent as oysters and enticingly plump. These were the tongues of the married men, who'd already donated their semen—in abundance—to the lucky women taxing the sofa cushions across the room. The wives and mothers who were nursing other complaints by now, of insufficient sleep and stalled careers—complaints that to Tomasina were desperate wishes.

At this point, I should introduce myself. I'm Wally Mars. I'm an old friend of Tomasina's. Actually, I'm an old boyfriend. We went out for three months and seven days in the spring of 1985. At the time, most of Tomasina's friends were sur-prised that she was dating me. They said what she did when she saw my name on the ingredient list. They said, "Wally

Mars?" I was considered too short (I'm only five feet four), and not athletic enough. Tomasina loved me, though. She was crazy about me for a while. Some dark hook in our brains, which no one could see, linked us up. She used to sit across the table, tapping it and saying, "What else?" She liked to hear me talk.

She still did. Every few weeks she called to invite me to lunch. And I always went. At the time all this happened, we made a date for a Friday. When I got to the restaurant, Tomasina was already there. I stood behind the hostess station for a moment, looking at her from a distance and getting ready. She was lounging back in her chair, sucking the life out of the first of the three cigarettes she allowed herself at lunch. Above her head, on a ledge, an enormous flower arrangement exploded into bloom. Have you noticed? Flowers have gone multicultural, too. Not a single rose, tulip, or daffodil lifted its head from the vase. Instead, jungle flora erupted: Amazonian orchids, Sumatran flytraps. The jaws of one flytrap trembled, stimulated by Tomasina's perfume. Her hair was thrown back over her bare shoulders. She wasn't wearing a top—no, she was. It was flesh-colored and skintight. Tomasina doesn't exactly dress corporate, unless you could call a brothel a kind of corporation. What she has to display was on display. (It was on display every morning for Dan Rather, who had a variety of nicknames for Tomasina, all relating to Tabasco sauce.) Somehow, though, Tomasina got away with her chorus-girl outfits. She toned them down with her maternal attributes: her homemade lasagna, her hugs and kisses, her cold remedies.

At the table, I received both a hug and a kiss. "Hi, hon!" she said, and pressed herself against me. Her face was all lit up. Her left ear, inches from my cheek, was a flaming pink. I could feel its heat. She pulled away and we looked at each other.

"So," I said. "Big news."

"I'm going to do it, Wally. I'm going to have a baby."

We sat down. Tomasina took a drag on her cigarette, then funneled her lips to the side, expelling smoke.

"I just figured, Fuck it," she said. "I'm forty. I'm an adult. I can do this." I wasn't used to her new teeth. Every time she opened her mouth it was like a flashbulb going off. They looked good, though, her new teeth. "I don't care what people think. People either get it or they don't. I'm not going to raise it all by myself: my sister's going to help. And Diane. You can babysit, too, Wally, if you want."

"Me?"

"You can be an uncle." She reached across the table and squeezed my hand. I squeezed back.

"I hear you've got a list of candidates on a recipe," I said.

"What?"

"Diane told me she sent you a recipe."

"Oh, that." She inhaled. Her cheeks hollowed out.

"And I was on it or something?"

"Old boyfriends." Tomasina exhaled upward. "All my old boyfriends."

Just then the waiter arrived to take our drink order.

Tomasina was still gazing up at her spreading smoke. "Martini up very dry two olives," she said. Then she looked at the waiter. She kept looking. "It's Friday," she explained. She ran her hand through her hair, flipping it back. The waiter smiled.

"I'll have a martini, too," I said. The waiter turned and looked at me. His eyebrows rose and then he turned back to Tomasina. He smiled again and went off.

As soon as he was gone, Tomasina leaned across the table to whisper in my ear. I leaned, too. Our foreheads touched. And then she said, "What about him?"

"Who?"

"*Him.*"

She indicated with her head. Across the restaurant, the waiter's tensed buns retreated, dipping and weaving.

"He's a waiter."

"I'm not going to marry him, Wally. I just want his sperm."

"Maybe he'll bring some out as a side dish."

Tomasina sat back, stubbing out her cigarette. She pondered me from a distance, then reached for cigarette number two. "Are you going to get all hostile again?"

"I'm not being hostile."

"Yes, you are. You were hostile when I told you about this and you're acting hostile now."

"I just don't know why you want to pick the waiter."

She shrugged. "He's cute."

"You can do better."

"Where?"

"I don't know. A lot of places." I picked up my soup spoon. I saw my face in it, tiny and distorted. "Go to a sperm bank. Get a Nobel Prize winner."

"I don't just want smart. Brains aren't everything." Tomasina squinted, sucking in smoke, then looked off dreamily. "I want the whole package."

I didn't say anything for a minute. I picked up my menu. I read the words *Fricassée de Lapereau* nine times. What was bothering me was this: the state of nature. It was becoming clear to me—clearer than ever—what my status was in the state of nature: it was low. It was somewhere around hyena. This wasn't the case, as far as I knew, back in civilization. I'm a catch, pragmatically speaking. I make a lot of money, for one thing. My IRA is pumped up to $254,000. But money doesn't count, apparently, in the selection of semen. The waiter's tight buns counted for more.

"You're against the idea, aren't you?" Tomasina said.

"I'm not against it. I just think, if you're going to have a baby, it's best if you do it with somebody else. Who you're in love with." I looked up at her. "And who loves you."

"That'd be great. But it's not happening."

"How do you know?" I said. "You might fall in love with somebody tomorrow. You might fall in love with somebody six months from now." I looked away, scratching my cheek. "Maybe you've already met the love of your life and don't even know it." Then I looked back into her eyes. "And then you realize it. And it's too late. There you are. With some stranger's baby."

Tomasina was shaking her head. "I'm forty, Wally. I don't have much time."

"I'm forty, too," I said. "What about me?"

She looked at me closely, as though detecting something in my tone, then dismissed it with a wave. "You're a man. You've got time."

After lunch, I walked the streets. The restaurant's glass door launched me into the gathering Friday evening. It was four thirty and already getting dark in the caverns of Manhattan. From a striped chimney buried in the asphalt, steam shot up into the air. A few tourists were standing around it, making low Swedish sounds, amazed by our volcanic streets. I stopped to watch the steam, too. I was thinking about exhaust, anyway, smoke and exhaust. That school bus of Tomasina's? Looking out one window was my kid's face. Our kid's. We'd been going out three months when Tomasina got pregnant. She went home to New Jersey to discuss it with her parents and returned three days later, having had an abortion. We broke up shortly after that. So I sometimes thought of him, or her, my only actual, snuffed-out offspring. I thought about him right then. What would the kid have looked like? Like me, with buggy eyes and potato nose? Or like Tomasina? Like her, I decided. With any luck, the kid would look like her.

For the next few weeks I didn't hear anything more. I tried to put the whole subject out of my mind. But the city wouldn't let me. Instead, the city began filling with babies. I saw them in elevators and lobbies and out on the sidewalk. I saw them straitjacketed into car seats, drooling and ranting. I saw babies in the park, on leashes. I saw them on the subway, gazing at me with sweet, gummy eyes over the shoulders of Dominican nannies. New York was no place to be having babies. So why was everybody having them? Every fifth person on the street toted a pouch containing a bonneted larva. They looked like they needed to go back inside the womb.

Mostly you saw them with their mothers. I always wondered who the fathers were. What did they look like? How big were they? Why did they have a kid and I didn't? One night I saw a whole Mexican family camping out in a subway car. Two small children tugged at the mother's sweatpants while the most recent arrival, a caterpillar wrapped in a leaf, suckled at the wineskin of her breast. And across from them, holding the bedding and the diaper bag, the progenitor sat with open legs. No more than thirty, small, squat, paint-spattered, with the broad flat face of an Aztec. An ancient face, a face of stone, passed down through the centuries into those overalls, this hurtling train, this moment.

The invitation came five days later. It sat quietly in my mailbox amid bills and catalogues. I noticed Tomasina's return address and ripped the envelope open. On the front of the invitation a champagne bottle foamed out the words:

nant!

preg

ting

get

I'm

Inside, cheerful green type announced, "On Saturday, April 13, Come Celebrate Life!"

The date, I learned afterward, had been figured precisely. Tomasina had used a basal thermometer to determine her times of ovulation. Every morning before getting out of bed, she took her resting temperature and plotted the results on a graph. She also inspected her underpants on a daily basis. A clear, albumeny discharge meant that her egg had dropped. She had a calendar on the refrigerator, studded with red stars. She was leaving nothing to chance.

I thought of canceling. I toyed with fictitious business trips and tropical diseases. I didn't want to go. I didn't want there to be parties like this. I asked myself if I was jealous or just conservative and decided both. And then, of course, in the end, I did go. I went to keep from sitting at home thinking about it.

Tomasina had lived in the same apartment for eleven years. But when I got there that night it looked completely different. The familiar speckled pink carpeting, like a runner of olive loaf, led up from the lobby, past the same dying plant on the landing, to the yellow door that used to open to my key. The same mezuzah, forgotten by the previous tenants, was still tacked over the threshold. According to the brass marker, 2-A, this was still the same high-priced one-bedroom I'd spent ninety-eight consecutive nights in almost ten years ago. But when I knocked and then pushed open the door I didn't recognize it. The only light came from candles scattered around the living room. While my eyes adjusted, I groped my way along the wall to the closet—it was right where it used to be—and hung up my coat. There was a candle burning on a nearby chest, and, taking a closer look, I began to get some idea of the direction Tomasina and Diane had gone with the party decorations. Though inhumanly large, the candle was nevertheless an exact replica of the male member in proud erection, the detailing almost hyperrealistic, right down to the tributaries of veins and the sandbar of the scrotum. The phallus's fiery tip illuminated two other objects on the table: a clay facsimile of an ancient Canaanite fertility goddess of the type sold at feminist bookstores and New Age emporiums, her womb domed, her breasts bursting; and a package of Love incense, bearing the silhouette of an entwined couple.

I stood there as my pupils dilated. Slowly the room bodied forth. There were a lot of people, maybe as many as seventy-five. It looked like a Halloween party. Women who all year secretly wanted to dress sexy *had* dressed sexy. They wore low-cut bunny tops or witchy gowns with slits up the sides. Quite a few were stroking the candles provocatively or fooling around with the hot wax. But they weren't young. Nobody was young. The men looked the way men have generally looked for the past twenty years: under threat yet agreeable. They looked like me.

Champagne bottles were going off, just like on the invitation. After every pop a woman shouted, "Ooops, I'm pregnant!" and everyone laughed. Then I did recognize something: the music. It was Jackson Browne. One of the things I used to find endearing about Tomasina was her antiquated and sentimental record collection. She still had it. I could remember dancing to this very album with her. Late one night, we just took off our clothes and started dancing all alone. It was one of those spontaneous living-room dances you have at the beginning of a relationship. On a hemp rug we twirled each other around, naked and graceless in secret, and it never happened again. I stood there, remembering, until someone came up from behind.

"Hey, Wally."

I squinted. It was Diane.

"Just tell me," I said, "that we don't have to watch."

"Relax. It's totally PG. Tomasina's going to do it later. After everybody's gone."

"I can't stay long," I said, looking around the room.

"You should see the baster we got. Four ninety-five, on sale at Macy's basement."

"I'm meeting someone later for a drink."

"We got the donor cup there, too. We couldn't find anything with a lid. So we ended up getting this plastic toddler's cup. Roland already filled it up."

Something was in my throat. I swallowed.

"Roland?"

"He came early. We gave him a choice between a *Hustler* and a *Penthouse*."

"I'll be careful what I drink from the refrigerator."

"It isn't in the refrigerator. It's under the sink, in the bathroom. I was worried somebody *would* drink it."

"Don't you have to freeze it?"

"We're using it in an hour. It keeps."

I nodded, for some reason. I was beginning to be able to see clearly now. I could see all the family photographs on the mantel. Tomasina and her dad. Tomasina and her mom. The whole Genovese clan up in an oak tree. And then I said, "Call me old-fashioned but . . ." and trailed off.

"Relax, Wally. Have some champagne. It's a *party*."

The bar had a bartender. I waved off the champagne and

asked for a glass of scotch, straight. While I waited, I scanned the room for Tomasina. Out loud, though pretty quietly, I said, with bracing sarcasm, "Roland." That was just the kind of name it would have to be. Someone out of a medieval epic. "The Sperm of Roland." I was getting whatever enjoyment I could out of this when suddenly I heard a deep voice somewhere above me say, "Were you talking to me?" I looked up, not into the sun, exactly, but into its anthropomorphic representation. He was both blond and orange, *and* large, and the candle behind him on the bookshelf lit up his mane like a halo.

"Have we met? I'm Roland DeMarchelier."

"I'm Wally Mars," I said. "I thought that might be you. Diane pointed you out to me."

"Everybody's pointing me out. I feel like some kind of prize hog," he said, smiling. "My wife just informed me that we're leaving. I managed to negotiate for one more drink."

"You're married?"

"Seven years."

"And she doesn't mind?"

"Well, she didn't. Right now I'm not so sure."

What can I say about his face? It was open. It was a face used to being looked at, looked into, without flinching. His skin was a healthy apricot color. His eyebrows, also apricot, were shaggy like an old poet's. They saved his face from being too boyish. It was this face Tomasina had looked at. She'd looked at it and said, "You're hired."

"My wife and I have two kids. We had trouble getting pregnant the first time, though. So we know how it can be. The anxiety and the timing and everything."

"Your wife must be a very open-minded woman," I said. Roland narrowed his eyes, making a sincerity check—he wasn't stupid, obviously (Tomasina had probably unearthed his SAT scores). Then he gave me the benefit of the doubt. "She says she's flattered. I know I am."

"I used to go out with Tomasina," I said. "We used to live together."

"Really?"

"We're just friends now."

"It's good when that happens."

"She wasn't thinking about babies back when we went out," I said.

"That's how it goes. You think you have all the time in the world. Then boom. You find you don't."

"Things might have been different," I said. Roland looked at me again, not sure how to take my comment, and then gazed across the room. He smiled at someone and held up his drink. Then he was back to me. "That didn't work. My wife wants to go." He set down his glass and turned to leave. "Nice to meet you, Wally."

"Keep on plugging," I said, but he didn't hear me, or pretended not to.

I'd already finished my drink, so I got a refill. Then I went in search of Tomasina. I shouldered my way across the room and squeezed down the hall. I stood up straight, showing off my suit. A few women looked at me, then away. Tomasina's bedroom door was closed, but I still felt entitled to open it.

She was standing by the window, smoking and looking out. She didn't hear me come in, and I didn't say anything. I just stood there, looking at her. What kind of dress should a girl wear to her Insemination Party? Answer: The one Tomasina had on. This wasn't skimpy, technically. It began at her neck and ended at her ankles. Between those two points, however, an assortment of peepholes had been ingeniously razored into the fabric, revealing a patch of thigh here, a glazed hip bone there; up above, the white sideswell of a breast. It made you think of secret orifices and dark canals. I counted the shining patches of skin. I had two hearts, one up, one down, both pumping.

And then I said, "I just saw Secretariat."

She swung around. She smiled, though not quite convincingly. "Isn't he gorgeous?"

"I still think you should have gone with Isaac Asimov." She came over and we kissed cheeks. I kissed hers, anyway. Tomasina kissed mostly air. She kissed my semen aura.

"Diane says I should forget the baster and just sleep with him."

"He's married."

"They all are." She paused. "You know what I mean."

I made no sign that I did. "What are you doing in here?"

She took two rapid-fire puffs on her cigarette, as though to fortify herself. Then she answered, "Freaking out."

"What's the matter?"

She covered her face with her hand. "This is *depressing*, Wally. This isn't how I wanted to have a baby. I thought this party would make it fun, but it's just depressing." She dropped her hand and looked into my eyes. "Do you think I'm crazy? You do, don't you?"

Her eyebrows went up, pleading. Did I tell you about Tomasina's freckle? She has this freckle on her lower lip like a piece of chocolate. Everybody's always trying to wipe it off.

"I don't think you're crazy, Tom," I said.

"You don't?"

"No."

"Because I trust you, Wally. You're mean, so I trust you."

"What do you mean I'm mean?"

"Not *bad* mean. Good mean. I'm not crazy?"

"You want to have a baby. It's natural."

Suddenly Tomasina leaned forward and rested her head

on my chest. She had to lean down to do it. She closed her eyes and let out a long sigh. I put my hand on her back. My fingers found a peephole and I stroked her bare skin. In a warm, thoroughly grateful voice, she said, "You get it, Wally. You totally get it."

She stood up and smiled. She looked down at her dress, adjusting it so that her navel showed, and then took my arm.

"Come on," she said. "Let's go back to the party."

I didn't expect what happened next. When we came out, everybody cheered. Tomasina held on to my arm and we started waving to the crowd like a couple of royals. For a minute I forgot about the purpose of the party. I just stood arm in arm with Tomasina and accepted the applause. When the cheers died down, I noticed that Jackson Browne was still playing. I leaned over and whispered to Tomasina, "Remember dancing to this song!"

"Did we dance to this?"

"You don't remember?"

"I've had this album forever. I've probably danced to it a thousand times." She broke off. She let go of my arm.

My glass was empty again.

"Can I ask you something, Tomasina?"

"What?"

"Do you ever think about you and me?"

"Wally, don't." She turned away and looked at the floor. After a moment, in a reedy, nervous voice, she said, "I was really screwed up back then. I don't think I could have stayed with anybody."

I nodded. I swallowed. I told myself not to say the next thing. I looked over at the fireplace, as though it interested me, and then I said it: "Do you ever think about our kid?"

The only sign that she'd heard me was a twitch next to her

left eye. She took a deep breath, let it out. "That was a long time ago."

"I know. It's just that when I see you going to all this trouble I think it could be different sometimes."

"I don't think so, Wally." She picked a piece of lint off the shoulder of my jacket, frowning. Then she tossed it away. "God! Sometimes I wish I was Benazir Bhutto or somebody."

"You want to be prime minister of Pakistan?"

"I want a nice, simple, arranged marriage. Then after my husband and I sleep together he can go off and play polo."

"You'd like that?"

"Of course not. That would be horrible." A tress fell into her eyes and she backhanded it into place. She looked around the room. Then she straightened up and said, "I should mingle."

I held up my glass. "Be fruitful and multiply," I said. And Tomasina squeezed my arm and was gone.

I stayed where I was, drinking from my empty glass to have something to do. I looked around the room for any women I hadn't met. There weren't any. Over at the bar, I switched to champagne. I had the bartender fill my glass three times. Her name was Julie and she was majoring in art history at Columbia University. While I was standing there, Diane stepped into the middle of the room and clinked her glass. Other people followed and the room got quiet.

"First of all," Diane began, "before we kick everyone out of here, I'd like to make a toast to tonight's oh-so-generous donor, Roland. We conducted a nationwide search and, let me tell you, the auditions were *grueling*." Everybody laughed. Somebody shouted, "Roland left."

"He left? Well, we'll toast his semen. We've still got that." More laughter, a few drunken cheers. Some people, men and women both now, were picking up the candles and waving them around.

"And, finally," Diane went on, "finally, I'd like to toast our soon-to-be-expecting—knock on wood—mother. Her courage in seizing the means of production is an inspiration to us all." They were pulling Tomasina out onto the floor now. People were hooting. Tomasina's hair was falling down. She was flushed and smiling. I tapped Julie on the arm, extending my glass. Everyone was looking at Tomasina when I turned and slipped into the bathroom.

After shutting the door, I did something I don't usually do. I stood and looked at myself in the mirror. I stopped doing that, for any prolonged period, at least twenty years ago. Staring into mirrors was best at around thirteen. But that night I did it again. In Tomasina's bathroom, where we'd once showered and flossed together, in that cheerful, brightly tiled grotto, I presented myself to myself. You know what I was thinking? I was thinking about nature. I was thinking about hyenas again. The hyena, I remembered, is a fierce predator. Hyenas even attack lions on occasion. They aren't much to look at, hyenas, but they do OK for themselves. And so I lifted my glass. I lifted my glass and toasted myself: "Be fruitful and multiply."

The cup was right where Diane had said it would be. Roland had placed it, with priestly care, on top of a bag of cotton balls. The toddler cup sat enthroned on a little cloud. I opened it and inspected his offering. It barely covered the bottom of the cup, a yellowish scum. It looked like rubber cement. It's terrible, when you think about it. It's terrible that women need this stuff. It's so paltry. It must make them crazy, having everything they need to create life but this one meager leaven. I rinsed Roland's out under the faucet. Then I checked to see that the door was locked. I didn't want anybody to burst in on me.

•

That was ten months ago. Shortly after, Tomasina got pregnant. She swelled to immense proportions. I was away on business when she gave birth in the care of a midwife at St. Vincent's. But I was back in time to receive the announcement:

Tomasina Genovese proudly announces
the birth of her son,
Joseph Mario Genovese,
on January 15, 1996.
5 lbs. 3 oz.

The small size alone was enough to clinch it. Nevertheless, bringing a Tiffany spoon to the little heir the other day, I settled the question as I looked down into his crib. The potato nose. The buggy eyes. I'd waited ten years to see that face at the school-bus window. Now that I did, I could only wave goodbye.

1995

EARLY MUSIC

As soon as he came in the front door, Rodney went straight to the music room. That was what he called it, wryly but not without some hope: the music room. It was a small, dogleg-shaped fourth bedroom that had been created when the building was cut up into apartments. It qualified as a music room because it contained his clavichord.

There it stood on the unswept floor: Rodney's clavichord. It was apple green with gold trim and bore a scene of geometric gardens on the inside of its lifted lid. Modeled on the Bodechtel clavichords built in the 1790s, Rodney's had come from the Early Music Shop, in Edinburgh, three years ago. Still, resting there majestically in the dim light—it was winter in Chicago—the clavichord looked as though it had been waiting for Rodney to play it not only for the nine and a half hours since he'd left for work but for a couple of centuries at least.

You didn't need that big a room for a clavichord. A clavichord wasn't a piano. Spinets, virginals, fortepianos, clavichords, and even harpsichords were relatively small instruments. The eighteenth-century musicians who'd played them were small. Rodney was big, however—six feet three. He sat down gently on the narrow bench. Carefully he slid his knees under the keyboard. With closed eyes he began to play from memory a Sweelinck prelude.

Early music is rational, mathematical, a little bit stiff, and so was Rodney. He'd been that way long before he'd ever seen a clavichord or written a doctoral dissertation (unfinished) on temperament systems during the German Reformation. But Rodney's immersion in the work of Bach père et fils had only fortified his native inclinations. The other piece of furniture in the music room was a small teak desk. In its drawers and pigeonholes were the super-organized files Rodney kept: health-insurance records; alphabetized appliance manuals along with warranties; the twins' immunization histories, birth certificates, and Social Security cards; plus three years' worth of monthly budgets stipulating household expenses down to the maximum allowed for heating (Rodney kept the apartment a bracing 58 degrees). A little cold weather was good for you. Cold weather was like Bach: it sorted the mind. On top of the desk was this month's folder, marked "FEB '05." It contained three credit-card statements with horrendous running balances and the ongoing correspondence from the collection agency that was dunning Rodney for defaulting on his monthly payments to the Early Music Shop.

His back was straight as he played; his face twitched. Behind closed eyelids, his eyeballs fluttered in time with the quick notes.

And then the door swung open and Imogene, who was six, shouted in her longshoreman's voice:

"Daddy! Dinner!"

Having completed this task, she slammed the door shut again. Rodney stopped. Looking at his watch, he saw that he'd been playing—practicing—for exactly four minutes.

•

The house Rodney grew up in had been neat and tidy. They used to do that in those days. They used to house-clean. They, of course, meant she: a mother. All those years of vacuumed carpets and spick-and-span kitchens, of shirts that miraculously picked themselves up off the floor only to re-appear freshly laundered in the dresser drawer—the whole functioning efficiency that used to be a house was no more. Women had given all that up when they went to work.

Or even when they didn't. Rebecca, Rodney's wife, didn't work outside the home. She worked in the apartment, in a back bedroom. She didn't call it a bedroom. She called it an office. Rodney had a music room in which he played little music. Rebecca had an office in which she did little business. But she was there a lot, all day, while Rodney was at work at a real office in the city.

As he came out of the sanctuary of the music room, Rodney stepped around the cardboard boxes and rolls of bubble wrap and stray toys crowding the hall. He turned sideways to squeeze by the squad of winter coats hanging on the wall above crusty boots and single mittens. Moving into the living room, he stepped on something that felt like a mitten. But it wasn't. It was a stuffed mouse. Sighing, Rodney picked it up. A little bigger than a real mouse, this particular mouse was baby blue in color and wore a black beret. It appeared to have a cleft palate.

"You're supposed to be cute," Rodney said to the mouse. "Exert yourself."

The mice were what Rebecca did. They were part of a line called Mice 'n' Warm™, which included, at present, four "characters": Modernist Mouse, Boho Mouse, Surfer-Realist Mouse, and Flower-Power Mouse. Each artistic rodent was filled with aromatic pellets and was irresistibly squeezable. The selling point (still mainly theoretical) was that you could put these mice in the microwave and they would come out muffin-warm and smelling like potpourri.

Rodney carried the mouse in cupped hands, like an injured thing, into the kitchen.

"Escapee," he said, by way of greeting.

Rebecca looked up from the sink, where she was straining pasta, and frowned. "Throw that in the trash," she said. "It's a reject."

From the twins at the table came a cry of alarm. They didn't like the mice to meet untimely ends. Springing up, they rushed their father with clutching hands.

Rodney held Boho Mouse higher.

Immy, who had Rebecca's sharp chin along with her clear-eyed determination, climbed up on a chair. Tallulah, always the more instinctive and feral of the two, just grabbed Rodney's arm and started walking up his leg.

While this assault was under way, Rodney said to Rebecca, "Let me guess. It's the mouth."

"It's the mouth," Rebecca said. "And the smell. Smell it."

In order to do so, Rodney had to turn and pop the mouse into the microwave, hitting the warm-up button.

After twenty seconds, he took the warm mouse out and held it to his nose.

"It's not that bad," he said. "But I see what you mean. A little more armpit than would be ideal."

"It's supposed to be musk."

"On the other hand," said Rodney, "B.O. is perfect for a bohemian."

"I've got five kilos of musk-scented pellets," moaned Rebecca, "which are now useless."

Rodney crossed the kitchen and stepped on the trash-can pedal, raising the lid. He tossed the mouse in and let the trash can close. It felt good to toss the mouse. He wanted to do it again.

•

It had probably not been a wise move to buy the clavichord. For one thing, it cost a small fortune. And they didn't have a fortune of any size to spend. Also, Rodney had stopped playing professionally ten years earlier. After the twins were born, he'd stopped playing altogether. To drive all the way down to Hyde Park from Logan Square, and then to drive around and around looking for a place to park (Hyde Park, went the joke, you can't hide and you can't park), and then to unpeel his U. of Chicago ID from his wallet, holding a thumb over the ridiculously out-of-date photo while waving it at the security guard, in order to gain admittance to practice room 113, where for an hour, on the battered but not untuneful university clavichord, Rodney would work through a few bourrées and roundelays, just to keep a hand in—all that became too difficult after the kids were born. Back in the days when Rodney and Rebecca had both been pursuing a Ph.D. (back when they were childless and super-focused and surviving on yogurt and brewer's yeast), Rodney had spent three or four hours a day playing the department clavichord. The harpsichord next door had been in great demand. But the clavichord was always free. This was because it was a pedal clavichord, that rare beast, and no one liked to play it. It was a speculative replica of an early-eighteenth-century clavichord, and the pedal unit (which some lead-footed student had stomped on pretty thoroughly) was a little funky. But Rodney got used to it, and from then on the clavichord was like Rodney's own personal instrument, until he dropped out of the program and became a father and took a job on the North Side giving piano lessons at the Old Town School of Folk Music.

The thing about early music was nobody knew quite what it had sounded like. Disputes about how to tune a harpsichord or clavichord constituted a good part of the discipline. The question was "How had Bach tuned *his* harpsichord?" And nobody knew. People argued about what Johann Sebastian had meant by *wohltemperiert*. They tuned their instruments in a historically likely manner and studied the hand-drawn schematics on the title pages of various Bach compositions.

Rodney had intended to settle this question in his dissertation. He was going to figure out, once and for all, exactly how Bach had tuned his harpsichord, how his music had sounded at the time, and, therefore, *how it should be played now*. To do this, he would have to go to Germany. He would have to go, in fact, to East Germany (Leipzig) in order to examine the actual harpsichord on which Bach himself had composed and onto whose keyboard (so it was rumored) the Master had written his preferred markings. In the fall of 1987, with the help of a doctoral grant—and with Rebecca on a *Stiftung* at the Freie Universität—Rodney had set off for West Berlin. They lived in a two-room sublet near Savignyplatz featuring a sit-down shower and a toilet with a shelf. The leaseholder was a guy named Frank, from Montana, who'd come to Berlin to build sets for experimental theater. A married professor had also used the place to entertain his girlfriends. In the flannel-sheeted bed where Rebecca and Rodney had sex, they encountered miscellaneous pubic hairs. The professor's shaving equipment remained in the tiny, malodorous bathroom. On the toilet shelf their feces landed high and dry, ready for inspection. It would have been unbearable if they hadn't been twenty-six and poor and in love. Rodney and Rebecca washed the sheets and hung them out to dry on the balcony. They got used to the dinky tub. They continued to complain about, and be entirely grossed out by, the shelf.

West Berlin wasn't what Rodney had expected. It was nothing like early music. West Berlin was completely irrational and unmathematical, not stiff but loose. It was full of war widows, draft dodgers, squatters, anarchists. Rodney didn't like the cigarette smoke. The beer made him feel bloated. So he escaped, going as often as he could to the Philharmonie or the Deutsche Oper.

Rebecca had fared better. She'd become friendly with the people in the *Wohngemeinschaft* one floor above them. Wearing soft-soled Maoist shoes or ankle bracelets or ironic monocles, the six young Germans pooled their money, swapped partners, and held deep-throated conversations about Kantian ethics as it applied to traffic disputes. Every few months, one or another of them disappeared to Tunisia or India or returned to Hamburg to enter the family export business. At Rebecca's urging, Rodney politely attended their parties, but he always felt too scrubbed in their company, too apolitical, too blithely American.

In October, when he went to the East German Embassy to pick up his academic visa, Rodney was told that his request had been denied. The minor diplomat who relayed this news wasn't an Eastern Bloc functionary but a kind-looking, balding, nervous man, who seemed genuinely sorry. He himself was from Leipzig, he said, and as a child had attended the Thomaskirche, where Bach had been the director of choir and music. Rodney appealed to the American Embassy, in Bonn, but they were powerless to help. He made a frantic call to his advisor, Professor Breskin, back in Chicago, who was going through a divorce and was less than compassionate. In a sardonic voice he'd said, "Got any other dissertation ideas?"

The lindens along the Ku'damm lost their leaves. In Rodney's opinion, the leaves had never turned orange enough, red enough, to die. But this was how autumn was handled in Prussia. Winter, too, never quite got to be winter: rain, gray skies, scant snow—just a dampness that worked its way into Rodney's bones as he walked from church concert to church concert. He had six months left in Berlin and no idea how to fill them.

And then, in early spring, a wonderful thing had happened. Lisa Turner, the cultural attaché at the American
Embassy, invited Rodney to tour Germany, playing Bach, as
part of a *Deutsche-Amerikanische Freundschaft* program. For a
month and a half, Rodney traveled through mostly small
towns in Swabia, North Rhine–Westphalia, and Bavaria,
putting on concerts in local halls. He stayed in dollhouse-
size hotel rooms full of dollhouse knickknacks; he slept on
single beds under wonderfully soft duvets. Lisa Turner ac-
companied him, seeing to Rodney's every need and taking
particular care of his traveling companion. This wasn't Rebecca. Rebecca had stayed in Berlin to write the first draft of
her thesis. Rodney's companion was a clavichord, made by
Hass in 1761 and, then and now, the single most beautiful,
expressive, and finicky clavichord Rodney's trembling, de-
lighted hands had ever touched.

Rodney wasn't famous. But the Hass clavichord was. In
Munich, three separate newspaper photographers had shown
up before the concert at the Rathaus to take a picture of the
clavichord. Rodney stood behind it, a mere retainer.

That the audiences who came to see Rodney weren't
large, that the universally retired members of these audiences
were permanently stone-faced from years and years of faithfully enduring high culture, that fifteen minutes into a piece
by Scheidemann a third of the audience would be asleep,
their mouths open as though singing along or sustaining one
long complaint—none of that bothered Rodney. He was
getting paid, which had never happened before. The halls that
Lisa Turner optimistically rented were two- or three-hundred-
seat places. With twenty-five or sixteen or (in Heidelberg)
three people in attendance, Rodney had the feeling that he
was alone, playing for himself. He tried to hear the notes the
Master had played more than two hundred years earlier, to
catch them on the wind of the moment and reproduce them.

It was like bringing Bach back to life and going back in time simultaneously. This was what Rodney thought about as he played in those cavernous, echoing halls.

The Hass clavichord wasn't as thrilled as Rodney. The clavichord complained a lot. It didn't want to go back to 1761. It had done its work and wanted to rest, to retire, like the audience. The tangents broke and had to be repaired. A new key went dead every night.

Still, the early music rang out, prim and lurching and undeniably antique, and Rodney, its medium, like a man on a flying horse, maintained his balance on the stool. The keyboard rose and fell, thumped, and the music whirled on.

When he returned to Berlin in late May, Rodney found he had less enthusiasm for strict musicology. He wasn't sure anymore if he even wanted to be an academic. Instead of getting a Ph.D., he toyed with the idea of enrolling at the Royal Academy of Music, in London, and pursuing a performing career.

West Berlin, meanwhile, had been undoing and remaking Rebecca. In that walled, subsidized half-city, no one seemed to have a job. The comrades in the *Wohngemeinschaft* spent their time nurturing the sad orange trees on their concrete balcony. Volunteering at the Schwarzfahrer Theater, Rebecca played electrified accompaniment, half Kraftwerk, half Kurt Weill, for the antic, antinuclear goings-on onstage. Up late at night, sleeping ever later in the morning, she made little progress on her examination of Johann Georg Sulzer's *Allgemeine Theorie der schönen Künste* as it related to theoretical concepts of music listening in eighteenth-century Germany. To be specific, while Rodney was away Rebecca had managed to write five pages.

They had a wonderful year in Berlin, Rodney and Rebecca. But their doctoral research led them to the inescapable conclusion that they didn't want to be doctors of anything.

They moved back to Chicago and drifted. Rodney joined an early-keyboard group that gave intermittent concerts. Rebecca took up painting. They moved to Bucktown and, a year later, to Logan Square. They lived on next to nothing. They lived like Boho Mouse.

Rodney's fortieth birthday found him with the flu. He got out of bed with a fever of 103, called the school to cancel his lessons, then got back into bed.

In the afternoon, Rebecca and the girls brought in a weird-looking birthday cake. Through gummed-up eyelids, Rodney saw the lemon sponge cake of the soundboard, the marzipan of the keys, and the chocolate slab of the lid supported by a peppermint stick.

Rebecca's gift was a plane ticket to Edinburgh and a down payment made out to the Early Music Shop. "Do it," she said. "Just do it. You need it. We'll work it out. The mice are starting to sell."

That was three years ago. Now they were gathered around the gimpy-legged secondhand kitchen table, and Rebecca warned Rodney, "Don't answer the phone."

The twins were eating their usual naked pasta. The grown-ups, those gourmands, pasta with sauce.

"They called six times today."

"Who called?" asked Immy.

"Nobody," said Rebecca.

"The woman?" Rodney asked. "Darlene?"

"No. Somebody new. A man."

That didn't sound good. Darlene was almost family at this point. Considering all the letters she had sent, in ever-bolder typefaces, and all the phone calls she'd made, politely asking for money, then demanding money, and finally making threats—considering the persistent entitlement, Darlene was like an alcoholic sister or a cousin with a gambling addiction. Except that in this case she held the moral high ground. Darlene wasn't the one who owed $27,000 compounding at an interest rate of 18 percent.

Darlene, when she called, called from within the call-center honeycomb; in the background you could hear the buzz of numberless other worker bees. The job was to collect pollen. In that effort, they were beating their wings and, if need be, raising their stingers. Because he was a musician, Rodney heard all this acutely. Sometimes he drifted off and forgot all about the angry bee that was after him.

Darlene had ways of regaining his attention. Unlike a trolling telemarketer, she didn't make mistakes. She didn't mispronounce Rodney's name or mess up his address: she knew these by heart. Since it was easier to resist a stranger, the first time Darlene had called she'd introduced herself. She'd stated her mission and made it clear that she wasn't going away until she achieved it.

Now she had gone away.

"A man?" Rodney said.

Rebecca nodded. "A not very nice man."

Immy brandished her fork. "You said nobody called. How can a man be nobody?"

"I meant nobody you know, honey. Nobody you have to worry about."

Just then the cordless phone rang and Rebecca said, "Don't answer it."

Rodney took his napkin (which was in fact a paper towel) and folded it in his lap. In an elevated tone, he said for the girls' benefit, "People shouldn't call during dinner. It's impolite."

For the first two years, Rodney had kept up with the payments. But then he'd quit teaching at the Old Town School of Folk Music and had tried to go out on his own. Students came directly to his apartment, where he taught them on the clavichord (it was perfect preparation for the piano, he told their parents). For a while, Rodney made about twice as much as he'd been making before, but then the students began to drop out. No one liked the clavichord. It sounded weird, the kids said. Only a girl would play it, one boy said. In a panic, Rodney started renting a rehearsal room with a piano and holding lessons there, but soon he was making less than he'd made at Old Town. That was when he'd quit being a music teacher and taken his present job as a patients' records associate at an HMO.

By then, however, he'd defaulted on his payments to the Early Music Shop. The interest rate rose and then (fine print in the loan agreement) skyrocketed. After that, he could never catch up.

Darlene had threatened him with repossession, but so far it hadn't happened. And so Rodney continued to play the clavichord fifteen minutes in the morning and fifteen minutes at night.

"Some good news, though," Rebecca said, after the phone had stopped ringing. "I got a new client today."

"Great. Who?"

"Stationery store out in Des Plaines."

"How many mice they want?"

"Twenty. To start."

Rodney, who was capable of keeping straight the 1/6 comma fifths of Bach's keyboard bearing (F-C-G-D-A-E) from the pure fifths (E-B-F#-C#) and the devilish 1/12 comma fifths (C#-G#-D#-A#), had no trouble performing the following calculations in his head: Each Mice 'n' Warm mouse sold for $15. Rebecca's take was 40 percent. That came to $6 per mouse. Since each mouse cost roughly $3.50 to make, the profit on one mouse was $2.50. Times twenty came to fifty bucks.

He did another calculation: $27,000 divided by $2.50

came to 10,800. The stationery store wanted twenty mice to start. Rebecca would have to sell more than ten thousand to pay off the clavichord.

With lusterless eyes Rodney looked across the table at his wife.

There were lots of women with actual jobs around. Rebecca just didn't happen to be one of them. But whatever a woman did nowadays was called a job. A man sewing together stuffed mice was considered, at best, a poor provider, at worst, a loser. Whereas a woman with a master's and a near-Ph.D. in musicology who hand-stitched microwavable, sweet-smelling rodents was now considered (especially by her married female friends) an entrepreneur.

Of course, because of Rebecca's "job," she couldn't take care of the twins full-time. They were forced to hire a babysitter, whose weekly salary came to more than Rebecca brought in by selling the Mice 'n' Warm mice (which was why they could pay only the minimum amount on their credit cards, driving them even further into debt). Rebecca had offered many times to give up the mice and get a job that paid a steady salary. But Rodney, who knew what it was to love a useless thing, always said, "Give it another few years."

Why was what Rodney did a job and what Rebecca did not a job? First of all, Rodney made money. Second, he had to warp his personality to suit his employer. Third, he disliked it. That was a sure sign that it was a job.

"Fifty dollars," he said.

"What?"

"That's the profit on twenty mice. Before taxes."

"Fifty dollars!" cried Tallulah. "That's a lot!"

"It's just one account," Rebecca said.

Rodney felt like asking how many accounts she had *total*. He felt like asking for a monthly report showing liabilities and receivables. He was sure Rebecca had detailed financial information scrawled on the back of an envelope somewhere. But he didn't say anything, because the girls were there. He just got up and started to clear the table. "I've got to do the dishes," he said, as though it were news.

Rebecca herded the girls into the living room and sat them down before a rented DVD. Typically she used the half hour after dinner to phone her suppliers in China, where it was now tomorrow morning, or to call her mother, a sciatica sufferer. Alone at the kitchen sink, Rodney scraped plates and rinsed kefir-coated glasses. He fed the dragonlike disposal in its lair. A real musician would have had his hands insured. But what would it matter if Rodney stuck his fingers straight down the drain into the churning blades?

The smart thing to do would be to take out insurance first and *then* stick his hand down the disposal. That way he could pay off the clavichord and sit at it every night playing with his bandaged stump.

Maybe if he'd stayed in Berlin, if he'd gone to the Royal Academy, if he hadn't got married and had kids, maybe Rodney would still be playing music. He might be an internationally known performer, like Menno van Delft or Pierre Goy.

Opening the dishwasher, Rodney saw that it was full of standing water. The outflow tube had been improperly installed; the landlord had promised to fix it but never did. Rodney stared at the rust-colored tide for a while, as though he were a plumber and knew what to do, but in the end he filled the soap container, shut the door, and turned the dishwasher on.

The living room was empty by the time he came out. The DVD control screen played on the television, the loop of theme music repeating itself over and over. Rodney switched it off. He went down the hallway toward the bedrooms. The water was running in the bathtub and he could hear Rebecca's voice coaxing the twins in. He listened for his daughters' voices. This was the new music and he wanted to hear it, just for a minute, but the water was too loud.

On nights when Rebecca gave the girls a bath, it fell to Rodney to read them their bedtime story. He was on his way down the hallway to their room when he reached Rebecca's office. And here he did something he didn't normally do: he stopped. In general, when passing by Rebecca's office, Rodney made a habit of staring at the floor. It was better for his emotional equilibrium to let whatever went on in there go on without his seeing it. But tonight he turned and stared at the door. And then, raising his uninsured right hand, he pushed the door open.

From the back wall, massing around the long worktables and bumping up against the sewing machine, a huge raft of fabric bolts in pastel hues was making its way downstream across the floor. The logjam carried with it ribbon spools, leaking bags of perfumed pellets, stickpins, buttons. Balancing on the logs, some with the jaunty stance of lumberjacks, others terrified and clingy like flood victims, the four varieties of Mice 'n' Warm mice rode toward the falls of the marketplace.

Rodney stared at their little faces looking up with pitiful appeal or savoir faire. He stared for as long as he could bear it, which was about ten seconds. Then he turned and walked in hard shoes back down the hallway. He passed the bathroom without stopping to listen for Immy's and Lula's voices and he continued into the music room, where he shut the door behind him. After seating himself at the clavichord, he took a deep breath and began to play one part of a keyboard duet in E-flat by Müthel.

It was a difficult piece. Johann Gottfried Müthel, Bach's last pupil, was a difficult composer. He'd studied with Bach for only three months. And then he'd gone off to Riga to disappear into the Baltic twilight of his genius. Hardly anybody knew who Müthel was anymore. Except for clavichordists. For clavichordists, playing Müthel was a supreme achievement.

Rodney got off to a good start.

Ten minutes into the duet, Rebecca stuck her head in the door.

"The girls are ready for their story," she said.

Rodney kept playing.

Rebecca said it louder and Rodney stopped.

"You do it," he said.

"I have to make some calls."

With his right hand, Rodney played an E-flat scale. "I'm practicing," he said. He stared at his hand, as though he were a student learning to play scales for the first time, and he didn't stop staring until Rebecca had withdrawn her head from the doorway. Then Rodney got up and shut the door semi-violently. He came back to the clavichord and started the piece from the beginning.

Müthel hadn't written much. He composed only when the spirit moved him. That was like Rodney. Rodney played only when the spirit moved him.

It moved him now, tonight. For the next two hours, Rodney played the Müthel piece over and over.

He was playing well, with a lot of feeling. But he was also making mistakes. He soldiered on. Then, to make himself feel better, he finished off with Bach's French Suite in D minor, a piece he'd been playing for years and knew by heart.

Before long he was flushed and sweating. It felt good to play with such concentration and vigor again, and when he finally stopped, with the bell-like notes still ringing in his ears and off the low ceiling of the room, Rodney lowered his head and closed his eyes. He was remembering that month and a half, at twenty-six, when he'd played ecstatically and invisibly in empty West German concert halls. Behind him on the desk the phone rang, and Rodney swiveled and picked it up.

"Hello?"

"Good evening, am I speaking with Rodney Webber?"

Rodney realized his mistake. But he said, "This is he."

"My name is James Norris and I'm with Reeves Collection. I know you're familiar with our organization."

If you hung up, they called again. If you changed your phone number, they got the new one. The only hope was to make a deal, to stall, to make promises and buy some time.

"I'm afraid I'm well acquainted with your organization." Rodney was trying for the right tone, light but not insouciant or disrespectful.

"Formerly I believe you've been dealing with Ms. Darlene Jackson. She's been the person assigned to your case. Up until now. Now I'm in charge and I hope we can work something out."

"I hope so, too," said Rodney.

"Mr. Webber, I come in when things get complicated and I try to make them simple. Ms. Jackson offered you various payment plans, I see."

"I sent a thousand dollars in December."

"Yes, you did. And that was a start. But, according to our records, you had agreed to send two thousand."

"I couldn't get that much. It was Christmas."

"Mr. Webber, let's keep things simple. You stopped meeting your payments to our client, the Early Music Shop, over a year ago. So Christmas doesn't really have a whole lot to do with it, does it?"

Rodney hadn't enjoyed his conversations with Darlene. But now he saw that Darlene had been reasonable, pliable, in a way that this guy James wasn't. There was a quality in James's voice that wasn't so much menacing as obdurate: a stone wall of a voice.

"Your account is in arrears over payments for a musical instrument, is that right? What kind of instrument is it?"

"A clavichord."

"I'm not familiar with that instrument."

"I wouldn't expect you to be."

The man chuckled, taking no offense.

"Lucky for me, that's not my job, knowing about ancient instruments."

"A clavichord is a precursor to the piano," Rodney said. "Except it's played by tangents instead of hammers. My clavichord—"

"You see that right there, Mr. Webber? That's incorrect. It's not yours. The instrument still belongs to the Early Music Shop out of Edinburgh. You only have it on loan from them. Until you pay off that loan."

"I thought you might like to know the provenance," said Rodney. How had his diction got way up here, to these heights? Nothing complex: he just wanted to put James Norris of Reeves Collection in his place. Next Rodney heard himself say, "It's a copy, by Verwolf, of a style of clavichord made by a man named Bodechtel in 1790."

James said, "Let me get to my point."

But Rodney didn't let him. "This is what I do," Rodney said, and his voice sounded tight and strained, overtuned. "This is what I do. I'm a clavichordist. I need the instrument to make my living. If you take it back, I'll never be able to pay you back. Or pay the Early Music Shop."

"You can keep your clavichord. I'd be happy to let you keep it. All you have to do is pay for it, in full, by five p.m. tomorrow, with a certified check or wire transfer from your bank, and you can go on playing your clavichord for as long as you like."

Rodney's laugh was bitter. "Obviously I can't do that."

"Then by five p.m. tomorrow we're going to unfortunately have to come out and repossess the instrument."

"I can't get that much by tomorrow."

"This is the end of the line, Rodney."

"There's got to be some way—"

"Only one way, Rodney. Payment in full."

Clumsily, furiously, his hand like a brick trying to throw a brick, Rodney slammed down the phone.

For a moment he didn't move. Then he swiveled back around and placed his hands on the clavichord.

He might have been feeling for a heartbeat. He ran his fingers over the gold ornamentation and the tops of the frigid keys. It wasn't the most beautiful or distinguished clavichord he'd ever played. It couldn't compare to the Hass, but it was his, or it had been, and it was lovely and rapturous-sounding enough. Rodney would never have got it if Rebecca hadn't sent him to Edinburgh. He would never have known how deeply depressed he'd been or how happy the clavichord, for a time, would make him.

His right hand was playing the Müthel again.

Rodney knew he'd never been a first-rate musicologist. At best, he was a mediocre, if sincere, performer. With fifteen minutes' practice in the morning and fifteen minutes in the evening, he wasn't going to get any better.

There'd always been something a little pathetic about being a clavichordist. Rodney knew that. The Müthel he was playing, however, mistakes and all, still seemed beautiful, maybe more so for its obsolescence. He played for another minute. Then he placed his hands on the warm wood of the clavichord and, leaning forward, stared at the painted garden inside the lid.

It was after ten when he came out of the music room. The apartment was quiet and dark. Entering the bedroom, Rodney

didn't turn on the light, so as not to wake Rebecca. He undressed in the dark, feeling in the closet for a hanger.

In his underwear he shuffled to his side of the bed and
crawled in. On one elbow he leaned over to see if Rebecca
was awake. But then he realized that her side of the bed was
empty. She was still in her office, working.

Rodney collapsed onto his back. He lay immobile. There
was a pillow underneath him, in the wrong spot, but he
didn't have the energy to roll over and tug it out.

His situation wasn't really so different from anybody
else's. He'd only got to the end of the road a little earlier. But
it was the same for the rock stars and for the jazz musicians,
for the novelists and the poets (definitely for the poets); it was
the same for the business executives, the biologists, the computer programmers, the accountants, the flower arrangers.
Artist or nonartist, academic or nonacademic, Menno van
Delft or Rodney Webber, even for Darlene and James of the
Reeves Collection Agency: it didn't matter. No one knew
what the original music sounded like. You had to make an
educated guess and do the best you could. For whatever you
played there was no indisputable tuning or handwritten
schematic, and the visa you needed in order to see the Master's keyboard was always denied. Sometimes you thought
you heard the music, especially when you were young, and
then you spent the rest of your life trying to reproduce the
sound.

Everybody's life was early music.

He was still awake a half hour later, when Rebecca
came in.

"Can I turn on the light?" she asked.

"No," said Rodney.

She paused and said, "You practiced a long time."

"Practice makes perfect."

"Who called? Someone called."

Rodney said nothing.

"You didn't answer, did you? They've been calling later and later."

"I was practicing. I didn't answer."

Rebecca sat on the edge of the bed. She tossed something in Rodney's direction. He picked it up and squinted at it. The beret, the cleft palate. Boho Mouse.

"I'm going to quit," Rebecca said.

"What?"

"The mice. I'm giving up." She stood and began to undress, dropping clothes on the floor. "I should have finished my dissertation. I could have been a musicology professor. Now all I am is Mommy. Mommy, Mommy, Mommy. A mommy who makes stuffed animals." She went into the bathroom. Rodney heard her brushing her teeth, washing her face. She came out again and got into bed.

After a long silence, Rodney said, "You can't give up."

"Why not? You've always wanted me to."

"I changed my mind."

"Why?"

Rodney swallowed. "These mice are our only hope."

"You know what I did tonight?" Rebecca said. "First I took the mouse out of the trash. Then I unpicked the stitches and took out the musk pellets. And then I filled it with cinnamon pellets and stitched it back up. That's how I spent my evening."

Rodney held the mouse to his nose.

"Smells good," he said. "These mice are destined for greatness. You're going to make us a million bucks."

"If I make a million bucks," Rebecca said, "I'll pay off your clavichord."

"Deal," said Rodney.

"And you can quit your job and get back to playing music full-time." She rolled over and kissed his cheek, then rolled back and adjusted her pillows and blankets.

Rodney kept the stuffed mouse against his nose, inhaling its spicy aroma. He kept smelling the mouse even after Rebecca had fallen asleep. If the microwave had been nearby, Rodney would have fired up Boho Mouse to reconstitute its bouquet. But the microwave was down the hall, in the shabby kitchen, and so he just lay there, smelling the mouse, which by now was cold and almost scentless.

2005

TIMESHARE

My father is showing me around his new motel. I shouldn't call it a motel after everything he's explained to me but I still do. What it is, what it's going to be, my father says, is a timeshare resort. As he, my mother, and I walk down the dim hallway (some of the bulbs have burned out), my father informs me of the recent improvements. "We put in a new oceanfront patio," he says. "I had a landscape architect come in, but he wanted to charge me an arm and a leg. So I designed it myself."

Most of the units haven't been renovated yet. The place was a wreck when my father borrowed the money to buy it, and from what my mother tells me, it looks a lot better now. They've repainted, for one thing, and put on a new roof. Each room will have a kitchen installed. At present, however, only a few rooms are occupied. Some units don't even have doors. Walking by, I can see painting tarps and broken air conditioners lying on the floors. Water-stained carpeting curls back from the edges of the rooms. Some walls have holes in them the size of a fist, evidence of the college kids who used to stay here during spring break. My father plans to install new carpeting, and to refuse to rent to students. "Or if I do," he says, "I'll charge a big deposit, like three hundred bucks. And

I'll hire a security guard for a couple of weeks. But the idea is to make this place a more upscale kind of place. As far as the college kids go, piss on 'em."

The foreman of this renewal is Buddy. My father found him out on the highway, where day workers line up in the morning. He's a little guy with a red face and makes, for his labor, five dollars an hour. "Wages are a lot lower down here in Florida," my father explains to me. My mother is surprised at how strong Buddy is for his size. Just yesterday, she saw him carrying a stack of cinder blocks to the Dumpster. "He's like a little Hercules," she says. We come to the end of the hallway and enter the stairwell. When I take hold of the aluminum banister, it nearly rips out of the wall. Every place in Florida has these same walls.

"What's that smell?" I ask.

Above me, hunched over, my father says nothing, climbing.

"Did you check the land before you bought this place?" I ask. "Maybe it's built over a toxic dump."

"That's Florida," says my mother. "It smells that way down here."

At the top of the stairs, a thin green runner extends down another darkened hallway. As my father leads the way, my mother nudges me, and I see what she's been talking about: he's walking lopsided, compensating for his bad back. She's been after him to see a doctor but he never does. Every so often, his back goes out and he spends a day soaking in the bathtub (the tub in room 308, where my parents are staying temporarily). We pass a maid's cart, loaded with cleaning fluids, mops, and wet rags. In an open doorway, the maid stands, looking out, a big black woman in blue jeans and a smock. My father doesn't say anything to her. My mother says hello brightly and the maid nods.

At its middle, the hallway gives onto a small balcony. As soon as we step out, my father announces, "There it is!" I think he means the ocean, which I see for the first time, storm-colored and uplifting, but then it hits me that my father never points out scenery. He's referring to the patio. Red-tiled, with a blue swimming pool, white deck chairs, and two palm trees, the patio looks as though it belongs to an actual seaside resort. It's empty but, for the moment, I begin to see the place through my father's eyes—peopled and restored, a going concern. Buddy appears down below, holding a paint can. "Hey, Buddy," my father calls down, "that tree still looks brown. Have you had it checked?"

"I had the guy out."

"We don't want it to die."

"The guy just came and looked at it."

We look at the tree. The taller palms were too expensive, my father says. "This one's a different variety."

"I like the other kind," I say.

"The royal palms? You like those? Well, then, after we get going, we'll get some."

We're quiet for a while, gazing over the patio and the purple sea. "This place is going to get all fixed up and we're going to make a million dollars!" my mother says.

"Knock on wood," says my father.

Five years ago, my father actually made a million. He'd just turned sixty and, after working all his life as a mortgage banker, went into business for himself. He bought a condominium complex in Fort Lauderdale, resold it, and made a big profit. Then he did the same thing in Miami. At that point, he had enough to retire on but he didn't want to. Instead, he bought a new Cadillac and a fifty-foot powerboat. He bought a twin-engine airplane and learned to fly it. And then he flew around the country, buying real estate, flew to California, to the Bahamas, over the ocean. He was his own boss and his temper improved. Later, the reversals began. One of his developments in North Carolina, a ski resort, went bankrupt. It turned out his partner had embezzled $100,000. My father had to take him to court, which cost more money. Meanwhile, a savings and loan sued my father for selling it mortgages that defaulted. More legal fees piled up. The million dollars ran out fast and, as it began to disappear, my father tried a variety of schemes to get it back. He bought a company that made "manufactured homes." They were like mobile homes, he told me, only more substantial. They were prefabricated, could be plunked down anywhere but, once set up, looked like real houses. In the present economic situation, people needed cheap housing. Manufactured homes were selling like hotcakes.

My father took me to see the first one on its lot. It was Christmas, two years ago, when my parents still had their condominium. We'd just finished opening our presents when my father said that he wanted to take me for a little drive. Soon we were on the highway. We left the part of Florida I knew, the Florida of beaches, high-rises, and developed communities, and entered a poorer, more rural area. Spanish moss hung from the trees and the unpainted houses were made of wood. The drive took about two hours. Finally, in the distance, we saw the onion bulb of a water tower with OCALA painted on the side. We entered the town, passing rows of neat houses, and then we came to the end and kept on going. "I thought you said it was in Ocala," I said.

"It's a little farther out," said my father.

Countryside began again. We drove into it. After about fifteen miles, we came to a dirt road. The road led into an open, grassless field, without any trees. Toward the back, in a muddy area, stood the manufactured house.

It was true it didn't look like a mobile home. Instead of being long and skinny, the house was rectangular, and fairly wide. It came in three or four different pieces that were screwed together, and then a traditional-looking roof was put in place on top. We got out of the car and walked on bricks to get closer. Because the county was just now installing sewer lines out this far, the ground in front of the house—"the yard," my father called it—was dug up. Right in front of the house, three small shrubs had been planted in the mud. My father inspected them, then waved his hand over the field. "This is all going to be filled in with grass," he said. The front door was a foot and a half off the ground. There wasn't a porch yet but there would be. My father opened the door and we went inside. When I shut the door behind me, the wall rattled like a theater set. I knocked on the wall, to see what it was made of, and heard a hollow, tinny sound. When I turned around, my father was standing in the middle of the living room, grinning. His right index finger pointed up in the air. "Get a load of this," he said. "This is what they call a 'cathedral ceiling.' Ten feet high. Lotta headroom, boy."

Despite the hard times, nobody bought a manufactured home, and my father, writing off the loss, went on to other things. Soon I began getting incorporation forms from him, naming me vice president of Baron Development Corporation, or the Atlantic Glass Company, or Fidelity Mini-Storage Inc. The profits from these companies, he assured, would one day come to me. The only thing that *did* come, however, was a man with an artificial leg. My doorbell rang one morning and I buzzed him in. In the next moment, I heard him clumping up the stairs. From above, I could see the blond stubble on his bald head and could hear his labored breathing. I took him for a deliveryman. When he got to the top of the stairs, he asked if I was vice president of Duke Development. I said I guessed that I was. He handed me a summons.

It had to do with some legal flap. I lost track after a while. Meanwhile, I learned from my brother that my parents were living off savings, my father's IRA, and credit from the banks. Finally, he found this place, Palm Bay Resort, a ruin by the sea, and convinced another savings and loan to lend him the money to get it running again. He'd provide the labor and know-how and, when people started coming, he'd pay off the S&L and the place would be his.

After we look at the patio, my father wants to show me the model. "We've got a nice little model," he says. "Everyone who's seen it has been very favorably impressed." We come down the dark hallway again, down the stairs, and along the first-floor corridor. My father has a master key and lets us in a door marked 103. The hall light doesn't work, so we file through the dark living room to the bedroom. As soon as my father flips on the light, a strange feeling takes hold of me. I feel as though I've been here before, in this room, and then I realize what it is: the room is my parents' old bedroom. They've moved in the furniture from their old condo: the peacock bedspread, the Chinese dressers and matching headboard, the gold lamps. The furniture, which once filled a much bigger space, looks squeezed together in this small room. "This is all your old stuff," I say.

"Goes nice in here, don't you think?" my father asks.

"What are you using for a bedspread now?"

"We've got twin beds in our unit," my mother says. "This wouldn't have fit anyway. We've just got regular bedspreads now. Like in the other rooms. Hotel supply. They're OK."

"Come and see the living room," my father tells me, and I follow him through the door. After some fumbling, he finds a light that works. The furniture in here is all new and doesn't remind me of anything. A painting of driftwood on the beach hangs on the wall. "How do you like that painting? We got fifty of them from this warehouse. Five bucks a pop. And they're all different. Some have starfish, some seashells. All in a maritime motif. They're signed oil paintings." He walks to the wall and, taking off his glasses, makes out the signature: "Cesar Amarollo! Boy, that's better than Picasso." He turns his back to me, smiling, happy about this place.

I'm down here to stay a couple of weeks, maybe even a month. I won't go into why. My father gave me unit 207, right on the ocean. He calls the rooms "units" to differentiate them from the motel rooms they used to be. Mine has a little kitchen. And a balcony. From it, I can see cars driving along the beach, a pretty steady stream. This is the only place in Florida, my father tells me, where you can drive on the beach.

The motel gleams in the sun. Somebody is pounding somewhere. A couple of days ago, my father started offering complimentary suntan lotion to anyone who stays the night. He's advertising this on the marquee out front but, so far, no one has stopped. Only a few families are here right now, mostly old couples. There's one woman in a motorized wheel-chair. In the morning, she rides out to the pool and sits, and then her husband appears, a washed-out guy in a bathing suit and flannel shirt. "We don't tan anymore," she tells me. "After a certain age, you just don't tan. Look at Kurt. We've been out here all week and that's all the tan he is." Sometimes, too, Judy, who works in the office, comes out to sunbathe during her lunch hour. My father gives her a free room to

stay in, up on the third floor, as part of her salary. She's from
Ohio and wears her hair in a long braided ponytail, like a girl
in fifth grade.

At night, in her hotel-supply bed, my mother has been
having prophetic dreams. She dreamed that the roof sprung
a leak two days before it did so. She dreamed that the skinny
maid would quit and, next day, the skinny maid did. She
dreamed that someone broke his neck diving into the empty
swimming pool (instead, the filter broke, and the pool had
to be emptied to fix it, which she says counts). She tells me
all this by the swimming pool. I'm in it; she's dangling her
feet in the water. My mother doesn't know how to swim.
The last time I saw her in a bathing suit I was five years old.
She's the burning, freckled type, braving the sun in her straw
hat only to talk to me, to confess this strange phenomenon. I
feel as though she's picking me up after swimming lessons.
My throat tastes of chlorine. But then I look down and see the
hair on my chest, grotesquely black against my white skin,
and I remember that I'm old, too.

Whatever improvements are being made today are being
made on the far side of the building. Coming down to the
pool, I saw Buddy going into a room, carrying a wrench. Out
here, we're alone, and my mother tells me that it's all due to
rootlessness. "I wouldn't be dreaming these things if I had a
decent house of my own. I'm not some kind of gypsy. It's just
all this traipsing around. First we lived in that motel in
Hilton Head. Then that condo in Vero. Then that recording
studio your father bought, without any windows, which just
about killed me. And now this. All my things are in storage.
I dream about them, too. My couches, my good dishes, all our
old family photos. I dream of them packed away almost every
night."

"What happens to them?"

"Nothing. Just that nobody ever comes to get them."

•

There are a number of medical procedures that my parents are planning to have done when things get better. For some time now, my mother has wanted a face-lift. When my parents were flush, she actually went to a plastic surgeon who took photographs of her face and diagrammed her bone structure. It's not a matter of simply pulling the loose skin up, apparently. Certain facial bones need shoring up as well. My mother's upper palate has slowly receded over the years. Her bite has become misaligned. Dental surgery is needed to resurrect the skull over which the skin will be tightened. She had the first of these procedures scheduled about the time my father caught his partner embezzling. In the trouble afterward, she had to put the idea on hold.

My father, too, has put off two operations. The first is disk surgery to help the pain in his lower back. The second is prostate surgery to lessen the blockage to his urethra and increase the flow of his urine. His delay in the latter case is not motivated purely by financial considerations. "They go up there with that Roto-Rooter and it hurts like hell," he told me. "Plus, you can end up incontinent." Instead, he has elected to go to the bathroom fifteen to twenty times a day, no trip being completely satisfying. During the breaks in my mother's prophetic dreams, she hears my father getting up again and again. "Your father's stream isn't exactly magnificent anymore," she told me. "You live with someone, you know."

As for me, I need a new pair of shoes. A sensible pair. A pair suited to the tropics. Stupidly, I wore a pair of old black wingtips down here, the right shoe of which has a hole in the bottom. I need a pair of flip-flops. Every night, when I go out to the bars in my father's Cadillac (the boat is gone, the plane is gone, but we still have the yellow "Florida Special"

with the white vinyl top), I pass souvenir shops, their windows crammed with T-shirts, seashells, sunhats, coconuts with
painted faces. Every time, I think about stopping to get flip-
flops, but I haven't yet.

One morning, I come down to find the office in chaos. Judy,
the secretary, is sitting at her desk, chewing the end of her
ponytail. "Your father had to fire Buddy," she says. But before
she can tell me anything more, one of the guests comes in,
complaining about a leak. "It's right over the bed," the man
says. "How do you expect me to pay for a room with a leak
over the bed? We had to sleep on the floor! I came down to
the office last night to get another room but there was no one
here."

      Just then my father comes in with the tree surgeon. "I
thought you told me this type of palm tree was hardy."

      "It is."

      "Then what's the matter with it?"

      "It's not in the right kind of soil."

      "You never told me to change the soil," my father says,
his voice rising.

      "It's not only the soil," the tree surgeon says. "Trees are
like people. They get sick. I can't tell you why. It might have
needed more water."

      "We watered it!" my father says, shouting now. "I had the
guy water it every goddamn day! And now you tell me it's
dead?" The man doesn't reply. My father sees me. "Hey there,
buddy!" he says heartily. "Be with you in a minute."

      The man with the leak begins explaining his trouble to
my father. In the middle, my father stops him. Pointing at
the tree surgeon, he says, "Judy, pay this bastard." Then he
goes back to listening to the man's story. When the man

finishes, my father offers him his money back and a free room for the night.

Ten minutes later, in the car, I learn the outlandish story. My father fired Buddy for drinking on the job. "But wait'll you hear *how* he was drinking," he says. Early that morning, he saw Buddy lying on the floor of unit 106, under the air conditioner. "He was supposed to be fixing it. All morning, I kept passing by, and every time I'd see Buddy lying under that air conditioner. I thought to myself, Jeez. But then this goddamn crook of a tree surgeon shows up. And he tells me that the goddamn tree he's supposed to be curing is dead, and I forgot all about Buddy. We go out to look at the tree and the guy's giving me all this bullshit—the climate this, the climate that—until finally I tell him I'm going to go call the nursery. So I come back to the office. And I pass 106 again. And there's Buddy still lying on the floor."

When my father got to him, Buddy was resting comfortably on his back, his eyes closed and the air-conditioner coil in his mouth. "I guess that coolant's got alcohol in it," my father said. All Buddy had to do was disconnect the coil, bend it with a pair of pliers, and take a drink. This last time he'd sipped too long, however, and had passed out. "I should have known something was up," my father says. "For the past week all he's been doing is fixing the air conditioners."

After calling an ambulance (Buddy remained unconscious as he was carried away), my father called the nursery. They wouldn't refund his money or replace the palm tree. What was more, it had rained during the night and no one had to tell him about leaks. His own roof had leaked in the bathroom. The new roof, which had cost a considerable sum, hadn't been installed properly. At a minimum, someone was going to have to retar it. "I need a guy to go up there and lay down some tar along the edges. It's the edges, see, where the

water gets in. That way, maybe I can save a couple of bucks."
While my father tells me all this, we drive out along A1A.
It's about ten in the morning by this point and the drifters
are scattered along the shoulder, looking for day work. You
can spot them by their dark tans. My father passes the first
few, his reasons for rejecting them unclear to me at first.
Then he spots a white man in his early thirties, wearing green
pants and a Disney World T-shirt. He's standing in the sun,
eating a raw cauliflower. My father pulls the Cadillac up
alongside him. He touches his electronic console and the
passenger window hums open. Outside, the man blinks, trying to adjust his eyes to see into the car's dark, cool interior.

At night, after my parents go to sleep, I drive along the strip
into town. Unlike most of the places my parents have wound
up, Daytona Beach has a working-class feel. Fewer old people,
more bikers. In the bar I've been going to, they have a real
live shark. Three feet long, it swims in an aquarium above
the stacked bottles. The shark has just enough room in its
tank to turn around and swim back the other way. I don't
know what effect the lights have on the animal. The dancers
wear bikinis, some of which sparkle like fish scales. They
circulate through the gloom like mermaids, as the shark
butts its head against the glass.

I've been in here three times already, long enough to
know that I look, to the girls, like an art student, that under
state law the girls cannot show their breasts and so must glue
wing-shaped appliqués over them. I've asked what kind of
glue they use ("Elmer's"), how they get it off ("just a little
warm water"), and what their boyfriends think of it (they
don't mind the money). For $10, a girl will take you by the
hand, past the other tables where men sit mostly alone, into
the back where it's even darker. She'll sit you down on a

padded bench and rub against you for the duration of two whole songs. Sometimes, she'll take your hands and will ask, "Don't you know how to dance?"

"I'm dancing," you'll say, even though you're sitting down.

At three in the morning, I drive back, listening to a country-and-western station to remind myself that I'm far from home. I'm usually drunk by this point but the trip isn't long, a mile at most, an easy cruise past the other waterfront real estate, the big hotels and the smaller ones, the motor lodges with their various themes. One's called Viking Lodge. To check in, you drive under a Norse galley, which serves as a carport.

Spring break's more than a month away. Most of the hotels are less than half full. Many have gone out of business, especially those farther out from town. The motel next to ours is still open. It has a Polynesian theme. There's a bar under a grass hut by the swimming pool. Our place has a fancier feel. Out front, a white gravel walkway leads up to two miniature orange trees flanking the front door. My father thought it was worth it to spend money on the entrance, seeing as that was people's first impression. Right inside, to the left of the plushly carpeted lobby, is the sales office. Bob McHugh, the salesman, has a blueprint of the resort on the wall, showing available units and timeshare weeks. Right now, though, most people coming in are just looking for a place to spend the night. Generally, they drive into the parking lot at the side of the building and talk to Judy in the business office.

It rained again while I was in the bar. When I drive into our parking lot and get out, I can hear water dripping off the roof of the motel. There's a light burning in Judy's room. I consider going up to knock on her door. Hi, it's the boss's son! While I'm standing there, though, listening to the dripping water and plotting my next move, her light goes off. And with it, it seems, every light around. My father's timeshare resort plunges into darkness. I reach out to put my hand on the hood of the Cadillac, to reassure myself with its warmth, and, for a moment, try to picture in my mind the way up, where the stairs begin, how many floors to climb, how many doors to pass before I get to my room.

"Come on," my father says. "I want to show you something."

He's wearing tennis shorts and has a racquetball racquet in his hand. Last week, Jerry, the current handyman (the one who replaced Buddy didn't show up one morning), finally moved the extra beds and draperies out of the racquetball court. My father had the floor painted and challenged me to a game. But, with the bad ventilation, the humidity made the floor slippery, and we had to quit after four points. My father didn't want to break his hip.

He had Jerry drag an old dehumidifier in from the office and this morning they played a few games.

"How's the floor?" I ask.

"Still a little slippy. That dehumidifier isn't worth a toot."

So it isn't to show me the new, dry racquetball court that my father has come to get me. It's something, his expression tells me, more significant. Leaning to one side (the exercise hasn't helped his back any), he leads me up to the third floor, then up another, smaller stairway that I haven't noticed before. This one leads straight to the roof. When we get to the top, I see that there's another building up here. It's pretty big, like a bunker, but with windows all around.

"You didn't know about this, did you?" my father says. "This is the penthouse. Your mother and I are going to move in up here soon as it's ready."

The penthouse has a red front door and a welcome mat. It sits in the middle of the tarred roof, which extends in every direction. From up here, all the neighboring buildings disappear, leaving only sky and ocean. Beside the penthouse, my father has set up a small hibachi. "We can have a cookout tonight," he says.

Inside, my mother is cleaning the windows. She wears the same yellow rubber gloves as when she used to clean the windows of our house back in the Detroit suburbs. Only two rooms in the penthouse are habitable at present. The third has been used as a storeroom and still contains a puzzle of chairs and tables stacked on top of one another. In the main room, a telephone has been installed beside a green vinyl chair. One of the warehouse paintings has been hung on the wall, a still life with seashells and coral.

The sun sets. We have our cookout, sitting in folding chairs on the roof.

"This is going to be nice up here," my mother says. "It's like being right in the middle of the sky."

"What I like," my father says, "is you can't see anybody. Private ocean view, right on the premises. A house this big on the water'd cost you an arm and a leg.

"Soon as we get this place paid off," he continues, "this penthouse will be ours. We can keep it in the family, down through the generations. Whenever you want to come and stay in your very own Florida penthouse, you can."

"Great," I say, and mean it. For the first time, the motel exerts an attraction for me. The unexpected liberation of the roof, the salty decay of the oceanfront, the pleasant absurdity of America, all come together so that I can imagine myself bringing friends and women up to this roof in years to come.

When it's finally dark, we go inside. My parents aren't

sleeping up here yet but we don't want to leave. My mother turns on the lamps.

I go over to her and put my hands on her shoulders.

"What did you dream last night?" I ask.

She looks at me, into my eyes. While she does this, she's not so much my mother as just a fellow human being, with troubles and a sense of humor. "You don't want to know," she says.

I go into the bedroom to check it out. The furniture has that motel look but, on the bureau, my mother has set up a photograph of me and my brothers. There's a mirror on the back of the bathroom door, which is open. In the mirror, I see my father. He's urinating. Or trying to. He's standing in front of the toilet, staring down with a blank look. He's concentrating on some problem I've never had to concentrate on, something I know is coming my way, but I can't imagine what it is. He raises his hand in the air and makes a fist. Then, as though he's been doing it for years, he begins to pound on his stomach, over where his bladder is. He doesn't see me watching. He keeps pounding, his hand making a dull thud. Finally, as though he's heard a signal, he stops. There's a moment of silence before his stream hits the water.

My mother is still in the living room when I come out. Over her head, the seashell painting is crooked, I notice. I think about fixing it, then think the hell with it. I go out onto the roof. It's dark now, but I can hear the ocean. I look down the beach, at the other high-rises lit up, the Hilton, the Ramada. When I go to the roof's edge, I can see the motel next door. Red lights glow in the tropical grass-hut bar. Beneath me, and to the side, though, the windows of our own motel are black. I squint down at the patio but can't see anything. The roof still has puddles from last night's storm and, when I step, I feel water gush up my shoe. The hole is getting bigger. I don't stay out long, just long enough to feel the world. When I turn back, I see that my father has come out into the living room again. He's on the phone, arguing with someone, or laughing, and working on my inheritance.

1997

FIND THE BAD GUY

We've owned this house for—what—twelve years now, I reckon. Bought it from an elderly couple, the De Rougemonts, whose aroma you can still detect around the place, in the master especially, and in the home office, where the old buzzard napped on summer days, and a little bit in the kitchen, still.

I remember going into people's houses as a kid and thinking, Can't they smell how they smell? Some houses were worse than others. The Pruitts next door had a greasy, chuckwagon odor, tolerable enough. The Willots, who ran that fencing academy in their rec room, smelled like skunk cabbage. You could never mention the smells to your friends, because they were part of it, too. Was it hygiene? Or was it, you know, glandular, and the way each family smelled had to do with bodily functions deep inside their bodies? The whole thing sort of turned your stomach, the more you thought about it.

Now *I* live in an old house that probably smells funny to outsiders.

Or used to live. At the present time, I'm in my front yard, hiding out between the stucco wall and the traveler palms.

There's a light burning up in Meg's room. She's my sugar

pie. She's thirteen. From my vantage point I can't make out
Lucas's bedroom, but as a rule Lucas prefers to do his homework downstairs, in the great room. If I were to sidle up to
the house, I'd more than likely spy Lucas in his school V-neck
and necktie, armed for success: graphing calculator (check),
St. Boniface iPad (check), Latin Quizlet (check), bowl of
Goldfish (check). But I can't go up there now on account of
it would violate the restraining order.

I'm not supposed to come any closer than fifty feet to my
lovely wife, Johanna. It's an emergency TRO (meaning tem-
porary), issued at night, with a judge presiding. My lawyer,
Mike Peekskill, is in the process of having it revoked. In
the meantime, guess what? Yours truly, Charlie D., still has
the landscape architect's plans from when Johanna and I
were thinking of replacing these palms with something less
jungly and prone to pests. So I happen to know for certain
that the distance from the house to the stucco wall is sixty-
three feet. Right now, I reckon I'm about sixty or sixty-one,
here in the vegetation. And, anyway, nobody can see me,
because it's February and already dark in these parts.

It's Thursday, so where's Bryce? Right. Trumpet lessons
with Mr. Talawatamy. Johanna'll be going to pick him up
soon. Can't stay here long.

If I were to leave my hideout and mosey around the side
of the house, I'd see the guest room, where I used to retreat
when Johanna and I were fighting real bad, and where, last
spring, after Johanna got promoted at Hyundai, I commenced
to putting the blocks to the babysitter, Cheyenne.

And if I kept going all the way into the backyard I'd come
face-to-face with the glass door I shattered when I threw that
lawn gnome through it. Drunk at the time, of course.

Yessir. Plenty of ammunition for Johanna to play Find the
Bad Guy at couples counseling.

It's not *cold* cold out, but it is for Houston. When I reach down to take my phone out of my boot, my hip twinges. Touch of arthritis.

I'm getting my phone to play Words with Friends. I started playing it over at the station, just to pass the time, but then I found out Meg was playing it, too, so I sent her a game invite.

In *mrsbieber vs. radiocowboy* I see that mrsbieber has just played *poop*. (She's trying to get my goat.) Meg's got the first *p* on a double-word space and the second on a double-letter space, for a total score of twenty-eight. Not bad. Now I play an easy word, *pall*, for a measly score of nine. I'm up fifty-one points. Don't want her to get discouraged and quit on me.

I can see her shadow moving around up there. But she doesn't play another word. Probably Skypeing or blogging, painting her nails.

Johanna and me—you say it "Yo-hanna," by the way, she's particular about that—we've been married twenty-one years. When we met I was living up in Dallas with my girlfriend at the time, Jenny Braggs. Back then I was consulting for only three stations, spread out over the state, so I spent most of every week on the road. Then one day I was up in San Antonio, at WWWR, and there she was. Johanna. Shelving CDs. She was a tall drink of water.

"How's the weather up there?" I said.

"Pardon me?"

"Nothing. Hi, I'm Charlie D. That an accent I hear?"

"Yes. I'm German."

"Didn't know they liked country music in Germany."

"They don't."

"Maybe I should consult over there. Spread the gospel. Who's your favorite country recording artist?"

"I am more into opera," Johanna said.

"I getcha. Just here for the job."

After that, every time I was down San Antone way, I

made a point of stopping by Johanna's desk. It was less nerve-racking if she was sitting.

"You ever play basketball, Johanna?"

"No."

"Do they have girls' basketball over there in Germany?"

"In Germany I am not that tall," Johanna said.

That was about how it went. Then one day I come up to her desk and she looks at me with those big blue eyes of hers, and she says, "Charlie, how good an actor are you?"

"Actor or liar?"

"Liar."

"Pretty decent," I said. "But I might be lying."

"I need a green card," Johanna said.

Roll the film: me emptying my water bed into the bathtub so I can move out, while Jenny Braggs weeps copious tears. Johanna and me cramming into a photo booth to take cute "early relationship" photos for our "scrapbook." Bringing that scrapbook to our immigration hearing, six months later.

"Now, Ms. Lubbock—do I have that right?"

"Lübeck," Johanna told the officer. "There's an umlaut over the *u*."

"Not in Texas there ain't," the officer said. "Now, Ms. Lubbock, I'm sure you can understand that the United States has to make certain that those individuals who we admit to a path of citizenship by virtue of their marrying U.S. citizens are really and truly married to those citizens. And so I'm going to have to ask you some personal questions that might seem a little intrusive. Do you agree to me doing that?"

Johanna nodded.

"When was the first time you and Mr. D.—" He stopped short and looked at me. "Hey, you aren't *the* Charlie Daniels, are you?"

"Nuh-uh. That's why I just go by the D. To avoid confusion."

"Because you sort of look like him."

"I'm a big fan," I said. "I take that as a compliment."

He turned back to Johanna, smooth as butter. "When was the first time you and Mr. D. had intimate sexual relations?"

"You won't tell my mother, will you?" Johanna said, trying to joke.

But he was all business. "Before you were married or after?"

"Before."

"And how would you rate Mr. D.'s sexual performance?"

"What do you think? Wonderful. I married him, didn't I?"

"Any distinguishing marks on his sex organ?"

"It says 'In God We Trust.' Like on all Americans."

The officer turned to me, grinning. "You got yourself a real spitfire here," he said.

"Don't I know it," I said.

Back then, though, we weren't sleeping together. That didn't happen till later. In order to pretend to be my fiancée, and then my bride, Johanna had to spend time with me, getting to know me. She's from Bavaria, Johanna is. She had herself a theory that Bavaria is the Texas of Germany. People in Bavaria are more conservative than your normal European leftist. They're Catholic, if not exactly God-fearing. Plus, they like to wear leather jackets and such. Johanna wanted to know everything about Texas, and I was just the man to teach her. I took her to SXSW, which wasn't the cattle call it is today. And oh my Lord if Johanna didn't look good in a pair of blue jeans and cowboy boots.

Next thing I know we're flying home to Michigan to meet my folks. (I'm from Traverse City, originally. Got to talking this way on account of living down here so long. My brother Ted gives me a hard time about it. I tell him you gotta talk the talk in the business I'm in.)

Maybe it was Michigan that did it. It was wintertime. I took Johanna snowmobiling and ice fishing. My mama would never have seen eye to eye on the whole green-card thing, so I just told her we were friends. Once we got up there, though, I overheard Johanna telling my sister that we were "dating." On perch night at the VFW hall, after drinking a few PBRs, Johanna started holding my hand under the table. I didn't complain. I mean, there she was, all six-foot-plus of her, healthy as can be and with a good appetite, holding my hand in hers, secret from everyone else. I'll tell you, I was happier than a two-peckered dog.

My mother put us in separate bedrooms. But one night Johanna came into mine, quiet as an Injun, and crawled into bed.

"This part of the Method acting?" I said.

"No, Charlie. This is real."

She had her arms around me, and we were rocking, real soft like, the way Meg did after we gave her that kitten, before it died, I mean, when it was just a warm and cuddly thing instead of like it had hoof and mouth, and went south on us.

"Feels real," I said. "Feels like the realest thing I ever did feel."

"Does this feel real, too, Charlie?"

"Yes, ma'am."

"And this?"

"Lemme see. Need to reconnoitre. Oh yeah. That's *real* real."

Love at fifteenth sight, I guess you'd call it.

I look up at my house and cogitate some—I don't rightly want to say what about. The thing is, I'm a successful man in the prime of life. Started DJ-ing in college, and, OK, my voice was fine for the 3:00-to-6:00 a.m. slot at Marquette, but out in the real world there was an upper limit, I'll admit. Never did land me a job in front of a microphone. Telemarketed instead. Then the radio itch got back into me and I started consulting. This was in the eighties, when you had your first country-rock crossovers. A lot of stations were slow to catch on. I told them who and what to play. Started out contracting for three stations and now I've got sixty-seven coming to me asking, "Charlie D., how do we increase our market share? Give us your crossover wisdom, Sage of the Sagebrush." (That's on my website. People have sort of picked it up.)

But what I'm thinking right now doesn't make me feel so sagelike. In fact, not even a hair. I'm thinking, How did this happen to me? To be out here in the bushes?

Find the Bad Guy is a term we learned at couples counseling. Me and Johanna saw this lady therapist for about a year, name of Dr. Van der Jagt. Dutch. Had a house over by the university, with separate paths to the front and the back doors. That way, people leaving didn't run into those showing up.

Say you're coming out of couples therapy and your next-door neighbor's coming in. "Hey, Charlie D.," he says. "How's it going?" And you say, "The missus has just been saying I'm verbally abusive, but I'm doing OK otherwise."

Naw. You don't want that.

Tell the truth, I wasn't crazy about our therapist being a woman, plus European. Thought it would make her partial to Johanna's side of things.

At our first session, Johanna and I chose opposite ends of the couch, keeping throw pillows between us.

Dr. Van der Jagt faced us, her scarf as big as a horse blanket.

She asked what brought us.

Talking, making nice, that's the female department. I waited for Johanna to start in.

But the same cat got her tongue as mine.

Dr. Van der Jagt tried again. "Johanna, tell me how you are feeling in the marriage. Three words."

"Frustrated. Angry. Alone."

"Why?"

"When we met, Charlie used to take me dancing. Once we had kids, that stopped. Now we both work full-time. We don't see each other all day long. But as soon as Charlie comes home he goes out to his fire pit—"

"You're always welcome to join me," I said.

"—and drinks. All night. Every night. He is married more to the fire pit than to me."

I was there to listen, to connect with Johanna, and I tried my best. But after a while I stopped paying attention to her words and just listened to her voice, the foreign sound of it. It was like if Johanna and I were birds, her song wouldn't be the song I'd recognize. It would be the song of a species of bird from a different continent, some species that nested in cathedral belfries or windmills, which, to my kind of bird, would be like, Well, la-di-da.

For instance, regarding the fire pit. Didn't I try to corral everyone out there every night? Did I ever say I *wanted* to sit out there alone? No, sir. I'd like us to be together, as a family, under the stars, with the mesquite flaming and popping. But Johanna, Bryce, Meg, and even Lucas—they never want to. Too busy on their computers or their Instagrams.

"How do you feel about what Johanna is saying?" Dr. Van der Jagt asked me.

"Well," I said. "When we bought the house, Johanna was excited about the fire pit."

"I never liked the fire pit. You always think that, because you like something, I like the same thing."

"When the real estate lady was showing us around, who was it said, 'Hey, Charlie, look at this! You're gonna love this'?"

"*Ja*, and you wanted a Wolf stove. You had to have a Wolf stove. But have you ever cooked anything on it?"

"Grilled those steaks out in the pit that time."

Right around there, Dr. Van der Jagt held up her soft little hand.

"We need to try to get beyond these squabbles. We need to find what's at the core of your unhappiness. These things are only on the surface."

We went back the next week, and the week after that. Dr. Van der Jagt had us fill out a questionnaire ranking our level of marital contentment. She gave us books to read: *Hold Me Tight*, which was about how couples tend to miscommunicate, and *The Volcano Under the Bed*, which was about overcoming sexual dry spells and made for some pretty racy reading. I took off the covers of both books and put on new ones. That way, people at the station thought I was reading Tom Clancy.

Little by little, I picked up the lingo.

Find the Bad Guy means how, when you're arguing with your spouse, both people are trying to win the argument. Who didn't close the garage door? Who left the Bigfoot hair clump in the shower drain? The thing you have to realize, as a couple, is that there *is* no bad guy. You can't win an argument when you're married. Because if you win, your spouse loses, and resents losing, and then you lose, too, pretty much.

Due to the fact that I was a defective husband, I started spending a lot of time alone, being introspective. What I did was go to the gym and take a sauna. I'd dropper some eucalyptus into a bucket of water, toss the water on the fake rocks, let the steam build up, then turn over the miniature hourglass, and, for however long it took to run out, I'd introspect. I liked to imagine the heat burning all my excess cargo away—I could stand to lose a few, like the next guy—until all that was left was a pure residue of Charlie D. Most other guys hollered that they were cooked after ten minutes and red-assed it out of there. Not me. I just turned the hourglass over and hunkered on down some more. Now the heat was burning away my real impurities. Things I didn't even tell anyone about. Like the time after Bryce was born and had colic for six straight months, when in order to keep from throwing him out the window what I did was drink a couple bourbons before dinner and, when no one was looking, treat Forelock as my personal punching bag. He was just a puppy then, eight or nine months. He'd always done *something*. A grown man, beating on my own dog, making him whimper so Johanna'd call out, "Hey! What are you doing?" and I'd shout back, "He's just faking! He's a big faker!" Or the times, more recent, when Johanna was flying to Chicago or Phoenix and I'd think, What if her plane goes down? Did other people feel these things, or was it just me? Was I evil? Did Damien know he was evil in *The Omen* and *Omen II*? Did he think "Ave Satani" was just a catchy soundtrack? "Hey, they're playing my song!"

My introspecting must have paid off, because I started noticing patterns. As a for instance, Johanna might come into my office to hand me the cap of the toothpaste I'd forgotten to screw back on, and, later, that would cause me to say *"Achtung!"* when Johanna asked me to take out the recycling, which would get Johanna madder than a wet hen, and before you know it we're fighting World War III.

In therapy, when Dr. Van der Jagt called on me to speak,

I'd say, "On a positive note this week, I'm becoming more aware of our demon dialogues. I realize that's our real enemy. Not each other. Our demon dialogues. It feels good to know that Johanna and I can unite against those patterns, now that we're more cognizant."

But it was easier said than done.

One weekend we had dinner with this couple. The gal, Terri, worked with Johanna over at Hyundai. The husband, name of Burton, was from out east.

Though you wouldn't know it to look at me, I was born with a shy temperament. To relax in a social context, I like to throw back a few margaritas. I was feeling OK when the gal, Terri, put her elbows on the table and leaned toward my wife, gearing up for some girl talk.

"So how did you guys meet?" Terri said.

I was involved with Burton in a conversation about his wheat allergy.

"It was supposed to be a green-card marriage," Johanna said.

"At first," I said, butting in.

Johanna kept looking at Terri. "I was working at the radio station. My visa was running out. I knew Charlie a little. I thought he was a really nice guy. So, *ja*, we got married, I got a green card, and, you know, *ja, ja*."

"That makes sense," Burton said, looking from one of us to the other, and nodding, like he'd figured out a riddle.

"What do you mean by that?" I asked.

"Charlie, be nice," Johanna said.

"I am being nice," I said. "Do you think I'm not being nice, Burton?"

"I just meant your different nationalities. Had to be a story behind that."

The next week at couples counseling was the first time I started the conversation.

"My issue is," I said. "Hey, I've got an issue. Whenever people ask how we met, Johanna always says she married me for a green card. Like our marriage was just a piece of theater."

"I do not," Johanna said.

"You sure as shooting do."

"Well, it's true, isn't it?"

"What I'm hearing from Charlie," Dr. Van der Jagt said, "is that when you do that, even though you might feel that you are stating the facts, what it feels like, for Charlie, is that you are belittling your bond."

"What am I supposed to say?" Johanna said. "Make up a story to say how we met?"

According to *Hold Me Tight*, what happened when Johanna told Terri about the green card was that my attachment bond was threatened. I felt like Johanna was pulling away, so that made me want to seek her out, by trying to have sex when we got home. Due to the fact that I hadn't been all that nice to Johanna during our night out (due to I was mad about the green-card thing), she wasn't exactly in the mood. I'd also had more than my fill of the friendly creature. In other words, it was a surly, drunken, secretly needy, and frightened life-mate who made the move across the memory foam. The memory foam being a point of contention in itself, because Johanna loves that mattress, while I'm convinced it's responsible for my lower lumbar pain.

That was our pattern: Johanna fleeing, me bloodhounding her trail.

I was working hard on all this stuff, reading and thinking. After about three months of counseling, things started getting rosier around La Casa D. For one thing, Johanna got that promotion I mentioned, from local rep to regional. We made it a priority to have some together time together. I agreed to go easier on the sauce.

Around about this same time, Cheyenne, the little gal who babysat for us, showed up one night smelling like a pigpen. Turned out her father had kicked her out. She'd moved in with her brother, but there were too many drugs there, so she left. Every guy who offered her a place to stay only wanted one thing, so finally Cheyenne ended up sleeping in her Chevy. At that point Johanna, who's a soft touch and throws her vote away on the Green Party, offered Cheyenne a room. What with Johanna traveling more, we needed extra help with the kids, anyway.

Every time Johanna came back from a trip, the two of them were like best friends, laughing and carrying on. Then Johanna'd leave and I'd find myself staring out the window while Cheyenne suntanned by the pool. I could count her every rib.

Plus, she liked the fire pit. Came down most every night.

"Care to meet my friend, Mr. George Dickel?" I said.

Cheyenne gave me a look like she could read my mind. "I ain't legal, you know," she said. "Drinking age."

"You're old enough to vote, ain't you? You're old enough to join the armed forces and defend your country."

I poured her a glass.

Seemed like she'd had some before.

All those nights out by the fire with Cheyenne made me forget that I was me, Charlie D., covered with sunspots and the marks of a long life, and Cheyenne was Cheyenne, not much older than the girl John Wayne goes searching for in *The Searchers*.

I started texting her from work. Next thing I know I'm taking her shopping, buying her a shirt with a skull on it, or a fistful of thongs from Victoria's Secret, or a new Android phone.

"I ain't sure I should be accepting all this stuff from you," Cheyenne said.

"Hey, it's the least I can do. You're helping me and Johanna out. It's part of the job. Fair payment."

I was half daddy, half sweetheart. At night by the fire we talked about our childhoods, mine unhappy long ago, hers unhappy in the present.

Johanna was gone half of each week. She came back hotel-pampered, expecting room service and the toilet paper folded in a V. Then she was gone again.

One night I was watching *Monday Night*. A Captain Morgan commercial came on—I get a kick out of those—put me in mind of having me a Captain Morgan and Coke, so I fixed myself one. Cheyenne wandered in.

"What you watching?" she asked.

"Football. Want a drink? Spiced rum."

"No, thanks."

"You know those thongs I bought you the other day? How they fit?"

"Real good."

"You could be a Victoria's Secret model, I swear, Cheyenne."

"I could not!" She laughed, liking the idea.

"Why don't you model one of them thongs for me. I'll be the judge."

Cheyenne turned toward me. All the kids were asleep. Fans were shouting on the TV. Staring straight into my eyes, Cheyenne undid the clasp of her cutoffs and let them fall to the floor.

I got down on my knees, prayerful-like. I mashed my face against Cheyenne's hard little stomach, trying to breathe her in. I moved it lower.

In the middle of it all, Cheyenne lifted her leg, Captain Morgan style, and we busted up.

Terrible, I know. Shameful. Pretty easy to find the bad guy here.

Twice, maybe three times. OK, more like seven. But then one morning Cheyenne opens her bloodshot teenage eyes and says, "You know, you could be my granddaddy."

Next she calls me at work, completely hysterical. I pick her up, we go down to the CVS for a home pregnancy test. She's so beside herself she can't even wait to get back home to use it. Makes me pull over, then goes down into this gulch and squats, comes back with mascara running down her cheeks.

"I can't have a baby! I'm only nineteen!"

"Well, Cheyenne, let's think a minute," I said.

"You gonna raise this baby, Charlie D.? You gonna support me and this baby? You're old. Your *sperm* are old. Baby might come out autistic."

"Where did you read that?"

"Saw it on the news."

She didn't need to think long. I'm anti-abortion but, under the circumstances, decided it was her choice. Cheyenne told me she'd handle the whole thing. Made the appointment herself. Said I didn't even need to go with her. All she needed was $3,000.

Yeah, sounded high to me, too.

Week later, I'm on my way to couples therapy with Johanna. We're coming up Dr. Van der Jagt's front path when my phone vibrates in my pocket. I open the door for Johanna and say, "After you, darlin'."

The message was from Cheyenne: "It's over. Have a nice life."

Never *was* pregnant. That's when I realized. I didn't care either way. She was gone. I was safe. Dodged another bullet.

And then what did I go and do? I walked into Dr. Van der Jagt's office and sat down on the couch and looked over at

Johanna. My wife. Not as young as she used to be, sure. But older and more worn out because of me, mainly. Because of raising my kids and doing my laundry and cooking my meals, all the while holding down a full-time job. Seeing how sad and tuckered out Johanna looked, I felt all choked up. And as soon as Dr. Van der Jagt asked me what I had to say, the whole story came rushing out of me.

I had to confess my crime. Felt like I'd explode if I didn't.

Which means something. Which means, when you get down to it, that the truth is true. The truth will out.

Up until that moment, I wasn't so sure.

When our fifty minutes was up, Dr. Van der Jagt directed us to the back door. As usual, I couldn't help keeping an eye out for anyone who might see us.

But what were we skulking around for, anyway? What were we ashamed of? We were just two people in love and in trouble, going to our Nissan to pick up our kids from school. Over in the Alps, when they found that prehistoric man frozen in the tundra and dug him out, the guy they call Ötzi, they saw that aside from wearing leather shoes filled with grass and a bearskin hat he was carrying a little wooden box that contained an ember. That's what Johanna and I were doing, going to marital therapy. We were living through an Ice Age, armed with bows and arrows. We had wounds from previous skirmishes. All we had if we got sick were some medicinal herbs. There was a flint arrowhead lodged in my left shoulder, which slowed me down some. But we had this ember box with us, and if we could just get it somewhere—I don't know, a cave, or a stand of pines—we could use this ember to reignite the fire of our love. A lot of the time, while I was sitting there stony-faced on Dr. Van der Jagt's couch, I was thinking about Ötzi, all alone out there, when he was killed. Murdered, apparently. They found a fracture in his skull. You have to realize that things aren't so bad nowadays as you might think. Human violence is way down since prehistoric times, statistically. If we'd lived when Ötzi did, we'd have to watch our backs anytime we took a saunter. Under those conditions, who would I want at my side more than Johanna, with her broad shoulders and strong legs and used-to-be-fruitful womb? She's been carrying our ember the whole time, for years now, despite all my attempts to blow it out.

At the car, wouldn't you know it, my key fob chose right then not to work. I kept pressing and pressing. Johanna stood on the gravel, looking small, for her, and crying, "I hate you! I hate you!" I watched my wife crying from what felt like a long way off. This was the same woman who, when we were trying to have Lucas, called me on the phone and said, like Tom Cruise in *Top Gun*, "I feel the need for seed!" I'd rush home from work, stripping off my vest and string tie as I hurried into the bedroom, sometimes leaving my cowboy boots on (though that didn't feel right, and I tried not to), and there would be Johanna, lying on her back with her legs and arms spread out in welcome, her cheeks fiery red, and I leapt and fell, and kept falling, it felt like, forever, down into her, both of us lost in the sweet, solemn business of making a baby.

So that's why I'm out here in the bushes. Johanna kicked me out. I'm living downtown now, near the theater district, renting a two-bedroom in the overpriced condos they built before the crash and now can't fill.

I'd wager I'm about sixty feet away from the house now. Maybe fifty-nine. Think I'll get closer.

Fifty-eight.

Fifty-seven.

How do you like that, Lawman?

I'm standing next to one of the floodlights when I remember that restraining orders aren't calculated in feet. They're in *yards*. I'm supposed to be staying fifty yards away!

Tarnation.

But I don't move. Here's why. If I'm supposed to be fifty yards away, that means I've been violating the restraining order for weeks.

I'm guilty already.

So, might as well get a little closer.

Up onto the front porch, for instance.

Just like I thought: front door's open. God damn it, Johanna! I think. Just leave the house wide open for any home invader to waltz right in, why don't you?

For a minute, it feels like old times. I'm angrier than a hornet, and I'm standing in my own house. A sweet urge of self-justification fills me. I know who the bad guy is here. It's Johanna. I'm just itching to go and find her and shout, "You left the front door open! *Again*." But I can't right now, because, technically, I'm breaking and entering.

Then the smell hits me. It's not the De Rougemonts. It's partly dinner—lamb chops, plus cooking wine. Nice. Partly, too, a shampoo smell from Meg's having just showered upstairs. Moist, warm, perfumey air is filtering down the staircase. I can feel it on my cheeks. I can also smell Forelock, who's too old to even come and greet his master, which under the circumstances is OK by me. It's all these smells at once, which means that it's our smell. The D.s! We've finally lived here long enough to displace the old-person smell of the De Rougemonts. I just didn't realize it before. I had to get kicked out of my own house to be able to come and smell this smell, which I don't think, even if I were a little kid with super-smelling abilities, would be anything other than pleasant.

Upstairs Meg runs out of her bedroom. "Lucas!" she shouts. "What did you do with my charger!"

"I didn't do anything," he says back. (He's up in his bedroom.)

"You took it!"

"I did not!"

"Yes, you did!"

"Mom!" Meg yells, and comes to the top of the stairs, where she sees me. Or maybe doesn't. She needs to wear her glasses. She stares down to where I'm standing in the shadows and she shouts, "Mom! Tell Lucas to give me back my charger!"

I hear something, and turn. And there's Johanna. When she sees me, she does a funny thing. She jumps back. Her face goes white and she says, "Guys! Stay upstairs!"

Hey, come on, I'm thinking. It's just me.

Johanna presses the speed dial on her phone, still backing away.

"You don't have to do that," I say. "Come on now, Jo-Jo."

She gets on with 911. I take a step toward her with my hand out. I'm not going to grab the phone. I just want her to hang up and I'll leave. But suddenly I'm holding the phone, Johanna's screaming, and, out of nowhere, something jumps me from behind, tackling me to the ground.

It's Bryce. My son.

He isn't at trumpet lessons. Maybe he quit. I'm always the last to know.

Bryce has got a rope in his hand, or an extension cord, and he's strong as a bull. He always did take after Johanna's side.

He's pressing his knee hard into my back, trying to hog-tie me with the extension cord.

"Got him, Mom!" he shouts.

I'm trying to talk. But my son has my face smashed down into the rug. "Hey, Bryce, lemme go," I say. "It's Pa. It's Pa down here. Bryce? I'm not kidding now."

I try an old Michigan wrestling move, scissor kick. Works like a charm. I flip Bryce off me, onto his back. He tries to scramble away but I'm too fast for him.

"Hey, now," I say. "Who's your daddy now, Bryce? Huh? Who's your daddy?"

That's when I notice Meg, higher on the stairs. She's been frozen there the whole time. But when I look at her now she hightails it. Scared of me.

Seeing that takes all the fight out of me. *Meg? Sugar pie? Daddy won't hurt you.*

But she's gone.

"OK," I say. "Ah'mo leave now."

I turn and go outside. Look up at the sky. No stars. I put my hands in the air and wait.

After bringing me to headquarters, the officer removed my handcuffs and turned me over to the sheriff, who made me empty my pockets: wallet, cell phone, loose change, 5-Hour Energy bottle, and an Ashley Madison ad torn from some magazine. He had me put all that stuff in a ziplock and sign a form vouching for the contents.

It was too late to call my lawyer's office, so I called Peekskill's cell and left a message on his voice mail. I asked if that counted as a call. It did.

They took me down the hall to an interrogation room. After about a half hour, a guy I haven't seen before, detective, comes in and sits down.

"How much you had tonight?" he asks me.

"A few."

"Bartender at Le Grange said you came in around noon and stayed through happy hour."

"Yessir. Not gonna lie to you."

The detective pushes himself back in his chair.

"We get guys like you in here all the time," he says. "Hey, I know how you feel. I'm divorced, too. Twice. You think I don't want to stick it to my old lady sometimes? But you know what? She's the mother of my children. That sound corny to you? Not to me it doesn't. You have to make sure she's happy, whether you like it or not. Because your kids are going to be living with her and they're the ones that'll pay the price."

"They're my kids, too," I say. My voice sounds funny.

"I hear you."

With that, he goes out. I look around the room, making sure there isn't a two-way mirror, like on *Law & Order,* and when I'm satisfied I just hang my head and cry. When I was a kid, I used to imagine getting arrested and how cool I'd act. They wouldn't get nothing out of me. A real outlaw. Well, now I *am* arrested, and all I am is a guy with gray stubble on my cheeks, and my nose still bleeding a little from when Bryce mashed it against the rug.

There's a thing they've figured out about love. Scientifically. They've done studies to find out what keeps couples together. Do you know what it is? It isn't getting along. Isn't having money, or children, or a similar outlook on life. It's just checking in with each other. Doing little kindnesses for each other. At breakfast, you pass the jam. Or, on a trip to New York City, you hold hands for a second in a subway elevator. You ask "How was your day?" and pretend to care. Stuff like that really works.

Sounds pretty easy, right? Except most people can't keep it up. In addition to finding the bad guy in every argument, couples do this thing called the Protest Polka. That's a dance where one partner seeks reassurance about the relationship and approaches the other, but because that person usually does this by complaining or being angry, the other partner wants to get the hell away, and so retreats. For most people, this complicated maneuver is easier than asking, "How are your sinuses today, dear? Still stuffed? I'm sorry. Let me get you your saline."

While I'm thinking all this, the detective comes in again and says, "OK. Vamoose."

He means I'm getting out. No argument from me. I follow him down the hall to the front of headquarters. I expect to see Peekskill, which I do. He's shooting the breeze with the desk sergeant, using cheerful profanities. No one can say "you motherfucker" with more joie de vivre than Counselor Peekskill. None of this surprises me at all. What surprises me is that standing a few feet behind Peekskill is my wife.

"Johanna's declining to press charges," Peekskill tells me, when he comes over. "Legally, that doesn't mean shit because the restraining order's enforced by the state. But the police don't want to charge you with anything if the wife's not going to be behind it. I gotta tell you, though, this isn't going to help you before the judge. We may not be able to get this thing revoked."

"Never?" I say. "I'm within fifty yards of her right now."

"True, but you're in a police station."

"Can I talk to her?"

"You want to talk to her? I don't advise that right now."

But I'm already crossing the precinct lobby.

Johanna is standing by the door, her head down.

I'm not sure when I'm going to see her again, so I look at her real hard.

I look at her but feel nothing.

I can't even tell if she's pretty anymore.

Probably she is. At social functions, other people, men, anyway, are always saying, "You look familiar. You didn't used to be a Dallas cheerleader, did you?"

I look. Keep looking. Finally, Johanna meets my eye.

"I want to be a family again," I say.

Her expression is hard to read. But the feeling I get is that Johanna's young face is lying under her new, older face, and that the older face is like a mask. I want her younger face to come out not only because it was the face I fell in love with but because it was the face that loved me back. I remember how it crinkled up whenever I came into a room.

No crinkling now. More like a Halloween pumpkin, with the candle gone out.

And then she tells me what's what. "I tried for a long time, Charlie. To make you happy. I thought if I made more money it would make you happy. Or if we got a bigger house. Or if I just left you alone so you could drink all the time. But none of these things made you happy, Charlie. And they didn't make me happy, either. Now that you've moved out, I'm sad. I am crying every night. But, as I now know the truth, I can begin to deal with it."

"This isn't the only truth there is," I say. It sounds more vague than I want it to, so I spread my arms wide—like I'm hugging the whole world—but this only ends up seeming even vaguer.

I try again. "I don't want to be the person I've been," I say. "I want to change." This is meant sincerely. But, like most sincerities, it's a little threadbare. Also, because I'm out of practice being sincere, I still feel like I'm lying.

Not very convincing.

"It's late," Johanna says. "I'm tired. I'm going home."

"Our home," I say. But she's halfway to her car already.

•

I don't know where I'm walking. Just wandering. I don't much want to go back to my apartment.

After me and Johanna bought our house, we went over to meet the owners, and you know what the old guy did to me? We were walking out to see the mechanical room—he wanted to explain about servicing the boiler—and he was walking real slow. Then right quick he turned around and looked at me with his old bald head, and he said, "Just you wait."

His spine was all catty-whompered. He could only shuffle along. So, in order to stave off the embarrassment of being closer to death than me, he hit me with that grim reminder that I'd end up just like him someday, shuffling around this house like an invalid.

Thinking of Mr. De Rougement, I all of a sudden figure out what my problem is. Why I've been acting so crazy.

It's death. *He's* the bad guy.

Hey, Johanna. I found him! It's death.

I keep on walking, thinking about that. Lose track of time.

When I finally look up, I'll be god-darned if I ain't in front of my house again! On the other side of the street, in legal territory, but still. My feet led me here out of habit, like an old plug horse.

I take out my phone again. Maybe Meg played a word while I was in jail.

No such luck.

When a new word comes on Words with Friends, it's a beautiful sight to see. The letters appear out of nowhere, like a sprinkle of stardust. I could be anywhere, doing anything, but when Meg's next word flies through the night to skip and dance across my phone, I'll know she's thinking of me, even if she's trying to beat me.

When Johanna and I first went to bed, I was a little in-timidated. I'm not a small man, but on top of Johanna? Sort of a *Gulliver's Travels*–type situation. It was like Johanna had fallen asleep and I'd climbed up there to survey the scene. Beautiful view! Rolling hills! Fertile cropland! But there was only one of me, not a whole town of Lilliputians throwing ropes and nailing her down.

But it was strange. That first night with Johanna, and more and more every night after, it was like she shrank in bed, or I grew, until we were the same size. And little by little that equalizing carried on into the daylight. We still turned heads. But it seemed as though people were just looking at us, a single creature, not two misfits yoked at the waist. *Us.* Together. Back then, we weren't fleeing or chasing each other. We were just seeking, and every time one of us went looking, there the other was, waiting to be found.

We found each other for so long before we lost each other. *Here I am!* we'd say, in our heart of hearts. *Come find me.* Easy as putting a blush on a rainbow.

2013

THE ORACULAR VULVA

Skulls make better pillows than you'd think. Dr. Peter Luce (the famous sexologist) rests his cheek on the varnished parietal of a Dawat ancestor, he's not sure whose. The skull tips back and forth, jawbone to chin, as Luce himself is gently rocked by the boy on the next skull over, rubbing his feet against Luce's back. The pandanus mat feels scratchy against his bare legs.

It's the middle of the night, the time when, for some reason, all the yammering jungle creatures shut up for a minute. Luce's specialty isn't zoology. He's paid scant attention to the local fauna since coming here. He hasn't told anybody on the team, but he's phobic about snakes and so hasn't wandered too far from the village. When the others go off to hunt boar or chop sago, Luce stays in to brood on his situation. (Specifically, his ruined career, but there are other complaints.) Only one brave, drunken night, going to pee, did he venture away from the longhouses to stand in the dense vegetation for roughly thirty-five seconds before getting creeped out and hurrying back. He doesn't know what goes on in the jungle and he doesn't care. All he knows is that every night at sundown the monkeys and birds start screaming and then, about 1 p.m. New York time—to which his luminous

wristwatch is still faithfully set—they stop. It gets perfectly
quiet. So quiet that Luce wakes up. Or sort of wakes up. His
eyes are open now, at least he thinks they are. Not that it makes
any difference. This is the jungle during the new moon. The
darkness is total. Luce holds his hands in front of his face,
palm to nose, unable to see it. He shifts his cheek on the skull,
causing the boy to stop rubbing momentarily and let out a
soft, submissive cry.

Wetly, like a vapor—he's definitely awake now—the jungle invades his nostrils. He's never smelled anything like it
before. It's like mud and feces mixed with armpit and worm,
though that doesn't quite cover it. There's also the scent of
wild pig, the cheesy whiff of six-foot orchids, and the corpse
breath of carnivorous flytraps. All around the village, from the
swampy ground up to the tops of trees, animals are eating
each other and digesting with open, burping mouths.

Evolution has no consistent game plan. While famous for
remaining true to certain elegant forms (Dr. Luce likes to
point out, for instance, the structural similarity between
mussels and the female genitalia), it can also, on a whim, im-
provise. That's what evolution is: a scattershot of possibilities,
proceeding not by successive improvements but just by
changes, some good, some bad, none thought out beforehand.
The marketplace—that is, the world—decides. So that here,
on the Casuarina Coast, the flowers have evolved traits that
Luce, a Connecticut boy, doesn't associate with flowers,
though botany isn't his specialty either. He thought flowers
were supposed to smell *nice*. To attract bees. Here it's something different. The few lurid blooms he's unwisely stuck his
snout into have smelled pretty much like death. There's always a little pool of rainwater inside the cup (actually diges-
tive acid) and a winged beetle being eaten away. Luce'll snap
his head back, holding his nose, and then, in the bushes somewhere, he'll hear a few Dawat laughing their heads off.

These ruminations are interrupted by the puling of the boy on the next skull over. *"Cemen,"* the boy cries out. *"Ake cemen."* There's silence, a few Dawat muttering to themselves in dreams, and then, just like every night, Luce feels the kid's hand come snaking into his shorts. He grabs it gently by the wrist, fishing for his penlight with his other hand. He switches it on and the pale beam illuminates the boy's face. He's resting his cheek on a skull, too (his grandfather's, to be precise), which is stained a dark orange from years of hair and skin oil. Beneath his kinky hair the boy's eyes are wide, frightened by the light. He looks a little like a young Jimi Hendrix. His nose is wide and flat, his cheekbones prominent. His full lips have a permanent pout from speaking the explosive Dawat language. *"Ake cemen,"* he goes again, which is maybe a word. His trapped hand makes another lunge for Luce's midsection, but Luce redoubles his grip.

So, then, the other complaints: Having to do fieldwork at his age, for one thing. Getting mail yesterday for the first time in eight weeks, ripping open the soggy packet with excitement only to find, right on the cover of *The New England Journal of Medicine*, Pappas-Kikuchi's spurious study. And, more immediately, the kid.

"Come on now," Luce says. "Go back to sleep."

"Cemen. Ake cemen!"

"Thanks for the hospitality, but no thanks."

The kid turns and looks into the darkness of the hut, and when he turns back the penlight beam shows tears welling in his eyes. He's scared. He tugs at Luce, bowing his head and pleading. "You ever hear of a thing called professional ethics, kid?" Luce says. The boy stops, looking at him, trying to understand, then starts tugging again.

The kid's been after him for three straight weeks. It's not that he's in love or anything. Among the many rare characteristics of the Dawat—not the precise biological oddity that has brought Luce and his team to Irian Jaya but a related anthropological one—is that the tribe maintains strict segregation between the sexes. The village is laid out in a dumbbell shape, thinning in the middle with a longhouse at either end. The men and boys sleep in one longhouse; the women and girls in the other. Dawat males consider contact with females highly polluting, and so have organized social structures to limit exposure as much as possible. Dawat men, for instance, go into the women's longhouse only for the purpose of procreation. They do what they have to do quickly and then leave. According to Randy, the anthropologist who speaks Dawat, the Dawat word for "vagina" translates literally as "that thing which is truly no good." This, of course, incensed Sally Ward, the endocrinologist who came along to analyze plasma hormone levels, and who has little tolerance for so-called cultural differences and out of sheer disgust and justified anger has been denigrating the field of anthropology to Randy's face whenever she gets the chance. Which isn't often because, by tribal law, she has to stay down at the other end of the village. What it's like over there, Luce has no idea. The Dawat have erected an earthwork between the two areas, a mud wall about five feet high with spears jutting up. Impaled on the spears are oblong green gourds that at first looked refreshingly festive to Luce, like Venetian lanterns, until Randy explained that the gourds are only stand-ins for the human heads of yesteryear. At any rate, you can't see much over the earthwork, and there's only a little pathway where the women leave food for the men and through which the men go, once a month, to mount their wives for three and a half minutes.

As papal as the Dawat appear to be in reserving sex for procreation, they are a hard sell for the local missionaries. They're not exactly celibate in the Longhouse of Men. Dawat boys live with their mothers until they're seven years old, at which point they come to live with the men. For the next eight years the boys are coerced into fellating their elders. With the denigration of the vagina in Dawat belief comes the exaltation of the male sexual parts, and especially of semen, which is held to be an elixir of stunning nutritive power. In order to become men, to become warriors, boys must ingest as much semen as possible, and this, nightly, daily, hourly, they do. Their first night in the longhouse, Luce and his assistant, Mort, were taken aback, to say the least, when they saw the sweet little boys going dutifully from man to man as if bobbing for apples. Randy just sat taking notes. After all the men had been satisfied, one of the chieftains, in what no doubt was a show of hospitality, barked something at two boys, who then came over to the American scientists. "That's OK," Mort had said to his kid. "I'm good." Even Luce felt himself breaking out into a sweat. Around the hut, the boys went about their business either cheerfully or with mild resignation, like kids back home doing chores. It impressed upon Luce once again the fact that sexual shame was a social construct, completely relative to culture. Still, *his* culture was American, specifically Anglo-Irish lapsed Episcopalian, and he refused the Dawat offer graciously, that night and, now, this.

The irony, however, wasn't lost on him that he, Dr. Peter Luce, director of the Sexual Disorders and Gender Identity Clinic, past general secretary of the Society for the Scientific Study of Sex (SSSS), champion of the open investigation of human sexual behavior, opponent of prudishness, scourge of inhibition, and crusader for physical delights of all kinds, should find himself, halfway around the world in the erotic jungle, feeling so uptight. In his annual address to the society in 1969, Dr. Luce had reminded the assembled sexologists of the historical conflict between scientific research and common morality. Look at Vesalius, he said. Look at Galileo. Always practical, Luce had advised his listeners to travel to

foreign countries where so-called aberrant sexual practices
were tolerated and consequently easier to study (sodomy in
Holland, for instance, and prostitution in Phuket). He prided
himself on his open mind. To him, human sexuality was
like a great big Bruegel painting and he loved watching all
the action. Luce tried not to make value judgments about the
sundry clinically documented paraphilias, and only when they
were patently injurious (as with pedophilia and rape) did he
object. This tolerance went even further when dealing with
another culture. The blow jobs being performed in the Longhouse of Men might upset Luce if they were happening at
the YMCA on West Twenty-third Street, but here he feels he
has no right to condemn. It doesn't help his work. He isn't
here as a missionary. Given the local mores, these boys aren't
likely to be warped by their oral duties. They aren't growing
up to be typical heterosexual husbands, anyway. They just
move from being givers to being receivers, and everyone's
happy.

But then why does Luce get so upset every time the kid
starts rubbing his feet against his back and making his little
mating calls? It might have something to do with the increas-
ingly anxious sound of the calls themselves, not to mention
the kid's worried expression. It may be that if the kid doesn't
pleasure the foreign guests he's in for some kind of punish-
ment. Luce can't explain the kid's fervor any other way. Is
white semen believed to possess special power? Unlikely,
given the way Luce, Randy, and Mort look these days. They
look like hell: greasy-haired, dandruffy. The Dawat probably
think that all white men are covered with heat rashes. Luce
longs for a shower. He longs to put on his cashmere turtle-
neck, his ankle boots, and his suede blazer and go out for a
whiskey sour. After this trip, the most exotic he wants to get
is dinner at Trader Vic's. And if all goes well, that's how it's

going to be. Him and a mai tai with a parasol in it, back in Manhattan.

Up until three years ago—until the night Pappas-Kikuchi blindsided him with her fieldwork—Dr. Peter Luce was considered the world's leading authority on human intersexuality. He was the author of a major sexological work, *The Oracular Vulva*, which was standard reading in a variety of disciplines ranging from genetics and pediatrics to psychology. He had written a column of the same name for *Playboy* from August 1969 to December 1973, in which the conceit was that a personified and all-knowing female pudendum answered the queries of male readers with witty and sometimes sibylline responses. Hugh Hefner had come across Peter Luce's name in the newspaper in an article about a demonstration for sexual freedom. Six Columbia students had staged an orgy in a tent on the main green, which the cops broke up, and when he was asked what he thought about such activity on campus, Assistant Professor Peter Luce, thirty-four, had been quoted as saying, "I'm in favor of orgies wherever they happen." That caught Hef's eye. Not wanting to replicate Xaviera Hollander's "Call Me Madam" column in *Penthouse*, Hefner saw Luce's column as being devoted to the scientific and historic side of sex. Thus, in her first three issues, the Oracular Vulva delivered disquisitions on the erotic art of the Japanese painter Hiroshi Yamamoto, the epidemiology of syphilis, and the custom of the berdache among the Navajo, all in the ghostly, rambling style that Luce modeled on his aunt Rose Pepperdine, who used to lecture him on the Bible while soaking her feet in the kitchen. The column proved popular, though intelligent queries were always hard to come by, the readership being more interested in the

"Playboy Advisor"'s cunnilingus tips or remedies for premature ejaculation. Finally, Hefner told Luce to screw it and write his own questions, which he did.

Peter Luce had appeared on *Phil Donahue* in 1987, along with two intersex persons and a transsexual, to discuss both the medical and psychological aspects of these conditions. On that program Phil Donahue said, "Ann Parker was born and raised a girl. You won the Miss Miami Beach Contest in 1968 in good old Dade County, Florida? Boy, wait till they hear this. You lived as a woman to the age of twenty-nine and then you switched to living as a man. He has the anatomical characteristics of both a man and a woman. If I'm lyin', I'm dyin'."

He also said, "Here's what's not so funny. These live, irreplaceable sons and daughters of God, human beings all, want you to know, among other things, that that's exactly what they are, human beings."

Luce's interest in intersexuality had begun nearly thirty years ago, when he was still a resident at Mount Sinai. A sixteen-year-old girl had come in to be examined. Her name was Felicity Kennington, and his first glimpse of her had inspired some unprofessional thoughts. She was very good-looking, Felicity Kennington, slender and bookish, with glasses, which always killed him.

Luce examined her with a grave face and concluded, "You've got lentigines."

"What?" the girl asked, alarmed.

"Freckles." He smiled. Felicity Kennington smiled back. Luce remembered that his brother asked him one night, with a lot of suggestive eyebrow movement, if he didn't sometimes get turned on examining women, and that he'd responded with the old line about how you're so caught up in your work that you don't even notice. He had no trouble noticing Felicity Kennington, her pretty face, her pink gums and child-size teeth, her shy white legs that she kept crossing and uncrossing as she sat on the examining table. The thing he didn't notice was her mother, sitting in the corner of the room.

"Lissie," the woman broke in, "tell the doctor about the pain you've been having."

Felicity blushed, looking down at the floor. "It's in my—it's just below my stomach."

"What kind of pain?"

"There's kinds?"

"A sharp pain or dull?"

"Sharp."

At that point in his career, Luce had given a total of eight pelvic exams. The one he gave to Felicity Kennington still ranks as one of the most difficult. First, there was the problem of his terrible attraction. He was only twenty-five himself. He was nervous; his heart throbbed. He dropped the speculum and had to go out for another. The way Felicity Kennington turned her face away and bit her lower lip before parting her knees made him literally dizzy. Second, the mother's watching him the whole time didn't make it any easier. He'd suggested that she wait outside, but Mrs. Kennington had replied, "I'll stay here with Lissie, thank you." Third, and worst of all, was the pain he seemed to cause Felicity Kennington with everything he did. The speculum wasn't even halfway in before she cried out. Her knees vised, and he had to give up. Next, he tried merely to palpate her genitals but as soon as he pressed she shrieked again. Finally, he had to get Dr. Budekind, a gynecologist, to complete the examination while he looked on, his stomach in knots. The gynecologist looked at Felicity for no more than fifteen seconds, then took Luce across the hall.

"What's the matter with her?"

"Undescended testes."

"What!"

"Looks like andrenogenital syndrome. Ever seen one before?"

"No."

"That's what you're here to do, right? Learn."

"That girl has testes?"

"We'll know in a little while."

The tissue mass up inside Felicity Kennington's inguinal canal turned out to be, when they put a sample under the microscope, testicular. At that time—this was in 1961—such a fact designated Felicity Kennington as male. Since the nineteenth century, medicine had been using the same primitive diagnostic criterion of sex formulated by Edwin Klebs way back in 1876. Klebs had maintained that a person's gonads determined sex. In cases of ambiguous gender, you looked at the gonadal tissue under the microscope. If it was testicular, the person was male; if ovarian, female. But there were problems inherent in this method. And these became clear to Luce when he saw what happened to Felicity Kennington in 1961. Even though she looked like a girl and thought of herself as a girl, because she possessed male gonads Budekind declared her to be a boy. The parents objected. Other doctors were consulted—endocrinologists, urologists, geneticists—but they couldn't agree, either. Meanwhile, as the medical community vacillated, Felicity began to go through puberty. Her voice deepened. She grew sparse tufts of light brown facial hair. She stopped going to school and soon stopped leaving the house altogether. Luce saw her one last time, when she came in for another consultation. She wore a long dress and a scarf that tied under her chin, covering most of her face. In one nail-bitten hand she carried a copy of *Jane Eyre*. Luce bumped into her at the drinking fountain. "Water tastes like rust," she said, looking up at him with no

recognition and hurrying away. A week later, with her father's
.45 automatic, she killed herself.

"Proves she was a boy," Budekind said in the cafeteria
the next day.

"What do you mean?" said Luce.

"Boys kill themselves with guns. Statistically. Girls use less
violent methods. Sleeping pills, carbon monoxide poisoning."

Luce never spoke to Budekind again. His meeting with
Felicity Kennington was a watershed moment. From then
on, he dedicated himself to making sure that something like
that never happened to anyone again. He threw himself
into the study of intersex conditions. He read everything
available on the subject, which wasn't much. And the more
he studied and the more he read, the more he became convinced that the sacred categories of male and female were, in
fact, shams. With certain genetic and hormonal conditions,
it was just plain impossible to say what sex some babies were.
But humans had historically resisted the obvious conclusion.
Confronted with a baby of uncertain sex, the Spartans would
leave the infant on a rocky hillside and walk quickly away.
Luce's own forebears, the English, didn't even like to mention the subject and might never have done so, had the nui-
sance of enigmatic genitalia not thrown a wrench into the
smooth workings of inheritance law. Lord Coke, the great
English jurist of the seventeenth century, tried to clear up
the matter of who'd get the landed estate by declaring that a
person should "be either male or female, and it shall succeed
according to the kind of sex which doth prevail." Of course,
he didn't specify a method for determining which sex *did*
prevail. It took the German Klebs to come along and begin
the task. Then, a hundred years later, Peter Luce finished it.

In 1965, Luce published an article called "Many Roads
Lead to Rome: Sexual Concepts of Human Hermaphroditism." In twenty-five pages, Luce argued that gender is

determined by a variety of influences: chromosomal sex; gonadal sex; hormones; internal genital structures; external genitals; and, most important, the sex of rearing. Often a patient's gonadal sex didn't determine his or her gender identity. Gender was more like a native tongue. Children learned to speak Male or Female, the way they learned to speak English or French.

The article made a big splash. Luce could still remember how, in the weeks following its publication, people gave him a new quality of attention: women laughed at his jokes more, made it known they were available, even on a few occasions showed up at his apartment wearing not a hell of a lot; his phone rang more often; the people on the other end were people he didn't know but who knew him; they had offers and beguilements; they wanted him to review papers, serve on panels, appear at the San Luis Obispo Snail Festival to judge an escargot contest, most snails being, after all, diecious. Within months, pretty much everyone had given up Klebs's criterion for Luce's criteria.

On the strength of this success, Luce was given the opportunity to open a psychohormonal unit at Columbia-Presbyterian Hospital. In a decade of solid, original research, he made his second great discovery: that gender identity is established very early on in life, at about the age of two. After that, his reputation reached the stratosphere. The funding flowed in, from the Rockefeller Foundation, the Ford Foundation, and the NIH. It was a great time to be a sexologist. The Sexual Revolution had opened a brief window of opportunity for the enterprising sex researcher. It was a matter of national interest, for a few years there, to get to the bottom of the mystery of the female orgasm. Or to plumb the psychological reasons that certain men exhibited themselves on the street. In 1968, Dr. Luce opened the Sexual Disorders and Gender Identity Clinic, and it soon became the foremost facility in the world for the study and treatment of conditions of ambiguous gender. Luce treated everybody: the web-necked teens with Turner's syndrome; the leggy beauties with androgen insensitivity; the surly Klinefelter's cases, who, without exception, either broke the water cooler or tried to punch out a nurse. When a baby was born with ambiguous genitalia, Dr. Luce was called in to discuss the matter with the shocked parents. Luce got transsexuals, too. Everybody came to the clinic; at his disposal Luce had a body of research material—of living, breathing specimens—that no scientist had ever had before.

It was 1968, and the world was going up in flames. Luce held one of the torches. Two thousand years of sexual tyranny were ending in the blaze. Not one coed in his behavioral-cytogenetics lecture course wore a bra to class. Luce wrote op-ed pieces for the *Times* calling for the revision of the penal code regarding socially harmless and nonviolent sex offenders. He handed out pro-contraceptive pamphlets at coffeehouses in the Village. That was how it went in science. Every generation or so, insight, diligence, and the necessities of the moment came together to lift a scientist's work out of the academy and into the culture at large, where it gleamed, a beacon of the future.

From deep in the jungle, buzzing in, a mosquito skims past Luce's left ear. It's one of the jumbo models. He never sees them, only hears them, at night, screaming like airborne lawn mowers. He closes his eyes, wincing, and in another moment, sure enough, feels the insect land in the blood-fragrant skin below his elbow. It's so big it makes a noise landing, like a raindrop. Luce tilts his head back, squeezing his eyes shut, and says, "Aye-yah." He's dying to swat the bug but he can't; his hands are busy keeping the kid away from his belt. He can't

see a thing. On the ground next to his skull the penlight
sputters out its weak flame. Luce dropped it in the scuffle
that's still in progress. Now it lights up a ten-inch cone of
the mat. No help at all. Plus, the birds have started up again,
signaling the approach of morning. Luce is in an alert fetal
position, on his back, holding a twiglike ten-year-old Dawat
wrist in each hand. From the position of the wrist he esti-
mates that the kid's head is somewhere in the air over his
navel, lolling forward probably. He keeps making these
smacking sounds that are very depressing to listen to.

"Aye-yah."

The stinger's in. The mosquito thrusts, wiggles its hips
contentedly, then settles down and starts to drink. Luce has
had typhus vaccinations that felt more gentle. He can feel the
suction. He can feel the bug gaining weight.

A beacon of the future? Who's he kidding? Luce's work
casts no more light today, it turns out, than that penlight on
the floor. No more light than the new moon not shining
above the jungle's canopy.

There's no need for him to read Pappas-Kikuchi's article
in *The New England Journal of Medicine*. He heard it all before, in person. Three years ago, at the annual convention
of the SSSS, he had arrived late to the last day's talk.

"This afternoon," Pappas-Kikuchi was saying when he
came in, "I'd like to share the results of a study our team just
completed in southwestern Guatemala."

Luce sat in the back row, careful about his pants. He was
wearing a Pierre Cardin tuxedo. Later that night, the SSSS
was presenting him with a lifetime-achievement award. He
took a minibar bottle of J&B out of his satin-lined pocket
and sipped it discreetly. He was already celebrating.

"The village is called San Juan de la Cruz," Pappas-
Kikuchi continued. Luce scanned what he could of her behind the podium. She was attractive, in a schoolteacherly

way. Soft, dark eyes, bangs, no earrings or makeup, and glasses. In Luce's experience, it was exactly these modest, unsexual-seeming women who proved to be the most passionate in bed, whereas women who dressed provocatively were often unresponsive or passive, as if they had used up all their sexual energy in display.

"Male pseudohermaphrodites with five-alpha-reductase deficiency syndrome who were raised as females serve as exceptional test cases for studying the effects of testosterone and the sex of rearing in the establishment of gender identity," Pappas-Kikuchi continued, reading from her paper now. "In these cases, decreased production of dihydrotestosterone in utero causes the external genitalia of the affected male fetuses to be highly ambiguous in appearance. Consequently, at birth many affected newborns are considered to be female and are raised as girls. However, prenatal, neonatal, and pubertal exposure to testosterone remains normal."

Luce took another swig of the old J&B and threw his arm over the seat next to him. Nothing Pappas-Kikuchi was saying was news. Five-alpha-reductase deficiency had been extensively studied. Jason Whitby had done some fine work with 5αR pseudohermaphrodites in Pakistan.

"The scrotum of these newborns is unfused, so that it resembles the labia," Pappas-Kikuchi soldiered on, repeating what everyone already knew. "The phallus, or micropenis, resembles a clitoris. A urogenital sinus ends in a blind vaginal pouch. The testes most often reside in the abdomen or inguinal canal, though occasionally they are found hypertrophied in the bifid scrotum. Nevertheless, at puberty, definite virilization occurs, as plasma testosterone levels are normal."

How old was she? Thirty-two? Thirty-three? Would she be coming to the awards dinner? With her frumpy blouse and buttoned-up collar, Pappas-Kikuchi reminded Luce of a girlfriend he'd had back in college. A classics major who wore Byronic white shirts and unbecoming woolen knee socks. In bed, however, his little Hellenist had surprised him. Lying on her back, she'd put her legs over his shoulders, telling him that this was Hector and Andromache's favorite position.

Luce was remembering the moment ("I'm Hector!" he'd shouted out, tucking Andromache's ankles behind his ears) when Dr. Fabienne Pappas-Kikuchi announced, "Therefore, these subjects are normal, testosterone-influenced *boys* who, due to their feminine external genitalia, are mistakenly reared as girls."

"What did she say?" Luce snapped back to attention. "Did she say 'boys'? They're not boys. Not if they weren't raised as boys, they're not."

"The work of Dr. Peter Luce has long been held as gospel in the study of human hermaphroditism," Pappas-Kikuchi now asserted. "Normative, in sexological circles, is his notion that gender identity is fixed at an early age of development. Our research," she paused briefly, "refutes this."

A small popping sound, of a hundred and fifty mouths simultaneously opening, bubbled up through the auditorium's air. Luce stopped in mid-sip.

"The data our team collected in Guatemala will confirm that the effect of pubertal androgens on five-alpha-reductase pseudohermaphrodites is sufficient to cause a change in gender identity."

Luce couldn't remember much after that. He was aware of being very hot inside his tuxedo. Of quite a few heads turning around to look at him, then only a few heads, then none. At the podium, Dr. Pappas-Kikuchi ran through her data, endlessly, endlessly. "Subject number seven changed to male gender but continues to dress as a woman. Subject number twelve has the affect and mannerisms of a man and engages in sexual activity with village women. Subject number twenty-five married a woman and works as a butcher, a traditionally male occupation. Subject number thirty-five was married to a man who left the marriage after a year, at which point the subject assumed a male gender identity. A year later, he married a woman."

The awards ceremony went on as scheduled later that night. Luce, anesthetized on more scotch in the hotel bar and wearing an Aetna sales rep's blue blazer that he'd mistaken for his tuxedo jacket, had walked to the podium to an absolute minimum of applause and accepted his lifetime achievement award—a crystal lingam and yoni, hot-glued onto a silver-plated base—which later looked quite beautiful catching the lights of the city as it fell twenty-two floors from his balcony to shatter in the hotel's circular drive. Even then, he was looking west, out over the Pacific, toward Irian Jaya and the Dawat. It took him three years to get research grants from the NIH, the National Foundation, the March of Dimes, and Gulf and Western, but now he's here, amid another isolated flowering of the $5\alpha R$ mutation, where he can put Pappas-Kikuchi's theory and his own to the test. He knows who'll win. And when he does, the foundations will begin funding his clinic the way they used to. He can stop subcontracting the back rooms to dentists and that one chiropractor. It's only a matter of time. Randy has persuaded the tribal elders to allow the examinations to go forward. As soon as dawn breaks, they'll be led out to the separate camp where the "turnim-men" live. The mere existence of the local term shows that Luce is right and that cultural factors can affect gender identity. It's the kind of thing Pappas-Kikuchi would gloss right over.

Luce's hands and the kid's are all tangled up. It's like they're playing a game. First Luce covered his belt buckle. Then the kid put his hand over Luce's hand. Then Luce put his hand over the kid's hand. And now the kid covers the whole stack. All these hands struggle, gently. Luce feels tired. The jungle is still quiet. He'd like to get another hour of sleep before the morning cry of the monkeys. He's got a big day ahead.

The B-52 buzzes by his ear again, then circles back and goes up his left nostril. "Jesus!" He pulls his hands free and covers his face, but by then the mosquito has taken off again, brushing by his fingers. Luce is half sitting up on the pandanus mat now. He keeps his face covered, because it gives him some kind of comfort, and he just sits there in the dark, feeling suddenly exhausted and sick of the jungle and smelly and hot. Darwin had it easier on HMS *Beagle*. All he had to do was listen to sermons and play whist. Luce isn't crying, but he feels like it. His nerves are shot. As if from far away, he feels the pressure of the boy's hands again. Undoing his belt. Struggling with the technological puzzle of the zipper. Luce doesn't move. He just keeps his face covered, there in total darkness. A few more days and he can go home. His swanky bachelor pad on West Thirteenth Street awaits him. Finally, the boy figures it out. And it's very dark. And Dr. Peter Luce is open-minded. And there's nothing you can do, after all, about local customs.

1999

CAPRICIOUS GARDENS

> I was asking myself these questions, weeping all the while with the most bitter sorrow in my heart, when all at once I heard the singsong voice of a child . . . I stemmed my flood of tears and stood up, telling myself that this could only be a divine command to open my book of Scripture and read the first passage on which my eyes should fall. —Saint Augustine

In Ireland, in summer, four people come out to a garden in search of food.

The back door of a large house opens and a man steps out. His name is Sean. He is forty-three years old. He moves away from the house, then glances behind him as two other figures materialize, Annie and Maria, American girls. There is a pause before the next person appears, a gap in the procession, but at last Malcolm arrives. He steps onto the grass tentatively, as if afraid he will sink.

But already they can all see what has happened.

Sean said: "It's my wife's fault, all of this. It's a perfect expression of her inner character. To go to all the trouble of digging and planting and watering and then to forget about it completely in a few days' time. It's unforgivable."

"I've never seen a garden quite so overrun," said Malcolm. He addressed the remark to Sean, but Sean didn't reply to it. He was busy looking at the American girls, who, in one identical motion, had put their hands on their hips. The precision of their movements, so perfectly synchronized and yet unintentional, unnerved him. It was a bad omen. Their movements seemed to say: "We are inseparable."

That was unfortunate because one of the girls was beautiful and the other was not. Less than an hour before, on his way home from the airport (he had just returned from Rome), Sean had seen Annie walking by the side of the road, alone. The house he was returning to had been closed up for a month, ever since his wife, Meg, had gone off to France, or Peru. They had lived apart for years, each occupying the house only when the other was away, and Sean dreaded returning after long absences. The smell of his wife was everywhere, rose from armchairs when he sat in them, made him remember days of bright scarves and impeccable sheets.

When he saw Annie, however, he knew immediately how to brighten his homecoming. She wasn't hitchhiking, but was wearing a backpack; she was a pretty traveler with unwashed hair, and he suspected his offer of a spare room would surpass the ditch or clammy bed-and-breakfast she would find to stay in that night. At once he stopped his car beside her and leaned across the seat to roll down the passenger's window. As he leaned he took his eyes off her, but when he looked up again, already bestowing his capricious invitation, he saw not only Annie but another girl, a companion, who had appeared out of nowhere. The newcomer wasn't attractive in the least. Her hair was short, revealing the squarish shape of her skull, and the thick lenses of her glasses glinted so that he couldn't see her eyes.

In the end Sean was forced to invite the regrettable Maria along as well. The girls climbed into his car like affectionate

sisters, having stowed their backpacks in the trunk, and Sean
sped off down the road. When he arrived at his house,
however, he encountered another surprise. There, on the front
steps, with his head in his hands, was his old friend Malcolm.

Malcolm stood at the edges of the garden, eyeing its neglect.
The garden was mostly dirt. Brambles covered the back por-
tion and, in the front, there was nothing but a row of brown
flowers crushed by the rain. Sean blamed it all on his wife.
"She thinks of herself as having a green thumb," he joked, but
Malcolm didn't laugh. The garden made him think of his
own marriage. Only five weeks earlier, his wife, Ursula, had
left him for another man. Their marriage had been unhappy
for some time; Malcolm knew that Ursula was discontented
with him and their life together, but he had never imagined
she could fall in love with someone else. After she was gone,
he fell into despair. Unable to sleep, beset by crying jags, he
began to drink to excess. On one occasion, he had driven to
a scenic outlook and got out of his car to stand at the edge of a
cliff. Even then, he knew he was being dramatic and that he
lacked the courage to throw himself off. Nevertheless, he
remained at the cliff's edge for almost an hour.
     The next day, Malcolm had taken a leave from his job
and had begun to travel, hoping to find, in freedom of movement, freedom from pain. Quite by chance he had found
himself in the town where he remembered his old friend
Sean lived. Wandering the streets, his shirt spotted with coffee, he had made his way to Sean's house, knocked on the
door, and found no one at home.
     He had been there less than fifteen minutes when he
looked up to see Sean striding down the front path with a girl
on either side of him. The vision filled Malcolm with envy.
Here was his friend, surrounded by youth and vitality (the

girls were laughing musical laughs), and here was he, sitting
on the doorstep, surrounded by nothing but the specters of
old age, loneliness, and despair.

The situation grew worse from there. Sean greeted him
quickly, as though they had seen each other only last week,
and Malcolm immediately sensed he was in the way. With a
flourish Sean opened the door and led them on a tour of the
house. He showed the girls where they would sleep, and indicated a bedroom in another wing that Malcolm could have.
After that, Sean took them into the kitchen. He and the girls
searched the cabinets to see what there was to eat. All they
found was a plastic bag of black beans and, in the refrigerator,
a stick of butter, a shriveled lemon, and a desiccated clove of
garlic. That was when Sean suggested they go out to the
garden.

Malcolm followed them outside. And now he stood apart,
wishing he could take the failure of his own marriage as
lightly as Sean took the failure of his. He wished he could
put Ursula behind him, lock her memory in a box and bury
it deep in the earth, far beneath the soil he now turned up
with the toe of his left shoe.

Sean stepped into the garden and kicked at the brambles. He
had forgotten the cupboards would be bare, he had nothing
to offer his guests now, and he had two more guests than he
wanted. He gave one last kick, disgusted with everything,
but this time his foot caught on a network of brambles, pulling them up in the air. They lifted as a lid lifts off a box and
underneath, hiding against the wall, was a clump of artichokes.
"Hold on," he said, seeing them. "Hold on one minute." He
took a few steps toward them. He bent and touched one. Then
he turned, looking back at Annie. "Do you know what this is?"
he asked her. "It's Divine Providence. The good Lord made

my wife plant these poor artichokes and then made her forget about them, so that we, in our need, would find them. And eat."

A few of the artichokes were blooming. Annie hadn't known that artichokes could bloom but there they were, as purple as thistles, only larger. The idea of eating them made her happy. Everything about the evening made her happy, the house, the garden, her new friend, Sean. For a month she and Maria had been traveling through Ireland, staying in youth hostels where they had to sleep on cots in rooms crowded with other girls. She was tired of the budget accommodations, of the meager meals scraped together in the hostel kitchens, and of the other girls rinsing out their socks and underwear in the bathroom sinks and hanging them on the bunk beds to dry. Now, thanks to Sean, she could sleep in a big bedroom with lots of windows and a canopy bed.

"Come look," Sean said, beckoning her with his hand, and she stepped into the garden. They bent over together. A tiny gold cross slipped out of her T-shirt and hung, swinging. "My God, you're Catholic," he said. "Yes," said Annie. "And Irish?" She nodded, smiling. He lowered his voice as he grasped one of the artichokes and presented it to her. "That makes us practically family, my dear."

If Sean perceived the implications of the girls' body language, even more so did Maria. For it wasn't true that the two of them had put their hands on their hips simultaneously without meaning to. Annie had started the movement and Maria had mirrored her. She did this in order to proclaim the very message of inseparability that Sean had read. Maria wanted to inhabit Annie's being as closely and as intimately as possible, and so, in this instance, she transformed Annie and herself into two identical sculptures set side by side on the grass.

Maria had never had a friend like Annie before. She had never felt that someone understood her so well. Her life thus far had been like living in a town of mutes, where no one spoke to her but only stared. It seemed to Maria that she had never heard the sound of another human voice, until that Sunday in March, at the library of the college they went to, when Annie had said for no reason at all: "You look all cozy in that chair."

At the back of the garden the artichokes lolled on their thick stems. Maria looked at Annie standing in them, running a hand through her thick hair. Maria was just as happy as Annie. She, too, responded to the stark beauty of Sean's stone house, and to the coolness of the evening air. But besides her delight in these surroundings there remained another bright spot that made her happy, a bright spot she returned to again and again in her thoughts. For the day before, in an empty train compartment, Annie had put her arms around Maria and had kissed her on the lips.

Annie's gold cross caught the light. Sean looked at it, thinking that it was impossible to guess what meaning circumstances might give to random things. It just so happened that, inside his as-yet unpacked suitcase, lay an object that, until this moment, he had foreseen no use for. But now, as the tiny cross glinted, his mind linked image to image, and he saw in the air before him the index finger of Saint Augustine.

It was his only souvenir of Rome. On his last day there, exploring the neighborhood around his hotel, Sean had come across a shop filled with religious statuary and artifacts. The proprietor, perhaps sensing from Sean's clothes that he had some money, had led him to a glass case to show him a thin, dusty piece of bonelike material that he insisted was the finger of the author of the "Confessions." Sean didn't believe him, but he had bought the relic anyway, because it amused him.

He led Annie farther back in the garden, away from Maria and Malcolm, who still hadn't ventured onto the dirt. He turned his back to them and asked, "Your friend isn't Catholic, is she?" "Episcopalian," Annie whispered. "Not good enough," said Sean. He frowned. "And Malcolm's an Anglican, I'm afraid." He put a finger to his lips as if he were deep in thought. "Why do you want to know?" Annie asked. Sean's attention returned to her. He gave her a sly look. But when he spoke it was to all of them: "We need to organize work details. Malcolm, perhaps you'd be good enough to pick these artichokes while we get the water boiling."

Malcolm looked disconsolate. "They have thorns," he said.

"Just prickles," said Sean, and with that he left the garden and started back toward the house.

Annie assumed that Sean meant all three of them would get the water boiling. She followed him into the kitchen, glancing back and smiling once at Maria, who hurried along after them, swinging her short arms. When they got inside, however, Sean looked at Maria and said, "If I remember correctly, my wife keeps the good silver upstairs in the hall chest. The red chest. In the bottom drawer, rolled up in a sheet. Could you get it, Maria? It would be nice at least to have good silverware." Maria hesitated before saying anything. Then she turned and asked Annie to come help her.

Annie didn't want to. She was fond of Maria but had found lately that Maria tended to smother her. Everywhere Annie went, Maria followed. On trains Maria sat squashed against her side. Yesterday, pressed between the metal compartment wall and Maria's stiff shoulder, Annie had finally gotten annoyed. She wanted to push Maria away and shout, "Let me breathe, will you!" She felt uncomfortably hot and was just about to nudge her when suddenly her annoyance subsided, replaced by a feeling of guilt. How could she get mad at Maria for simply sitting close to her? How could she return affection with peevishness? Annie felt ashamed, and though she was still uncomfortable pressed against Maria, she tried to ignore that. Instead, she leaned over and gave Maria a friendly peck on the lips.

Now Annie wanted to stay downstairs and help cook the meal. Sean interested her. He had the perfect life, didn't have to work, took trips to Rome whenever he wanted, and always came back to a beautiful country house. Annie had never met a person like Sean before, and what she most wanted out of life, at her age, was just that: newness, adventure. That was why she was glad when Sean said, "I'm afraid you'll have to go up by yourself, Maria. I need Annie's help here in the kitchen."

Gently, blindly, Malcolm picked the artichokes. It had grown dark in the garden; the sun had set behind the stone wall, and the only light came now from inside the house, illuminating a patch of lawn not far from where Malcolm knelt. There had been a time when he would never have done this sort of thing, get down on his knees and pick his own dinner, muddying his trousers, but such considerations seemed alien to him now. For weeks he hadn't been able to look himself in the mirror whereas usually his sophisticated appearance filled him with pride.

He ran his hands up the thick stems of the artichokes, snapping off the bulbs. This way he avoided the prickles. He worked slowly. The smell of the earth rose to his nostrils, damp and mineral. It was the first smell he had noticed in weeks, and there was something intoxicating about it. He could feel the coldness of the ground against his kneecaps.

In the dark the artichokes seemed to go on forever. As he picked them, and moved farther in, he kept encountering new stalks. He began to work a little faster, and after a time became completely absorbed in his work. He liked picking the artichokes. He slowed down. He didn't want the picking to end.

The front staircase was long and grand, and as soon as she began climbing it Maria ceased to mind her lonely errand. She felt free, far from home and all the disappointments of home. She liked her clothes, which were thick and baggy; she liked her short hair; she liked the fact that she and Annie were in a place where they couldn't be found, a place where they could act toward each other as they wished and not as society dictated. An old tapestry hung on the wall, a stag being torn by two threadbare dogs.

She came to the top of the stairs and went down the hallway looking for the red chest. There were chests all along the hall, most of them dark mahogany. Finally she found one somewhat redder than the others and knelt before it. She opened the bottom drawer. A roll of sheet lay inside, and, taking it out, she was surprised at how heavy it was. She laid the sheet on the floor and began to unroll it. She flipped it over and over again, the metal inside clinking together. Finally the last wrap came undone and there they were—knives, forks, spoons—all laid out in the same direction, glittering up at her.

Once he was alone with Annie, Sean took his time getting the water on the stove. He removed a metal pot from its hook on the wall. He brought it to the sink. He began filling it with water.

Through all this he was extremely aware of his actions and of the fact that Annie was watching him. When he reached up to unhook the pot from the wall he tried to make his movements as fluid as possible. He set the pot on the stove (gracefully) and turned to face her.

She was leaning back against the sink, her hands planted on either side of her, her body stretching in a delicate arc. She looked even more appealing than she had by the side of the road. "Since we're alone now, Annie," Sean said, "I can tell you a secret."

"I'm ready," she said.

"Do you promise to keep this quiet?"

"I promise."

He looked into her eyes. "How much do you know about Church history?"

"I went to catechism until I was thirteen."

"Then you're familiar with Saint Augustine?"

She nodded. Sean looked around the room as if to see if anyone were listening. Then he took a long pause, winked, and said: "I have his finger."

Annie was not so much interested in Saint Augustine's finger as in the fact that Sean was willing to tell her a secret. She listened to him devoutly, as if he were revealing a divine mystery.

When Annie flirted she didn't always admit to herself that she was flirting. Sometimes she preferred to suspend her mental faculties so that she could flirt, as it were, without her mind watching. It was as if her body and mind separated, her body stepping behind a screen to remove its clothing while her mind, on the other side of the screen, paid no attention.

With Sean now, in the kitchen, Annie began to flirt without admitting it to herself. He told her about his relic and said that, in consideration of the fact that she was Catholic, he would show it to her. "But you mustn't tell anyone. We don't want these heretics shouldering their way back into the true faith."

Annie agreed, laughing. She stretched her body even farther back. She knew that Sean was looking at her and, suddenly, dimly, she became aware that she enjoyed being looked at. She saw herself through his eyes: a willowy young woman, leaning back on her arms, her long hair falling behind her.

"Have you got a basket?" said Malcolm, coming into the doorway. His hands were covered with dirt and he was smiling for the first time that day.

"There can't be that many," Sean said.

"There are *hundreds*. I can't carry them all."

"Make two trips," said Sean. "Make three."

Malcolm looked at Annie leaning against the sink. The ivory comb in her hair gleamed as she turned her head toward him. He thought once again of Sean's ability to surround himself with youth and vitality. And so he said to her, "It's damned pleasant out in the garden, Annie. Why don't you come help me. Let old Sean boil the water."

He didn't give her a chance to refuse. He led her by the hand out the back door, waving goodbye to Sean with the other. "I've made a little pile," he said, once he had brought her into the garden. "It's a little wet but you get used to it." He knelt down by the pile of artichokes and looked up at her. In the light from the house he could make out her figure and the slopes and shadows of her face.

"Make a basket of your arms and I'll fill it," he said. Annie did as she was told, crossing her arms with the palms of her hands facing up. On his knees before her Malcolm began picking up the artichokes, placing them one by one in her arms, gently pressing them against her stomach. First there were five, then ten, then fifteen. As the number increased, Malcolm became more precise in the positions he chose for the artichokes. He furrowed his brow and fit each artichoke snugly into place among the rest, as if linking pieces of a puzzle. "Look at you," he said. "You've become a goddess of the harvest." And to him she was. She stood before him, slender and young, with a profusion of artichokes sprouting from her belly. He placed one last artichoke high up on her chest, accidentally pricking her.

"Oh, sorry!"

"I'd better take these in."

"Yes, by all means, take them in. We're going to have a feast!"

When Maria came into the kitchen and saw Sean standing over the stove, peering into the pot of water, she became uneasy. She of course understood quite well what Sean was up to. She saw the looks he gave Annie, noted the affected tones of his voice when he spoke to her. "You girls can have the blue bedroom," he had said, and his voice had tried to sound grand and generous.

She moved to set down the silverware on the kitchen counter but caught herself before doing so. It would make too much noise. Instead she stood holding it all, watching Sean from behind, quietly enjoying the fact that she was watching him without his knowing it.

The room she and Annie were staying in had only one bed. Maria had noticed that at once. When they first went in, carrying their backpacks, Maria had looked at the bed, noticing out of the corner of her eye that Annie was also looking at it. It had been a moment of unspoken understanding. The understanding said: "We are going to sleep tonight in the same bed!" But, in front of Sean and Malcolm, they couldn't say a word. They both knew what the other was thinking but they only said "This is great" and "Oh, a canopy bed. I used to have one of those!"

Malcolm knelt in the garden, savoring the vision of Annie as a goddess of the harvest. It had been a long time since he had felt such foolish delight. In the last years, at home, Ursula was often in a bad mood. Malcolm tried to find out what was bothering her, but his attempt only seemed to madden her further. After a while, he had stopped trying. They went about their daily lives communicating only when it was absolutely necessary.

Now he picked up the last few artichokes Annie had been unable to carry. He put them against his cheek to feel how cool they were. As he did this, he was overcome by a feeling he recognized from his undergraduate days when he had first met Sean, a feeling of the beauty of the world and, along with this, his duty, or destiny, to apprehend it, so that it would not go unnoticed before it passed away. Living with Ursula, fighting with her, had narrowed Malcolm's life to the point where he had lost this ability, this awareness. It wasn't her fault. It was nobody's fault.

Sean dropped the artichokes into the boiling water one by one. Annie was standing next to him. Their shoulders were touching. He could smell her skin, her hair.

At the table Maria was wiping off the silverware. She was hunched over, squinting at the spots, and rubbing her nose from time to time with the back of her hand. Some

artichokes were also on the table. Now and then Annie shut-
tled a new batch from table to stove, handing them carefully
to Sean, who dropped them into the enormous pot with the
eager abandon of a man tossing coins into a wishing well.

The sight was certainly a happy one, thought Malcolm as he
stepped into the doorway, holding his small charge of artichokes. The pot on the stove was steaming. Annie and Sean
were washing dust off plates exhumed from the cupboards.
On the far side of the kitchen Maria was stacking silverware
into neat piles. It was a scene of rustic simplicity—the vege-
tables harvested from the garden, the mammoth hissing stove,
the two American girls reminding Malcolm of all the country
girls he had ever glimpsed from train windows: slight figures
beckoning from side roads, paused on their bicycles. Everything spoke of simplicity, goodness, and health. Malcolm was
so struck by the scene that he couldn't bring himself to intrude
upon it. He could only stand in the shadows of the doorway,
looking in.

It occurred to him that they were about to partake of a
miraculous meal. Less than an hour ago they had stared at
the open, empty cupboards with disappointment and he had
thought they would end up in a pub, eating liver-and-onion
sandwiches amid the smoke and the noise. Now the kitchen
was full of food.

From the doorway, invisibly, he watched them. And the
longer he watched without their noticing, the stranger he
began to feel. He felt suddenly as though he had receded from
the reality of the kitchen onto another plane of existence, as
though now he were not looking at life but peering into it.
Wasn't he dead in some respects? Hadn't he come to the point
of despising life and throwing it away? At the sink Sean was
wringing out a yellow dish towel, Annie was melting the stick

of butter over the stove, at the table Maria was holding a silver spoon up to the light. But none of them, not one, recognized the significance of the meal they were about to share.

And so it was with the greatest joy that Malcolm felt his bulk finally ease forward (from out of the netherworld back into the dear sluggish atmosphere of earth). His face came into the light. He was smiling with the bliss of reprieve. There was still time left for him to speak.

Sean didn't notice Malcolm enter the kitchen because he was carrying the bowl of artichokes to the table. The artichokes were steaming; the steam was rising in his face, blinding him.

Annie didn't notice Malcolm enter the kitchen because she was thinking about what she would write home in her next letter. She would describe it all: the artichokes! the steam! the bright plates!

Malcolm entered, took his seat at the table, and deposited his artichokes on the floor beside his feet. At that moment the faces of the girls were indescribably beautiful. The face of his old friend Sean was also beautiful.

Annie wasn't paying attention when Malcolm began to speak. She heard his voice but his words had no meaning for her, were only sounds, in the distance. She was still calculating the total effect of a letter home, imagining her family around the table, her mother reading it with her glasses on, her little sisters acting bored and complaining. Other memories of home crowded in: the backyard grass full of crab apples, the kitchen entrance, in winter, lined with wet boots. Through the parade of these memories Malcolm's voice kept up its slow, steady rhythm, and gradually Annie began to pick out bits of what he was saying. He had gone on a drive. He had stopped above a cliff. He had stood looking down at the sea.

In the middle of the table the artichokes fumed on their platter. Annie reached out and touched one but it was too hot to eat. Next she glanced at Sean's profile and then at Maria's and saw that they were uncomfortable about something. Only then did the full import of what Malcolm was saying become clear to her. He was talking about suicide. His own.

The idea of this middle-aged, heavyset man throwing himself off a cliff struck Maria as comic. Malcolm's eyes were moist, she could see that, but the fact that his emotion was genuine only separated her further from him. Maybe it was true that he had contemplated killing himself, maybe it was true that now (as he insisted) this meal had brought him back to life, but it was a mistake to think that she, who hardly knew him, could share either his sorrow or his joy. For a moment Maria reproached herself for not being able to feel for Malcolm (in a voice full of emotion he was describing the "darkest days" immediately after his wife had left him), but the moment quickly passed. Maria admitted to herself that she felt nothing. She kicked Annie under the table. Annie began to smile but then covered her mouth with her napkin. Maria rubbed her foot against Annie's calf. Annie moved her leg away, and Maria couldn't find it again. She searched back and forth with her foot and waited for Annie to look at her again so that she could wink, but Annie kept looking down at her plate.

•

Sean watched as Malcolm began to stuff himself with artichokes. He had them all captive now and so began to speak
and eat at the same time. And what a time to pick! Nothing
could be so detrimental to the mood of romance (which was
the mood Sean was hoping to induce) than the mention of
death. Already he could see Annie cringing ever so slightly,
hunching her shoulders, pressing (no doubt) her lovely legs
together. Death, jumping off cliffs, why did Malcolm have
to talk of it now? As if it meant anything to them! Some
dramatic moment Malcolm had indulged in to convince himself he could feel love. And how much love had he felt? Hadn't
he recovered rather quickly? Five weeks! "I never thought I
would again enjoy a simple meal among friends," he was
saying, and Sean watched as, unbelievably, a tear slid crook-
edly down Malcolm's cheek. He was crying, plucking the
leaves off a huge artichoke (even in the swell of emotion he
had managed to take the biggest one), plucking off the leaves
and dipping them in the butter before putting them in his
mouth.

"We're too quick to reckon the value of our lives!" Malcolm
proclaimed to them, and it seemed that he had never been so
close to any group of people in his life. They were all silent,
hanging on his every word, and his emotion was stirring
him to eloquence he had never known. How often in life one
says unimportant things, he thought, trivial things, just to
pass the time. Only rarely does one get a chance to unburden
one's heart, to speak of the beauty and meaning of life, its
preciousness, and to have people listen! Just moments before
he had felt the agony of the dead barred from life, but now he
could feel the joy of language, of sharing intimate thoughts,
and his body vibrated pleasurably with the sound of his own
voice.

·

At his first opportunity Sean broke Malcolm's gloomy solil-
oquy by taking an artichoke from the platter and saying:
"Here's one for you, Annie. It's not too hot now."

"They're marvelous," said Malcolm, dabbing his eyes.

"You know how to eat them, Annie, don't you?" Sean
asked. "You just pick off the leaves, dip them in the butter,
and then scrape the meat off with your teeth." As he explained
this, Sean demonstrated, dipping a leaf in the butter and holding it to her mouth. "Go on, try it," he said. Annie opened
her mouth, put her lips around the leaf, and bit down softly.

"We have artichokes in America, you know, Sean," said
Maria, taking one herself. "We've eaten them before."

"I haven't," said Annie, chewing and smiling at Sean.

"You have too," said Maria. "I've seen you eat them. Lots
of times."

"Perhaps that was asparagus," said Sean, and he and Annie
laughed together.

The dinner proceeded. Sean noticed that Annie had an-
gled her body in his direction. Malcolm was eating silently,
his wet cheeks shining like the buttery artichoke he held in his
hand. One by one the artichokes were taken from the platter,
one by one stripped of their leaves. Sean kept handing Annie
bits of food, caressing her with simple specific considerations:
"One more? . . . some butter? . . . water?" Between mouth-
fuls he leveled his face in her direction, filling the air between
them with the warm odor of what he had eaten.

He was thinking of their upcoming tryst. The plan he had
arranged with her was this: after dinner he would suggest
backgammon; she would immediately agree and together
they would go downstairs to the game room; they would play
until the others went to sleep and then go up to view the relic
alone.

But just then Malcolm said: "Ladies, take a look at these two old men who sit before you. We're dear old friends, Sean and I. At Oxford we were inseparable."

Sean looked up to see Malcolm smiling warmly at him across the table. His eyes were still watering. He looked vulnerable and idiotic. But Malcolm went on: "I pray that your friendship, young as it is, survives so long." He was looking at the girls now, from one to the other. "Old friends," he murmured, "they're the best."

"Would anyone care to retire to the game room for some backgammon?" Sean asked aloud to the table, but especially, Annie knew, to her. She was just about to say yes when out of the corner of her eye she caught Maria looking at her. Annie knew that Maria was waiting for her reply. If she said yes, Maria would also say yes. Suddenly she knew the plan wouldn't work, Maria would never go up to sleep by herself. And so Annie spread her hands on the table, looked at her nails, and asked, "Maria, what do you feel like?"

"Oh, I don't know," Maria said.

"We can't all play," said Sean. "Only two of us, I'm afraid."

"Backgammon sounds lovely," said Malcolm. Annie shifted in her seat. She had hesitated too long. She had ruined everything.

"We have to be up early, anyway," said Maria.

"Well, we'll excuse you two travelers then," said Malcolm. "With profound regret."

"Perhaps it is getting a little late," said Sean.

"Nonsense!" said Malcolm. "The night's just beginning!" And with that he slid his chair from the table and stood resolutely up.

•

There was nothing Sean could do. He had no idea why Annie had deviated from their plan. He suspected he had been too forward during dinner, had given away his true motives, and scared her off. Whatever the reason, now there was nothing for him to do but stand up, disown the signals from his heart (registering despair) by smiling, and head for the basement door. As he descended the stairs with Malcolm behind him he tried unsuccessfully to hear what the girls were saying in the kitchen.

The game room was a long, narrow wainscotted room, with a billiard table in the middle and, at one end, a leather sofa facing a television set. Sean went immediately to the television and turned it on.

"What about backgammon?" Malcolm asked.

"I've lost the mood," said Sean.

Malcolm looked at him uncertainly. "I hope you didn't mind my little oration," he said. "I'm afraid I monopolized the conversation."

Sean kept his eyes on the television. "I hardly noticed," he said.

"Sean likes you," Maria told Annie once they were alone.

"He does not."

"He does. I can tell."

"He's just being nice."

They were drying the last few dishes, standing elbow to elbow at the sink. "What did he say to you in the garden?"

"When?"

"In the garden. When he took you into the back."

"He told me I was the most beautiful girl he had ever seen and then he proposed marriage."

Maria was rinsing a plate. She held it under the water and said nothing.

"I'm kidding," said Annie. "He just talked about the soil, how hard it is to grow things here."

Maria started to scrub the plate, even though it was perfectly clean.

"I'm just kidding," Annie said again.

Annie wanted to take as long as possible washing the dishes. If Sean came back she could give him a sign to meet her later. But the plates were not very dirty, and there were only four of them, along with some glasses. Soon everything was done. "I'm exhausted," Maria said. "Aren't you exhausted?"

"No."

"You look exhausted."

"I'm not."

"What should we do now?"

Annie could think of no reason for staying in the kitchen. She could go downstairs but Malcolm would be there. He would be everywhere, all night. He would never go to sleep again, he was so happy to be alive. So at last she said, "There's nothing to do. I guess I'll go to bed."

"I'll go up with you," Maria said.

"Let's not watch television, Sean," said Malcolm. "We haven't had a chance to talk all night. We haven't talked for twenty years!"

"I haven't watched television for two weeks," said Sean.

Malcolm laughed, agreeably. "Sean," he said, "it's no use. You can't hide from me. Especially tonight." He waited for a response but received none. He felt monumentally calm. He could say whatever he had to say, without embarrassment, and he peered at his friend, wondering why Sean, on the contrary, was so withdrawn. But in the next moment it came to him. Sean's imperviousness was much too perfect. It was a sham. Inside his shell Sean was lonely too, and grieved for his failed marriage as Malcolm himself did. That was the reason he surrounded himself with jokes and the young women.

Malcolm was surprised he hadn't realized this before. His sight now in every way was sharper. He looked at his friend and felt great sympathy for him. And then he said: "Tell me about Meg, Sean. There's no reason to be ashamed. I'm in the same boat, you know."

This time Sean did turn and meet his gaze. His manner was still stiff, it was difficult for him, but at last he began: "Not the same boat, Malcolm. Not at all. I left Meg. Meg didn't leave me."

Malcolm looked away, down at the floor.

"And she took it badly, I'm afraid," Sean continued. "She stepped in front of a train."

"She tried to kill herself?" Malcolm asked. "Oh, my God!"

"Didn't just try. Succeeded."

"Meg's dead?"

"Yes, she is. That's why the garden is in such a state."

"Sean, I'm so sorry. Why didn't you say something?"

"I haven't been able to talk about it," Sean said.

This revenge pleased Sean. Malcolm had spoiled his evening but now Sean had control over him, could make him believe whatever he liked. Malcolm laid his head back against the sofa and Sean said, "Quite a coincidence, your showing up here tonight. And telling that story. Almost as if something sent you here."

"I had no idea," Malcolm said softly. Sean continued to stare at his friend, filled with the power of being able to create a world for Malcolm to live in, where nothing happened by chance and where even suicides harmonized.

He left Malcolm sitting on the couch and made his way toward the stairs.

When Maria went into the bathroom to brush her teeth, Annie tiptoed to the bedroom doorway. She heard nothing. The house was quiet. All she could hear was Maria swirling water in her mouth and spitting it into the sink. She stepped into the hall. Again she heard nothing. Then Maria came out of the bathroom. She had her glasses off and was squinting at the bed.

Sean reached the kitchen to find it empty. He cursed himself for ever suggesting backgammon, cursed Malcolm for getting in the way, cursed Annie for betraying their plan. It was not to be, no matter what he did. The house, the artichokes, the relic, none of these had been enough. He thought of his wife, dancing in some tropic zone, and then he saw himself as he was, alone, in a cold house, his desires thwarted.

He walked back to the basement door and listened. The television was still on. Malcolm was still sitting before it, thunderstruck. Sean turned away, determined to leave Malcolm there all night, but as soon as he did so he stopped where he was. For in front of him, wearing nothing but a man's long T-shirt, was Annie.

Upstairs, ears pricked, Maria was waiting for Annie to come back to bed. Annie had just gotten into bed when suddenly she crawled out again, saying she was going downstairs for a glass of water. "Drink from the tap in the bathroom," Maria suggested, but Annie said, "I want a glass."

After all this time, even after the kiss on the train, Annie was still shy. She was so nervous, she had gotten into bed and jumped right out again. Maria knew exactly what was going through her friend's mind. She crossed her arms behind her head. She stared up at the decorative plasterwork of the ceiling and felt the weight of her body sinking into the mattress, the pillows. A great calm came over her, a solidity, a sense that now, at last, her wishes were going to come true and all she had to do was wait.

Malcolm stood up and turned off the television. He moved across the room to the billiard table. He took out a ball, rolled it across the felt, and watched it career off the sides of the table. He caught it again and repeated the action. The ball made soft thumps against the cushions.

He was thinking about what Sean had told him. He was wondering what it all meant.

To get away before Malcolm came up, Sean led Annie to his study. On the way, he picked up his suitcase, which he had left in the front hall. Once he had closed the door of the study behind them, he told Annie in a whisper to be absolutely silent. Then, with an air of solemnity, he bent down to open his suitcase. As he released the metal latch, he was aware that Annie's naked thighs were only inches from his face. He wanted to reach out and take hold of her legs, to pull her toward him and fit his face into the bowl of her hips. But he didn't do that. He only took out a gray woolen sock from which he extracted a thin yellow bone less than three inches long.

"Here it is," he said, showing it to her. "Direct from Rome. Saint Augustine's index finger."

"How long ago did he live, again?"

"Fifteen hundred years."

Annie put out her hand and touched the sliver of bone, as Sean gazed at her lips, cheeks, eyes, hair.

Annie knew he was about to kiss her. She always knew when men were about to kiss her. Sometimes she made it difficult for them, moved away or asked them questions. Other times she merely pretended not to notice, as she did now, examining the saint's finger.

Then Sean said, "I was afraid our little meeting wasn't going to happen."

"It was hard getting away from the heretics," said Annie.

Malcolm came into the kitchen, looking for Sean. All he found were the plates the girls had thoughtfully washed, stacked next to the sink. He strolled about the kitchen, warmed his hands by the smoldering fire, and, seeing that the artichokes he had left on the floor were still there, set them on the table. Only after doing all these things did he go to the kitchen window and look out to the backyard.

When Maria saw them they were bent over something, their heads almost touching. Immediately she understood what had happened. Annie had come down to get a glass of water and Sean had waylaid her. She had arrived just in the nick of time to save her friend from an awkward situation.

"What's that?" she said, and boldly, triumphantly, walked into the room.

Maria's voice was the voice of the fate he could not escape. At the very moment of victory, as his desires were just about to

be satisfied (he and Annie were cheek to cheek), Sean heard
Maria's voice and his hopes shrank before it. He said nothing.
All he did was stand mute as Maria approached him and took
the relic into her cold hand.

"It's Saint Augustine's finger," Annie offered in explanation.

Maria examined the bone a moment, then handed it back
to Sean and said, simply, "No way." The girls turned (together)
and moved toward the door. "Good night," they said, and,
motionless, Sean heard their voices blend into an excruciating
unison.

"You didn't believe him, did you?" Maria asked once they
were alone in their room. Annie made no reply, only got into
bed and closed her eyes. Maria switched off the light and
fumbled through the darkness. "I can't believe you could fall
for that. The finger of Saint Augustine!" She laughed. "Guys
will do anything." She crawled into bed and pulled the covers
over her, then lay staring into the dark, thinking about the
trickery of men.

"Annie," she whispered, but her friend didn't reply. Maria
moved closer. "Annie," she said, a little more loudly. She
moved farther across the sheets. She touched her hip to Annie's
hip. And called again: "Annie."

But her friend didn't return her greeting, or amplify the
pressure of hip on hip. "I'm going to sleep!" Annie said, and
turned away.

Sean was left holding the counterfeit finger of an illustrious
saint. In the hallway he thought he heard the girls giggle.
Next came the sound of their feet on the stairs, the creak and
knock of the bedroom door closing, and then—silence.

The bone was coated with a film of white powder that flaked onto his open palm. He wanted to fling the bone across the room, or drop it and crush it beneath his heel, but something deterred him. Because as he stared at the bone he began to feel as though someone were watching him. He looked around the room but no one was there. When he looked back at the bone, a curious thing happened. The finger appeared to be pointing at him. As though it were still attached to a living person, or was infused with intelligence, and was accusing him, condemning him.

Fortunately, the feeling lasted only an instant. In the next moment the finger stopped pointing. It became just a bone again.

The moon had risen, and, in its light, Malcolm could make out the garden, a pale blue circle at the end of the grass. He looked back at the remaining artichokes lying on the table. Then he walked to the back door, opened it, and went out.

The garden was in even worse condition than before. The dead flowers, which had been in a row, were now trampled, dug up, and scattered. Footprints were everywhere. Signs of violence had replaced the serenity of neglect.

Malcolm saw the imprints of his own shoes, large and deep. Then he noticed the smaller treads of Annie's tennis shoes. He stepped into the garden and placed his feet over her treads, enjoying how thoroughly his shoes covered them. By this time, he had stopped wondering what had become of Sean. He was unaware of the location of the others inside the house, of Maria on one side of the bed, of Annie on the other, of Sean in his study staring at the twig of bone. Malcolm forgot his friends a moment, while he stood in the garden that Meg, his twin, had planted and left behind. Meg was gone, had given up, but he was still here. He was thinking that what he needed was a house and a garden of his own. He was imagining himself pruning rosebushes and picking beans. It seemed to him that happiness, with such a simple change, would come at last.

1988

GREAT EXPERIMENT

"If you're so smart, how come you're not rich?"

It was the city that wanted to know. Chicago, refulgent in early-evening, late-capitalist light. Kendall was in a penthouse apartment (not his) of an all-cash building on Lake Shore Drive. The view straight ahead was of water, eighteen floors below. But if you pressed your face to the glass, as Kendall was doing, you could see the biscuit-colored beach running down to Navy Pier, where they were just now lighting the Ferris wheel.

The gray Gothic stone of the Tribune Tower, the black steel of the Mies building just next door—these weren't the colors of the new Chicago. Developers were listening to Danish architects who were listening to nature, and so the latest condominium towers were all going organic. They had light green façades and undulating rooflines, like blades of grass bending in the wind.

There had been a prairie here once. The condos told you so.

Kendall was gazing at the luxury buildings and thinking about the people who lived in them (not him) and wondering what they knew that he didn't. He shifted his forehead against the glass and heard paper crinkling. A yellow Post-it was stuck to his forehead. Piasecki must have come in while Kendall was napping at his desk and left it there.

The Post-it said: "Think about it."

Kendall crumpled it up and threw it in the wastebasket. Then he went back to staring out the window at the glittering Gold Coast.

For sixteen years now, Chicago had given Kendall the benefit of the doubt. It had welcomed him when he arrived with his "song cycle" of poems composed at the Iowa Writers' Workshop. It had been impressed with his medley of high-IQ jobs the first years out: proofreader for *The Baffler*; Latin instructor at the Latin School. For someone in his early twenties to have graduated summa cum laude from Amherst, to have been given a Michener grant, and to have published, one year out of Iowa City, an unremittingly bleak villanelle in the *TLS*, all these things were marks of promise, back then. If Chicago had begun to doubt Kendall's intelligence when he turned thirty, he hadn't noticed. He worked as an editor at a small publishing house, Great Experiment, which published five titles per year. The house was owned by Jimmy Boyko, now eighty-two. In Chicago, people remembered Jimmy Boyko more from his days as a State Street pornographer back in the sixties and seventies and less from his much longer life as a free-speech advocate and publisher of libertarian books. It was Jimmy's penthouse that Kendall worked out of, Jimmy's high-priced view he was presently taking in. He was still mentally acute, Jimmy was. He was hard of hearing, but if you raised your voice to talk about what was going on in Washington the old man's blue eyes gleamed with ferocity and undying rebellion.

Kendall pulled himself away from the window and walked

back to his desk, where he picked up the book that was lying there. The book was Alexis de Tocqueville's *Democracy in America*. Tocqueville, from whom Jimmy had got the name for Great Experiment Books, was one of Jimmy's passions. One evening six months ago, after his nightly martini, Jimmy had decided that what the country needed was a super-abridged version of Tocqueville's seminal work, culling all of the predictions the Frenchman had made about America, but especially those that showed the Bush administration in its worst light. So that was what Kendall had been doing for the past week, reading through *Democracy in America* and picking out particularly salient bits. Like the opening, for instance: "Among the novel objects that attracted my attention during my stay in the United States, nothing struck me more forcibly than the general equality of condition among the people."

"How damning is that?" Jimmy had shouted, when Kendall read the passage to him over the phone. "What could be *less* in supply, in Bush's America, than equality of condition!"

Jimmy wanted to call the little book *The Pocket Democracy*. After his initial inspiration had worn off, he'd handed the project to Kendall. At first, Kendall had tried to read the book straight through. But after a while he began skipping around. Both Volumes I and II contained sections that were unspeakably boring: methodologies of American jurisprudence, examinations of the American system of townships. Jimmy was interested only in the prescient moments. *Democracy in America* was like the stories parents told adult children about their younger selves, descriptions of personality traits that had become only more ingrained over time, or of oddities and predilections that had been outgrown. It was curious to read a Frenchman writing about America when America was small, unthreatening, and admirable, when it was still something underappreciated that the French could claim and champion, like serial music or the novels of John Fante.

> In these, as in the forests of the Old World, destruction was perpetually going on. The ruins of vegetation were heaped upon one another; but there was no laboring hand to remove them, and their decay was not rapid enough to make room for the continual work of reproduction. Climbing plants, grasses, and other herbs forced their way through the mass of dying trees; they crept along their bending trunks, found nourishment in their dusty cavities and a passage beneath the lifeless bark. Thus decay gave its assistance to life.

How beautiful that was! How wonderful to imagine what America had been like in 1831, before the strip malls and the highways, before the suburbs and the exurbs, back when the lakeshores were "embosomed in forests coeval with the world." What had the country been like in its infancy? Most important, where had things gone wrong and how could we find our way back? How did decay give its assistance to life?

A lot of what Tocqueville described sounded nothing like the America Kendall knew. Other judgments seemed to part a curtain, revealing American qualities too intrinsic for him to have noticed before. The growing unease Kendall felt at being an American, his sense that his formative years, during the Cold War, had led him to unthinkingly accept various national pieties, that he'd been propagandized as efficiently as a kid growing up in Moscow at the time, made him want, now, to get a mental grip on this experiment called America.

Yet the more he read about the America of 1831, the more Kendall became aware of how little he knew about the America of today, 2005, what its citizens believed, and how they operated.

Piasecki was a perfect example. At the Coq d'Or the other night, he had said, "If you and I weren't so honest we could make a lot of money."

"What do you mean?"

Piasecki was Jimmy Boyko's accountant. He came on Fridays, to pay bills and handle the books. He was pale, perspirey, with limp blond hair combed straight back from his oblong forehead.

"He doesn't check anything, OK?" Piasecki said. "He doesn't even know how much money he has."

"How much *does* he have?"

"That's confidential information," Piasecki said. "First thing they teach you at accounting school. Zip your lips."

Kendall didn't press. He was leery of getting Piasecki going on the subject of accounting. When Arthur Andersen had imploded, in 2002, Piasecki, along with eighty-five thousand other employees, had lost his job. The blow had left him slightly unhinged. His weight fluctuated, he chewed diet pills and Nicorette. He drank a lot.

Now, in the shadowy, red-leather bar, crowded with happy-hour patrons, Piasecki ordered a scotch. So Kendall did, too.

"Would you like the executive pour?" the waiter asked.

Kendall would never be an executive. But he could have the executive pour. "Yes," he said.

For a moment they were silent, staring at the television screen, tuned to a late-season baseball game. Two newfangled Western Division teams were playing. Kendall didn't recognize the uniforms. Even baseball had been adulterated.

"I don't know," Piasecki said. "It's just that, once you've been screwed like I've been, you start to see things different. I grew up thinking that most people played by the rules. But after everything went down with Andersen the way it did—I mean, to scapegoat an entire company for what a few bad apples did on behalf of Ken Lay and Enron . . ." He didn't finish the thought. His eyes grew bright with fresh anguish.

The tumblers, the minibarrels of scotch, arrived at their table. They finished the first round and ordered another. Piasecki helped himself to the complimentary hors d'oeuvres.

"Nine people out of ten, in our position, they'd at least *think* about it," he said. "I mean, this fucking guy! How'd he make his money in the first place? On twats. That was his angle. Jimmy pioneered the beaver shot. He knew tits and ass were over. Didn't even bother with them. And now he's some kind of saint? Some kind of political activist? You don't buy that horseshit, do you?"

"Actually," Kendall said, "I do."

"Because of those books you publish? I see the numbers on those, OK? You lose money every year. Nobody reads that stuff."

"We sold five thousand copies of *The Federalist Papers*," Kendall said in defense.

"Mostly in Wyoming," Piasecki countered.

"Jimmy puts his money to good use. What about all the contributions he makes to the ACLU?" Kendall felt inclined to add, "The publishing house is only one facet of what he does."

"OK, forget Jimmy for a minute," Piasecki said. "I'm just saying, look at this country. Bush–Clinton–Bush–maybe Clinton. That's not a democracy, OK? That's a dynastic monarchy. What are people like us supposed to do? What would be so bad if we just skimmed a little cream off the top? Just a little skimming. I fucking hate my life. Do I think about it? Yeah. I'm already convicted. They convicted all of us and took away our livelihood, whether we were honest or not. So I'm thinking, if I'm guilty already, then who gives a shit?"

When Kendall was drunk, when he was in odd surroundings like the Coq d'Or, when someone's misery was on
display in front of him, in moments like this, Kendall still felt
like a poet. He could feel the words rumbling somewhere in
the back of his mind, as though he still had the diligence to
write them down. He took in the bruise-colored bags under
Piasecki's eyes, the addictlike clenching of his jaw muscles,
his bad suit, his corn-silk hair, and the blue Tour de France
sunglasses pushed up on his head.

"Let me ask you something," Piasecki said. "How old are
you?"

"Forty-five," Kendall said.

"You want to be an editor at a small-time place like Great
Experiment the rest of your life?"

"I don't want to do anything for the rest of my life,"
Kendall said, smiling.

"Jimmy doesn't give you health care, does he?"

"No," Kendall allowed.

"All the money he's got and you and me are both free-
lance. And you think he's some kind of social crusader."

"My wife thinks that's terrible, too."

"Your wife is smart," Piasecki said, nodding with approval. "Maybe I should be talking to her."

The train out to Oak Park was stuffy, grim, almost penal in its
deprivation. It rattled on the tracks, its lights flickering. During moments of illumination Kendall read his Tocqueville.
"The ruin of these tribes began from the day when Europeans
landed on their shores; it has proceeded ever since, and we are
now witnessing its completion." With a jolt, the train reached
the bridge and began crossing the river. On the opposite shore,
glass-and-steel structures of breathtaking design were canti-
levered over the water, all aglow. "Those coasts, so admirably

adapted for commerce and industry; those wide and deep rivers; that inexhaustible valley of the Mississippi; the whole continent, in short, seemed prepared to be the abode of a great nation yet unborn."

His cell phone rang and he answered it. It was Piasecki, calling from the street on his way home.

"You know what we were just talking about?" Piasecki said. "Well, I'm drunk."

"So am I," Kendall said. "Don't worry about it."

"I'm drunk," Piasecki repeated, "but I'm serious."

Kendall had never expected to be as rich as his parents, but he'd never imagined that he would earn so little or that it would bother him so much. After five years working for Great Experiment, he and his wife, Stephanie, had saved just enough money to buy a big fixer-upper in Oak Park, without being able to fix it up.

Shabby living conditions wouldn't have bothered Kendall in the old days. He'd liked the converted barns and underheated garage apartments Stephanie and he had lived in before they were married, and he liked the just appreciably nicer apartments in questionable neighborhoods they lived in *after* they were married. His sense of their marriage as countercultural, an artistic alliance committed to the support of vinyl records and Midwestern literary quarterlies, had persisted even after Max and Eleanor were born. Hadn't the Brazilian hammock as diaper table been an inspired idea? And the poster of Beck gazing down over the crib, covering the hole in the wall?

Kendall had never wanted to live like his parents. That had been the whole idea, the lofty rationale behind the snow-globe collection and the flea-market eyewear. But as the children

got older, Kendall began to compare their childhood un-
favorably with his own, and to feel guilty.

From the street, as he approached under the dark, dripping
trees, his house looked impressive enough. The lawn was
ample. Two stone urns flanked the front steps, leading up to
a wide porch. Except for paint peeling under the eaves, the
exterior looked fine. It was with the interior that the trouble
began. In fact, the trouble began with the word itself: *interior.*
Stephanie liked to use it. The design magazines she consulted
were full of it. One was even *called* it: *Interiors.* But Kendall
had his doubts as to whether their home achieved an authentic
state of interiority. For instance, the outside was always breaking in. Rain leaked through the master-bathroom ceiling.
The sewers flooded up through the basement drain.

Across the street, a Range Rover was double-parked, its
tailpipe fuming. As he passed, Kendall gave the person at
the wheel a dirty look. He expected a businessman or a styl-
ish suburban wife. But sitting in the front seat was a frumpy,
middle-aged woman, wearing a Wisconsin sweatshirt, talking
on her cell phone.

Kendall's hatred of SUVs didn't keep him from knowing
the base price of a Range Rover: $75,000. From the official
Range Rover website, where a husband up late at night could
build his own vehicle, Kendall also knew that choosing the
"Luxury Package" (preferably cashmere upholstery with navy
piping and burled-walnut dash) brought the price tag up to
$82,000. This was an unthinkable, a soul-crushing sum. And
yet, pulling into the driveway next to Kendall's was another
Range Rover, this belonging to his neighbor Bill Ferret. Bill
did something relating to software; he devised it, or marketed
it. At a backyard barbecue the previous summer, Kendall had
listened with a serious face as Bill explained his profession.
Kendall specialized in a serious face. This was the face he'd

trained on his high school and college teachers from his seat in the first row: the ever-alert, A-student face. Still, despite his apparent attentiveness, Kendall didn't remember what Bill had told him about his job. There was a software company in Canada named Waxman, and Bill had shares in Waxman, or Waxman had shares in Bill's company, Duplicate, and either Waxman or Duplicate was thinking of "going public," which apparently was a good thing to do, except that Bill had just started a third software company, Triplicate, and so Waxman, or Duplicate, or maybe both, had forced him to sign a "noncompete," which would last a year.

Munching his hamburger, Kendall had understood that this was how people spoke, out in the world—in the real world he himself lived in, though, paradoxically, had yet to enter. In this real world, there were things like custom software and ownership percentages and Machiavellian corporate struggles, all of which resulted in the ability to drive a heartbreakingly beautiful forest-green Range Rover up your own paved drive.

Maybe Kendall wasn't so smart.

He went up his front walk and into the house, where he found Stephanie in the kitchen, next to the open, glowing stove. She'd dumped the day's mail on the kitchen counter and was flipping through an architecture magazine. Kendall came up behind her and kissed the back of her neck.

"Don't get mad," Stephanie said. "The oven's only been on a few minutes."

"I'm not mad. I'm never mad."

Stephanie chose not to dispute this. She was a small, fine-boned woman who worked for a gallery of contemporary photography. She wore her hair in the same comp-lit page-boy she'd had the day they met, twenty-two years earlier, in an H.D. seminar. Since turning forty Stephanie had begun asking Kendall if she was getting too old to dress the way she did. But he answered truthfully that in her curated, second-hand outfits—the long parti-colored leather jacket or the drum majorette's skirt or the white fake fur Russian hat—she looked as great as ever.

The photos in the magazine Stephanie was looking at involved urban renovations. On one page a brick town house had had its back end blown out to make room for a boxy addition of glass; another showed a brownstone that had been gutted and now looked as bright and airy inside as a Soho loft. That was the ideal: to remain dutiful to a preservationist ethos while not depriving yourself of modern creature comforts. The handsome, affluent families who owned these houses were often pictured in carefree moments, eating breakfast or entertaining, their lives seemingly perfected by design solutions that made even turning on a light switch or running a bath a fulfilling, harmonious experience.

Kendall held his head next to Stephanie's as they looked at the photos. Then he said, "Where are the kids?"

"Max is at Sam's. Eleanor says it's too cold here, so she's sleeping over at Olivia's."

"You know what?" Kendall said. "Screw it. Let's just crank the heat."

"We shouldn't. Last month's bill was crazy."

"Keeping the oven open isn't any better."

"I know. It's freezing in here, though."

Kendall turned around to face the windows over the sink. When he leaned forward, he could feel cold air blowing through the panes. Actual currents.

"Piasecki said something interesting to me today."

"Who?"

"Piasecki. The accountant. From work. He said it's unbelievable that Jimmy doesn't give me health insurance."

"I've told you that."

"Well, Piasecki agrees with you."

Stephanie closed the magazine. Then she closed the oven door and turned off the gas. "We pay Blue Cross six thousand dollars per year. In three years, that's a new kitchen right there."

"Or we could spend it on heat," Kendall said. "And then our kids wouldn't abandon us. They would still love us."

"They still love you. Don't worry. They'll be back in the spring."

Kendall kissed his wife's neck once more as he exited the kitchen. He headed upstairs, first to use the bathroom and, second, to get a sweater, but as soon he entered the master bedroom he stopped in his tracks.

It wasn't the only master bedroom of its kind in Chicago. Across the country, the master bedrooms of more and more two-salaried, stressed-out couples were looking like this. With the twisted sheets and blankets on the bed, the pillows either mashed or denuded of their pillowcases to show saliva stains or spew feathers, and the socks and underpants littered like animal skins across the floor, the bedroom was like a den where two bears had recently hibernated. Or were hibernating still. In the far corner a hillock of dirty laundry rose three feet in the air. A few months ago, Kendall had gone to Bed Bath & Beyond to buy a wicker clothes hamper. After that, the family had conscientiously tossed their dirty wash into it. But soon the hamper filled up and they'd begun tossing their wash in its general direction. For all Kendall knew, the hamper might still be there, buried beneath the pyramid of laundry.

How had it happened in one generation? His parents' bedroom had never looked like this. Kendall's father had a dresser full of neatly folded laundry, a closet full of pressed suits and ironed shirts. Every night he had a perfectly made bed to climb into. Nowadays, if Kendall wanted to live as his own father had, he was going to have to hire a laundress and cleaning lady and a social secretary and a cook. He was going to have to hire a wife. Wouldn't that be great? Stephanie could use one, too. Everybody needed a wife, and no one had one anymore.

But to hire a wife Kendall needed to make more money. The alternative was to live as he did, in middle-class squalor, in married bachelorhood.

Like most honest people, Kendall sometimes fantasized about committing a crime. In the following days, however, he found himself indulging in criminal fantasies to a criminal degree. How did one embezzle if one wanted to embezzle well? What kind of mistakes did the rank amateurs make? How could you get caught and what were the penalties?

Quite amazing, to an embezzler-fantasist, was how instructive the daily newspapers were. Not only the lurid *Chicago Sun-Times*, with its stories of gambling-addicted accountants and Irish "minority" trucking companies. Much more instructive were the business pages of the *Tribune* or the *Times*. Here you found the pension-fund manager who'd siphoned off five million, or the Korean-American hedge-fund genius who vanished with a quarter billion of Palm Beach retiree money and who turned out to be a Mexican guy named Lopez. Turn the page and you read about the Boeing executive sentenced to four months in jail for rigging contracts with the Air Force. The malfeasance of Bernie Ebbers and Dennis Kozlowski claimed the front page, but it was the short articles on A21 or C15 detailing the quieter frauds, the scam artists working in subtler pigments, in found objects, that showed Kendall the extent of the general deceit.

At the Coq d'Or the next Friday, Piasecki said, "You know the mistake most people make?"

"What?"

"They buy a beach house. Or a Porsche. They red-flag themselves. They can't resist."

"They lack discipline," Kendall said.

"Right."

"No moral fiber."

"Exactly."

Wasn't scheming the way America worked? The *real* America that Kendall, with his nose stuck in *Rhyme's Reason*, had failed to notice? How far apart were the doings of these minor corporate embezzlers and the accounting fraud at Enron? And what about all the businesspeople who were clever enough *not* to get caught, who wriggled free from blame? The example set on high wasn't one of probity and full disclosure. It was anything but.

When Kendall was growing up, American politicians denied that the United States was an empire. But they weren't doing that anymore. They'd given up. Everyone knew about the empire now. Everyone was pleased.

And in the streets of Chicago, as in the streets of L.A., New York, Houston, and Oakland, the message was making itself known. A few weeks back, Kendall had seen the movie *Patton* on TV. He'd been reminded that the general had been severely punished for slapping a soldier. Whereas now Rumsfeld ran free from responsibility for Abu Ghraib. Even the president, who'd lied about WMD, had been reelected. In the streets, people got the point. Victory was what counted, power, muscularity, doublespeak if necessary. You saw it in the way people drove, in the way they cut you off, gave you the finger, cursed. Women and men alike, showing rage and toughness. Everyone knew what he wanted and how to get it. Everybody you met was nobody's fool.

One's country was like one's self. The more you learned about it, the more there was to be ashamed of.

•

Then again, it wasn't pure torture, living in the plutocracy. Jimmy was still out in Montecito, and every weekday Kendall had the run of his place. There were toadying doormen, invisible porters who hauled out the trash, a squad of Polish maids who came on Wednesday and Friday mornings to pick up after Kendall and scrub the toilet in the Moorish bathroom and tidy up the sunny kitchen where he ate his lunch. The co-op was a duplex. Kendall worked on the upper floor. Downstairs was Jimmy's "Jade Room," where he kept his collection of Chinese jade in museum-quality display cases. (If you had criminality in mind, a good place to start would be the Jade Room.)

In his office, whenever Kendall looked up from his Tocqueville, he could see the opalescent lake spreading out in all directions. The curious emptiness Chicago confronted, the way it just dropped off into nothing, especially at sunset or in the fog, was likely responsible for all the city's activity. The land had been waiting to be exploited. These shores so suited to industry and commerce had raised a thousand factories. The factories had sent vehicles of steel throughout the world, and now these vehicles, in armored form, were clashing for control of the petroleum that powered the whole operation.

Two days after his conversation with Piasecki, Kendall called his boss's landline in Montecito. Jimmy's wife, Pauline, answered. Pauline was his latest wife, and the one with whom he had found marital contentment. Jimmy had been married twice before, once to his college sweetheart, once to a Miss Universe thirty years his junior; Pauline was age-appropriate, a sensible woman with a kind manner, who ran the Boyko Foundation and spent her time giving away Jimmy's money.

After talking with Pauline a minute, Kendall asked if Jimmy was available and, a few moments later, Jimmy's loud voice came on. "What up, kiddo?"

"Hello, Jimmy, how are you?"

"Just got off my Harley. Rode all the way down to Ventura and back. Now my ass hurts but I'm happy. What's up?"

"Right," Kendall said. "So, I wanted to talk to you about something. I've been running the house for six years now. I think you've been happy with my work."

"I have been," Jimmy said. "No complaints."

"Given my performance, and given my tenure here, I wanted to ask if it might be possible to work out some kind of health-insurance coverage. I've—"

"Can't do it," Jimmy answered. The suddenness of his response was characteristic: it was the same kind of wall he'd put up all his life, a defense against the Polish kids who'd beat him up on his way home from school, against his own father, who'd told Jimmy he was a good-for-nothing who would never succeed in life, and, later on, against the vice cops who harassed the studio where Jimmy manufactured and sold his dirty magazines, against every business competitor who had tried to cheat him, and finally against the hypocrites and holier-than-thou politicians who undermined the First Amendment and wildly expanded the rights covered by the Second. "That was never part of your package. I'm running a nonprofit here, kiddo. Piasecki just sent me the statements. We're in the red this year. We're in the red *every* year. We publish all these important, foundational, patriotic books— essential books—and nobody buys them! The people in this country are asleep! We've got an entire nation on Ambien. Sandman Rove is blowing dust in everybody's eyes."

He went off on a tear, anathematizing Bush and Wolfo- witz and Perle, but then he must have felt bad about avoiding the subject at hand because he came back to it, softening his tone. "Listen, I know you've got a family. You have to do what's best for you. If you wanted to test your value out in the marketplace, I'd understand. I'd hate to lose you, Kendall, but I'd understand if you have to move on."

There was silence on the line.

Jimmy said, "You think about it." He cleared his throat. "So, since I've got you, tell me. How's *The Pocket Democracy* coming?"

Kendall wished he could remain businesslike. But he couldn't keep some bitterness out of his voice when he answered, "It's coming."

"When do you think you'll have something to show me?"

"No idea."

"What was that?"

"I've got no answer at the moment."

"Look, I'm running a business here," Jimmy said. "You think you're the first editor I've had? No. I hire young people and swap them out when they move on. As you may choose to do. That's how it works. No reflection on the job you've done, which has been first-rate. I'm sorry, kiddo. Let me know what you decide."

By the time Kendall hung up, the sun was setting. The water reflected the gray-blue of the darkening sky, and the lights of the water-pumping stations had come on, making them look like a line of floating gazebos. Kendall slumped in his desk chair, the Xeroxed pages of *Democracy in America* spread out on the desk around him. His left temple throbbed. He rubbed his forehead and looked down at the page in front of him:

I do not mean that there is any lack of wealthy individuals in the United States; I know of no country, indeed, where the love of money has taken stronger hold on the affections of men and where a profounder contempt is expressed for the theory of the permanent equality of property. But wealth circulates with inconceivable rapidity, and experience shows that it is rare to find two succeeding generations in the full enjoyment of it.

Kendall swiveled in his chair and grabbed the phone. He dialed Piasecki's number and, after a single ring, Piasecki answered.

"Meet me at the Coq d'Or," Kendall said.

"Now? What about?"

"I don't want to discuss it on the phone. I'll tell you when you get there."

This was how you did it. This was taking action. In an instant, everything could change.

In the fading light Kendall walked from Lakeshore up to the Drake Hotel and into the street entrance of the bar. He got a booth in the back, away from the guy in a tux playing piano, ordered a drink, and waited for Piasecki.

It took him a half hour to arrive. As soon as Piasecki sat down, Kendall stared across the table and smiled. "About that idea you had the other day," he said.

Piasecki gave him a sideways look. "You serious, or just playing around?"

"I'm curious."

"Don't fuck with me."

"I'm not," Kendall said. "I was just wondering. How would it work? Technically."

Piasecki leaned closer to be heard over the tinkling music. "I never said what I'm about to say, OK?"

"OK."

"If you do something like this, what you do is you set up a dummy company. You create invoices from this company.

Then Great Experiment pays these invoices. After a few years, you close the account and liquidate the company."

Kendall worked to understand. "But the invoices won't be for anything. Won't that be obvious?"

"When's the last time Jimmy checked the invoices for anything? He's eighty-two, for Christ's sake. He's out in California taking Viagra so he can bang some hooker. He's not thinking about the invoices. His mind is occupied."

"What if we get audited?"

This time it was Piasecki's turn to smile. "I like how you say 'we.' That's where *I* come in. If we get audited, who handles that? I do. I show the IRS the bills and the payments. Since our payments into the dummy company match the bills, everything looks fine. If we pay the right taxes on income, how is the IRS going to complain?"

It wasn't all that complicated. Kendall wasn't used to thinking this way, not just criminally but financially, but as his executive pour went down, he saw how it could work. He looked around the bar, at the businessmen boozing, making deals.

"I'm not talking about that much money," Piasecki was saying. "Jimmy's worth, like, eighty million. I'm talking maybe half a million for you, half a mil for me. Maybe, if things go smooth, a million each. Then we shut it down, cover our tracks, and move to Bermuda."

With burning, needy eyes Piasecki said, "Jimmy makes more than a million in the markets every four months. It's nothing to him."

"What if something goes wrong? I've got a family."

"And I don't? It's my family I'm thinking of. It's not like things are fair in this country. Things are *unfair*. Why should a smart guy like you not get a little piece of the pie? Are you scared?"

"Yes," Kendall said.

"If we do this, you *should* be scared. Just a little. Statistically, though, I'd put the chances of our getting caught at about one percent. Maybe less."

For Kendall it was exciting just to be having this conversation. Everything about the Coq d'Or, from the fatty appetizers to the Tin Pan Alley entertainment to the faux-Napoleonic decor, suggested that it was still 1926. Kendall and Piasecki were leaning conspiratorially together, like a couple of old-time gangsters. They'd seen the Mafia movies, so they knew how to do it. Criminality wasn't like poetry, where one movement succeeded another. The same scheming that had gone on in Chicago eighty years ago was going on now.

"I'm telling you, we could be in and out in two years," Piasecki was saying. "Do it nice and easy and leave no trail. Then we invest our money and do our part for the GDP."

What was a poet but a guy who lived in a fantasy world? Who dreamed instead of did. What would it be like to *do*? To apply your brain to the palpable universe of money instead of the intangible realm of words?

He would never tell Stephanie about any of this. He'd tell her he'd been given a raise. Simultaneous with this thought was another: renovating your kitchen wasn't a red flag. They could do the whole interior without attracting attention.

In his mind Kendall saw his fixer-upper as it would be a year or two from now: modernized, insulated, warm, his children happy, his wife repaid for everything she'd done for him.

Wealth circulates with inconceivable rapidity . . .

The full enjoyment of it . . .

"OK, I'm in," Kendall said.

"You're in?"

"Let me think about it."

That was sufficient for Piasecki for now. He lifted his glass. "To Ken Lay," he said. "My hero."

"What sort of business is this you're opening?"

"It's a storage facility."

"And you're?"

"The president. Co-president, actually."

"With Mr."—the lawyer, a squat woman with thatchlike hair, searched on the incorporation form—"Mr. Piasecki."

"That's right," Kendall said.

It was a Saturday afternoon. Kendall was in downtown Oak Park, in the lawyer's meager, diploma-lined office. Max was outside on the sidewalk, catching autumn leaves as they twirled to the ground. He ran back and forth, his arms outstretched.

"I could use some storage," the lawyer joked. "My kids' sports equipment is crazy. Snowboards, surfboards, tennis rackets, lacrosse sticks. I can barely fit my car into the garage."

"We do commercial storage," Kendall said. "Warehousing. For corporations. Sorry."

He hadn't even laid eyes on the place. It was up in the sticks, outside Kewanee. Piasecki had driven up there and leased the land. There was nothing on it but an old, weed-choked Esso station. But it had a legal address, and soon, as Midwestern Storage, a steady income.

Since Great Experiment sold few books, the publishing company had a lot of inventory on hand. In addition to storing them in their usual warehouse, in Schaumburg, Kendall would soon start sending a phantom number of books up to the facility in Kewanee. Midwestern Storage would charge Great Experiment for this service, and Piasecki would send the company checks. As soon as the incorporation forms were filed, Piasecki planned to open a bank account in Midwestern Storage's name. Signatories to this account: Michael J. Piasecki and Kendall Wallis.

It was all quite elegant. Kendall and Piasecki would own a legal company. The company would earn money legally, pay its taxes legally; the two of them would split the profit and claim it as business income on their tax returns. Who was ever to know that the warehouse housed no books because there *was* no warehouse?

"I just hope the old guy doesn't kick," Piasecki had said. "We've got to pray for Jimmy to stay healthy."

When Kendall had signed the required forms, the lawyer said, "OK, I'll file these papers for you Monday. Congratulations, you're the proud new owner of a corporation in the state of Illinois."

Outside, Max was still whirling beneath the falling leaves.

"How many did you catch, buddy?" Kendall asked.

"Twenty-two!" Max shouted.

Kendall looked up at the sky to watch the leaves, red and gold, spinning down toward the earth. He tucked the papers he was holding under his arm.

"Five more and we have to go home," Kendall said.

"Ten!"

"OK, ten. Ready? Leaf-catching Olympics starts—now!"

And now it was a Monday morning in January, the start of a new week, and Kendall was on the train again, reading about America: "There is one country in the world where the great social revolution that I am speaking of seems to have nearly reached its natural limits." Kendall had a new pair of shoes on, two-tone cordovans from the Allen Edmonds store on

Michigan Avenue. Otherwise, he looked the way he always did, same chinos, same shiny-elbowed corduroy jacket. Nobody on the train would have guessed that he wasn't the mild, bookish figure he appeared to be. No one would have imagined Kendall making his weekly drop-off at the mailbox outside the all-cash building (to keep the doormen from noticing the deposit envelopes addressed to the Kewanee bank). Seeing Kendall jotting figures in his newspaper, most riders assumed he was working out a Sudoku puzzle instead of estimating potential earnings from a five-year CD. Kendall in his editor-wear had the perfect disguise. He was like Poe's purloined letter, hidden in plain sight.

Who said he wasn't smart?

The fear had been greatest the first few weeks. Kendall would awaken at 3 a.m. with what felt like a battery cable hooked to his navel. What if Jimmy noticed the printing, shipping, and warehouse costs for the phantom books? What if Piasecki drunkenly confessed to a pretty bartender whose brother turned out to be a cop? Kendall's mind reeled with potential mishaps and dangers. How had he got into something like this with someone like that? In bed beside Stephanie, who was sleeping the sleep of the just, Kendall lay awake for hours, visions of jail time and perp walks filling his head.

It got easier after a while. Fear was like any other emotion. From an initial stage of passionate intensity, it slowly ebbed until it became routine and then barely noticeable. Plus, things had gone so well. Kendall drew up separate checks, one for the books they actually printed and another for the books he and Piasecki pretended to. On Friday, Piasecki entered these debits in his accounts against weekly income. "It looks like a profit-loss," he told Kendall. "We're actually saving Jimmy taxes. He should thank us."

"Why don't we let him in on it, then?" Kendall said.

Piasecki only laughed. "Even if we did, he's so out of it he wouldn't remember."

Kendall kept to his low-profile plan. As the bank account of Midwestern Storage slowly grew, the same beaten-up old Volvo remained in his driveway. The money stayed away from prying eyes. It showed only inside. In the *interior*. Every night when he came home, Kendall inspected the progress of the plasterers, carpenters, and carpet installers he'd hired. He was looking into additional interiors as well: the walled gardens of college-savings funds (the garden of Max, the garden of Eleanor); the inner sanctum of a SEP-IRA.

And there was something else hidden in his house: a wife. Her name was Arabella. She was from Venezuela and spoke little English. On her first day, confronted by the mountain of laundry in the master bedroom, she had shown neither shock nor horror. Just hauled load after load to the basement, washed and folded the laundry, and put it in their drawers. Kendall and Stephanie were thrilled.

At the lakefront co-op, Kendall did something he hadn't done in a long time: he did his job. He finished abridging *Democracy in America*. He FedExed the color-coded manuscript to Montecito and, the very next day, began writing proposals to bring other obscure books back into print. He sent two or three proposals per day, along with digital or hard copies of the texts in question. Instead of waiting for Jimmy to respond, Kendall called him repeatedly, and pestered him with questions. At first, Jimmy had taken Kendall's calls. But soon he began to complain about their frequency and, finally, he told Kendall to stop bothering him with minutiae and to deal with things himself. "I trust your taste," Jimmy said.

He hardly called the office at all anymore.

The train deposited Kendall at Union Station. Coming out onto Madison Street, he got into a cab (paying with untraceable cash) and had the driver let him out a block from the all-cash building. From there he trudged around the corner, looking as though he'd come on foot. He said hello to Mike, the doorman on duty, and made his way to the elevator.

The penthouse was empty. Not even a maid around. The elevator let you off on the lower floor, and as Kendall was going down the hall, on his way to the circular stairs to his office, he passed Jimmy's Jade Room. He tried the door. It wasn't locked. And so he stepped in.

He had no intention of stealing anything. That would be stupid. He just wanted to trespass, to add this minor act of insubordination to his much larger, Robin Hood–like act of rebellion. The Jade Room was like a room in a museum or an exclusive jewelry store, with beautifully carpentered walls filled with built-in shelves and drawers. At evenly spaced intervals lighted display cases contained pieces of jade. The stone wasn't dark green, as Kendall expected, but a light green. He remembered Jimmy telling him that the best jade, the rarest, was almost white in color, and that the most prized specimens were those carved from single pieces of stone.

The subjects of the carvings were hard to make out, the shapes so sinuous that at first Kendall thought the animals depicted were snakes or serpents. But then he recognized them as horses' heads. Long, tapering horses' heads enfolded upon themselves. Horses tucking their heads against their bodies as though in sleep.

He opened one of the drawers. Inside, on a bed of velvet, was another horse.

Kendall picked it up. Ran his finger along the line of the horse's mane. He thought about the artisan who'd fashioned this thing, some guy in China, sixteen hundred years ago, whose name no one knew anymore and who had died along with everyone else alive during the Jin Dynasty, but who, by looking at a living, breathing horse standing in a misty field somewhere in the Yellow River valley, had so *seen* the animal that he'd managed to render its form into this piece of precious stone, thereby making it even more precious. The human desire to do something useless like that, something exacting and skilled and downright crazy, was what had always excited Kendall, until it ceased to excite him because of his inability to do it himself. His inability to keep up the necessary persistence and to accept the shame of pursuing such a craft in a culture that not only didn't prize the discipline but openly ridiculed it.

Yet somehow this jade carver had succeeded. He would never know it, but this pale white somnolent horse that had lived long ago was still not dead, not yet, for here it was in Kendall's hand, softly lit by the recessed halogen bulbs in this jewelry cabinet of a room.

With something like veneration Kendall returned the horse head to its velvet drawer and closed it. Then he let himself out of the Jade Room and went upstairs to his office.

Shipping boxes filled the floor. The first editions of *The Pocket Democracy* had just come back from the printer—the real printer—and Kendall was in the process of sending copies to bookstore buyers and historical museum gift shops. He had just sat down at his desk and turned on his computer when his phone rang.

"Hey, kiddo. I just got the new book." It was Jimmy. "Looks fantastic! You did a helluva job."

"Thank you."

"What do the orders look like?"

"We'll know in a couple of weeks."

"I think we've got it priced right. And the format is perfect. Get these next to a cash register and we can up-sell these babies. The cover looks terrific."

"I think so, too."

"What about reviews?"

"It's a two-hundred-year-old book. Not exactly news."

"It's news that stays news. OK, ads," Jimmy said. "Send me a list of places you think can reach our audience. Not the fucking *New York Review of Books*. That's preaching to the converted. I want this book to get *out* there. This is important!"

"Let me think a little," Kendall said.

"What else was I going to—? Oh yeah! The bookmark! Great idea. People are going to love this. Promotes the book *and* our brand. You giving these out as promotional items or just in the books themselves?"

"Both."

"Perfect. What about making some posters, too? Each with a different quote from the book. I bet bookstores would use those for a display. Do some mock-ups and send them to me, will you?"

"Will do," Kendall said.

"I'm feeling optimistic. We might sell some books for once."

"Hope so."

"I'll tell you what," Jimmy said, "if this book does as well as I *think* it will, I'll give you health insurance."

Kendall hesitated. "That would be great."

"I don't want to lose you, kiddo. Plus, I'll be honest, it's a headache finding someone else."

This generosity wasn't grounds for reappraisal and regret. Jimmy had taken his sweet time, hadn't he? And the promise was phrased in the conditional. If, not when. No, Kendall thought to himself, just wait and see how things turn out. If Jimmy gives me insurance and a nice raise, then maybe I'll *think* about shutting Midwestern Storage down. But then and only then.

"Oh, one more thing," Jimmy said. "Piasecki sent me the accounts. The numbers look funny."

"Excuse me?"

"What are we doing printing thirty thousand copies of Thomas Paine? And why are we using *two* printers?"

At congressional hearings, or in courtrooms, the accused CEOs and CFOs followed one of two strategies: they either said they didn't know or they didn't remember.

"I don't remember why we printed thirty thousand," Kendall said. "I'll have to check the orders. As far as printers go, Piasecki handles that. Maybe someone offered us a better deal."

"The new printer is charging us a higher rate."

Piasecki hadn't told Kendall that. Piasecki had become greedy, jacked the price, and kept it to himself.

"Listen," Jimmy said, "send me the contact info for the new printer. And for that storage place up in wherever it is. I'm going to have my guy out here look into this."

Kendall sat forward in his chair. "What guy?"

"My accountant. You think I'd let Piasecki operate without oversight? No way! Everything he does gets double-checked out here. If he's pulling anything, we'll find out. Don't worry. And then that Polack's up shit creek."

Kendall's mind was racing. He was trying to come up with an answer that would prevent this audit, or delay it, but before he said anything, Jimmy continued, "Listen, kiddo, I'm going to London next week. The Montecito house'll be empty. Why don't you bring your family out here for a long weekend? Get out of that cold weather."

"I'll have to check with my wife," Kendall said tonelessly. "And the kids' school schedule."

"Take the kids out of school. It won't kill them."

"I'll talk to my wife."

"Anyway, you did good, kiddo. You boiled Tocqueville down to his essence. I remember when I first read this book. Must have been twenty-one, twenty-two. Blew me away."

In his vibrant, scratchy voice, Jimmy began to recite a

passage of *Democracy in America*. It was the passage Kendall had printed on the bookmarks and for which the small press was named: "In that land the great experiment of the attempt to construct society upon a new basis was to be made by civilized man," Jimmy said, "and it was there, for the first time, that theories hitherto unknown, or deemed impracticable, were to exhibit a spectacle for which the world had not been prepared by the history of the past."

Kendall stared out the window at the lake. It went on endlessly. But instead of finding relief and freedom from the view, he felt as if the lake, all those tons of cold, nearly freezing water, were closing in.

"That fucking kills me," Jimmy said. "Every time."

2008

FRESH COMPLAINT

By the time Matthew learns that the charges have been dropped—there will be no extradition or trial—he's been back in England for four months. Ruth and Jim have bought a house in Dorset, near the sea. It's a lot smaller than the house Matthew and his sister grew up in, when Ruth was married to their father. But it's full of things that Matthew remembers from his London childhood. As he climbs to the guest room at night or goes out the side door on his way to the pub, familiar objects leap out at him: the carved figurine of the Alpine hiker, in lederhosen, purchased on a family trip to Switzerland, in 1977; or those glass bookends that used to be in Dad's office, solid blocks of transparency, each containing a golden apple that, to his child's eyes, had appeared magically suspended. Now they're in the kitchen, holding up Ruth's cookbooks.

The side door opens onto a cobblestone lane that winds around the back of the neighboring houses, past a church and a cemetery, into the center of town. The pub is opposite a chemist's and an H&M outlet. Matthew's a regular there now. Other patrons sometimes ask why he's come back to England, but the reasons he gives—problems with his work visa and tax complications—seem to satisfy their curiosity. He worries that something about the case will pop up on the Internet, but so far nothing has. The town lies inland of the English Channel, 120 miles from London. PJ Harvey recorded *Let England Shake* in a church not far away. Matthew listens to the album on headphones while he walks on the moorlands, or runs errands in the car, if he can get Ruth's Bluetooth working. The lyrics of the songs, which are about ancient battles and the English dead, dark places of sacred memory, are his welcome back home.

Occasionally, as Matthew drives through the village, a flash goes off in his peripheral vision. A girl's bright blond hair. Or a group of students standing outside the nursing college, smoking cigarettes. He feels criminal just looking.

One afternoon he drives to the seaside. After parking the car, he sets out walking. The clouds, as they always do here, hang low in the sky. It's as if, having traveled across the ocean, they're surprised to find land beneath them, and haven't withdrawn to a respectable distance.

He follows the trail until it reaches the bluff. And it's then, as he looks west over the ocean, that the realization hits him.

He's free to go back now. He can see his children. It's safe to return to America.

Eleven months ago, early in the year, Matthew had been invited to give a lecture at a small college in Delaware. He took the Monday-morning train down from New York, where he lived with his wife, Tracy, who was American, and their two children, Jacob and Hazel. By three that afternoon he was in a coffee shop across from his hotel, waiting to be picked up by someone from the physics department and taken to the auditorium.

He'd chosen a table near the front window so that he could

be easily seen. While he drank his espresso, he went over his lecture notes on his computer, but soon got distracted by answering e-mail, and after that, by reading *The Guardian* online. He'd finished his coffee and was thinking of ordering a second when he heard a voice.

"Professor?"

A dark-haired girl in a baggy sweatshirt, carrying a backpack, was standing a few feet away. As soon as Matthew looked up at her, she raised her hands in surrender. "I'm not stalking you," she said. "I promise."

"I didn't think you were."

"Are you Matthew Wilks? I'm coming to your lecture today!"

She announced this as though Matthew had been hanging on the answer to this question. But then, seeming to realize that she needed to explain herself, she lowered her hands and said, "I go here. I'm a student." She pushed out her chest to show off the college seal on her sweatshirt.

Matthew didn't get recognized in public much. When it *did* happen, it was by colleagues of his—other cosmologists—and graduate students. Occasionally a reader, middle-aged or older. Never anybody like this.

The girl appeared to be Indian-American. She spoke and dressed like a typical American girl her age, and yet the clothes she had on, not only the sweatshirt but the black leggings, Timberland boots, and purple hiking socks, along with a general sense that clung to her of undergraduate uncleanliness, of the communal, dormitory existence she lived, didn't keep the extravagance of her face from making Matthew think of her genetic origins far away. The girl reminded him of a figure in a Hindu miniature. Her dark lips, her arching nose with its flared nostrils, and most of all her startling eyes, which were a color that might only exist in a painting where the artist could mix green and blue and yellow indiscriminately, made the girl look less like a college student from Delaware than a dancing gopi, or a child saint venerated by the masses.

"If you're coming to my lecture," Matthew managed to say while processing these impressions, "you must be a physics major."

The girl shook her head. "I'm only a freshperson. We don't have to declare until next year." She slipped off her backpack and set it down, as if settling in. "My parents want me to do something in science. And I'm interested in physics. I took AP Physics in high school. But I'm also thinking about going to law school, which would be more like humanities. Do you have any advice for me?"

It felt awkward to be sitting while the girl was standing. But asking her to sit would invite a longer conversation than Matthew had time or desire for. "My advice is to study whatever interests you. You've got time to make up your mind."

"That's what you did, right? At Oxford? You started studying philosophy but then switched to physics."

"That's right."

"I'd really like to hear how you combine all your interests," the girl said. "Because that's what I want to do. I mean, you're such a beautiful writer! The way you explain the Big Bang, or spontaneous inflation, it's almost like I can see it happening. Did you take a lot of literature courses in college?"

"I took some, yes."

"I'm literally addicted to your blog. When I heard you were coming to campus, I couldn't believe it!" The girl paused, staring and smiling. "Do you think we could get coffee or something while you're here, Professor?"

Bold as it was, this request didn't surprise Matthew all that much. Every class he taught had at least one pushy kid in it. Kids who'd been building their résumés since kindergarten. They wanted to meet for coffee or come to his office

hours, they wanted to network, hoping to line up recommen-
dations or internships down the line, or just to relieve for a
few minutes the anxiety of being the stressed-out, hyper-
competitive people the world had fashioned them to be. This
girl's intensity, her buzzing enthusiasm that came close to
nervousness, was a thing he recognized.

Matthew was away from home on business, with free
time on his hands. He didn't want to spend it serving as an
undergraduate advisor. "They're keeping me pretty busy
while I'm here," he said. "Full schedule."

"How long are you here for?"

"Just tonight."

"OK. Well, at least I'm coming to your talk."

"Right."

"I was going to come to your Q and A tomorrow morning but I have class," the girl said.

"You won't miss anything. I usually just repeat myself."

"I bet that is *so* not true," said the girl. She picked up her
backpack. She seemed on the point of leaving but then said,
"Do you need anyone to show you where the auditorium is?
I still get lost around here but I think I can find it. I'm going
there, obviously."

"They're sending someone to fetch me."

"OK. Now you think I *am* stalking you. It was nice
meeting you, Professor."

"Nice to meet you."

But still the girl didn't leave. She continued to look at
Matthew with her weird intensity that was also a vacancy.
From out of this vacancy, as if delivering a message from another realm, the girl suddenly said, "You're better-looking
in person than your photos."

"I'm not sure that's a compliment."

"It's a statement."

"I'm not sure it's good news, though. Given the Internet,

more people probably see photographs of me than my actual living self."

"I didn't say you looked *bad* in your photos, Professor," the girl said. And with a touch of hurt feelings, or an indication that their interchange had been, after all, a slight disappointment, the girl shouldered her backpack and walked away.

Matthew turned back to his laptop. Stared at the screen. Only when the girl had left the coffee shop and was passing by the front window did he glance up, conscientiously, to see what she looked like from behind.

It wasn't fair.

Even though a third of the kids at her school were Indian, Diwali wasn't an official holiday. They got off for Christmas and Easter, of course, and for Rosh Hashanah and Yom Kippur, but when it came to the Hindu or Muslim holidays there were only "accommodations." That meant teachers excused you from class but still assigned homework. And it meant that you were responsible for whatever material they went over that day.

Prakrti was going to miss four days. Almost a whole week and at the worst time possible: right before exams in math and history, and during her crucial junior year. The thought of it filled her with panic.

She'd pleaded with her parents to cancel the trip. She didn't understand why they couldn't celebrate the holiday at home like everyone else they knew. Prakrti's mother explained that she missed her family, her sister, Deepa, and her brothers, Pratul and Amitava. Her parents—Prakrti and Durva's grandparents—were getting older, too. Didn't Prakrti want to see Dadi and Dadu before they vanished from the earth?

Prakrti made no reply to this. She didn't know her grandparents well—saw them only on intermittent visits to what was, for her, a foreign country. It wasn't Prakrti's fault that her grandparents seemed strange and attenuated, and yet she knew that to publicize this fact would put her in a bad light.

"Just leave me here," she said. "I can take care of myself."

This didn't work either.

They flew out from Philadelphia International on a Monday night in early November. Sitting in the rear of the plane next to her little sister, Prakrti switched on the overhead light. Her plan was to read *The Scarlet Letter* on the way over and write the related essay on the flight back. But she couldn't concentrate. Hawthorne's symbolism felt as stuffy as the cabin's recirculated air; and though she sympathized with Hester Prynne, punished for doing what anyone would nowadays, as soon as the flight attendants served dinner Prakrti used the excuse to put down her tray table and watch a movie while she ate.

By the time they arrived in Kolkata, she was too jet-lagged to do homework. Too busy as well. Insisting that they shouldn't nap, Aunt Deepa took Prakrti, Durva, their cousin Smita and their mother shopping first thing. They went to a fancy new department store to buy utensils, silver forks, knives, and serving spoons; and, for the girls, gold and silver bangles. After that, they walked through a covered market, a kind of bazaar lined with stalls, to get the rice and vermillion powder. Back at the apartment, they began decorating for the holiday. Prakrti, Durva, and Smita were given the task of making Lakshmi's footprints. Barefoot, the three girls stepped into trays of moistened powder laid outside the front door. Carefully, they stepped out again, and made a path inside. They created two sets of footprints, one in red and one in white; and because Lakshmi was supposed to be bringing prosperity, they didn't miss a room, making footprints lead in and out of the kitchen, the living room, even the bathroom.

Rajiv, their other cousin, who was a year older than Prakrti, had two Xboxes in his bedroom. She spent the rest of the afternoon playing *Titanfall* with him, in multi-player mode. The apartment's Internet connection was super fast, and didn't glitch. On previous trips to India, Prakrti had pitied her cousins' obsolete computer equipment, but now, like Kolkata itself, they had leapt ahead of her. The city looked almost futuristic in places, especially compared with poor old Dover with its redbrick storefronts, its leaning telephone poles, its roads full of potholes.

Prakrti and Durva had packed their saris in plastic dry cleaner's bags to keep them from wrinkling. That night, for Dhanteras, they put them on. They slipped the new bangles on their arms and stood before the mirror, watching the metal catch the light.

As soon as it got dark, the family lit the diyas and placed them around the apartment—on the windowsills, coffee tables, in the center of the dining table, and on top of her uncle's stereo speakers. Music streamed from these black monoliths, as the family gathered around the dining table, and feasted, and sang bajahns.

All night long, relatives kept arriving. Some Prakrti recognized but most she didn't, though they knew all about her: that she was a top student, a member of the debating team, and even that she planned to apply for Early Decision to the University of Chicago next year. They agreed with her mother that Chicago was too far from Delaware, and also too cold. Did she really want to be so far away? Wouldn't she freeze?

A group of old women, white-haired and loud, wanted a piece of her, too. They clustered around her with their sagging breasts and bellies, and shouted questions in Bengali. Whenever Prakrti didn't understand something—which was most of the time—they shouted louder, only to give up, finally, and shake their heads, amused and appalled by her American ignorance.

Around midnight, jet lag caught up with her. Prakrti fell asleep on the couch. When she woke up, three old ladies were hovering over her, making comments.

"That is so creepy," Durva said, when Prakrti told her.

"I know, right?"

The next few days were just as crazy. They went to the temple, visited their uncles' families, exchanged gifts, and stuffed themselves with food. Some relatives observed every custom and ritual, others only a few, and still others treated the week like one long party and vacation. On the night of Diwali they went down to the water for the festivities. The river that ran through Kolkata, the Hooghly, which looked brown and sludgy during the daytime, was now, under a star-lit sky, transformed into a black and sparkling mirror. Thousands of people lined the bank. Despite the throngs, there was little jostling as people approached the water's edge to release their rafts of flowers. The crowd moved like a single organism, any lurch of activity in one direction compensated for by a retraction in another. The unity was impressive. On top of that, Prakrti's father explained to her that everything that was going into the water—the palm fronds, the flowers, even the candles themselves, which were made of beeswax—would decompose by tomorrow morning, the entire blazing ritual winking out and leaving no trace.

The glittery nonsense surrounding the holiday—Lakshmi, goddess of prosperity, gold and silver baubles, shining knives, forks, and serving spoons—all came down to this, to light and its brevity. You lived, you burned, you spread your little light—then poof. Your soul went into another body. That's what her mother believed. Her father doubted it, and Prakrti knew it wasn't true. She didn't plan on dying for a long time.

Before she did, she wanted to do something with her life. She put her arm around her little sister and together they watched their candles drift out until they became indistinguishable in the sea of flames.

If they'd left on the weekend, as scheduled, the trip would have been tolerable. But after Bhai Dooj, the last day of the festival, Prakrti's mother announced that she'd changed their tickets to stay a day longer.

Prakrti was so furious she could hardly sleep that night. The next morning, she came to breakfast in sweats and a T-shirt, her hair uncombed, her mood sullen.

"You can't wear that today, Prakrti," her mother said. "We're going out. Put on your sari."

"No."

"What?"

"It's all sweaty. I've worn it three times already. My choli smells."

"Go put it on."

"Why me? What about Durva?"

"Your sister's younger. A salwar kameez is fine for her."

When Prakrti came out in her sari, her mother was unsatisfied. She took her back to the bedroom to rewrap it herself. Next she inspected Prakrti's fingernails and tweezed her eyebrows. Finally—a new thing entirely—she applied kohl around Prakrti's eyes.

"Can you not?" Prakrti said, pulling away.

Her mother seized Prakrti's face with both hands. "Be still!"

A car was waiting outside. They drove for over an hour to the outside of the city, where they stopped before a compound with walls topped with razor wire.

A gatekeeper led them across a dirt courtyard into the house. They passed through a tiled entryway, up a flight of stairs, into a large room with tall windows on three sides and wicker-bladed fans on the ceiling. Despite the heat, the fans weren't running. The room was severely underfurnished, except in one corner, where a white-haired man in a Nehru jacket sat cross-legged on a mat. The kind of man you expected to encounter in India. A guru. Or a politician.

Across from him, a middle-aged couple occupied a small sofa. As Prakrti and her family came in, they waggled their heads in greeting.

Her parents sat opposite the couple. Durva was given a chair just behind. Prakrti was steered to a bench or platform—she didn't know what to call it—slightly apart from everyone else. The bench was made of sandalwood inlaid with ivory. It had a vaguely ceremonial air. As she sat down, she caught a whiff of herself—she was beginning to perspire in the heat. She wanted not to care. Had an urge even to inflict her body odor on all these people and embarrass her mother—but of course she couldn't. She was too mortified herself. Instead, she sat as still as possible.

During the conversation that followed, Prakrti heard her name spoken. But she was never directly addressed.

Tea was served. Indian sweets. After a week, Prakrti was sick of them. But she ate them to be polite.

She missed her phone. She wanted to text her friend Kylie and describe the torture she was presently undergoing. As the minutes passed on the hard bench, and servants came and went, other people passed along the corridor, peering in. The house appeared to contain dozens of people. Curious. Nosy.

By the time it was over, Prakrti had made a vow of silence. She got back into the car intending not to say another word to her parents until they got home. So it was left to Durva to ask, "Who were those people?"

"I told you," Prakrti's mother said. "The Kumars."

"Are we related to them?"

Her mother laughed. "Maybe one day." She looked out

the window, her face lit with a violent satisfaction. "They are the parents of the boy who wants to marry your sister."

Matthew talked for forty-five minutes, as requested. His topic, that day, was gravitational waves, in particular their recent detection by twin interferometers located at disparate locations in the continental United States. Wearing a lavalier, and pacing the stage in a navy jacket and jeans, Matthew explained that Einstein had theorized the existence of these waves almost a hundred years ago, but that proof had only been found this year. To aid his presentation, Matthew had come equipped with a digital simulation of the two black holes whose merging, in a galaxy 1.3 billion light-years away, had created the ripples that had passed invisibly and silently through the universe to register against the highly sensitive devices—in Livingston, Louisiana, and Hanford, Washington—that had been engineered for this purpose alone. "As acute as the ear of God," Matthew described them. "In fact, a lot better than that."

The auditorium was less than half full. Equally disheartening, most of the audience consisted of people in their seventies or eighties, retirees from the town who came to these lectures at the college because they were open to the public and given at a reasonable hour, and because they gave them something to talk about afterward at dinner.

At the book signing, those who remained bore avidly down on Matthew as he sat behind a table, armed with a Sharpie and a glass of wine. Many carried beige totes, the women wearing bright scarves and loose, forgiving sweaters, the men in shapeless chinos, all of them exuding anticipation and forbearance. It wasn't clear from what people said if they had read Matthew's book, or understood the science, but they definitely wanted their copies personalized. Most everyone was content to smile and say, "Thank you for coming to Dover!" as if he were doing it for free. Some men trotted out whatever they remembered from high school or college physics courses and tried to apply it to Matthew's talk.

A woman with white bangs and red cheeks stopped in front of Matthew. She'd recently been to England to research her genealogy, she said, and she gave him an extended account of the pertinent gravestones she'd located in various Anglican churchyards in Kent. This woman had just moved on when the girl from the coffee shop appeared.

"I don't have anything for you to sign," she said guiltlessly.

"That's all right. It's not required."

"I'm too poor to buy a book! College is so expensive!"

A little over an hour ago, the girl had struck Matthew as something of a bother. But now, drained by the procession of old, haggard faces, he gazed up at her with relief and gratitude. She'd taken off her baggy sweatshirt and now had on a little white top that left her shoulders bare.

"At least get yourself some wine," Matthew told her. "That's free."

"I'm not twenty-one yet. I'm nineteen. I'll be twenty in May."

"I don't think anyone will mind."

"Are you trying to ply me with liquor, Professor?" the girl said.

Matthew felt himself blushing. He tried to think of something to counter this impression, but because what the girl had said wasn't so far from the truth, nothing occurred to him.

Fortunately, the girl, in her hectic, excited way, had already moved on. "I know!" she said, her eyes growing wide.

"Could you sign a piece of paper for me? That way, I can paste it into your book."

"If you ever buy it."

"Right. First I have to graduate and pay off my college loans."

She had already swung her backpack onto the table. The motion released her smell, a light, clean scent, something like talcum.

Behind her, a dozen people were still in line. They didn't seem impatient but a few were staring to see what was holding things up.

The girl produced a small ringed notebook. Opening it, she searched for a blank page. As she did this, her black hair fell forward, curtaining them off from the people in line. And then a strange thing happened. The girl seemed to shiver. Some delicate or tormenting sensation traveled the length of her body. She lifted her eyes toward Matthew's, and as if giving in to an irresistible urge, she said in a strangled, elated voice, "Oh, God! Why don't you just sign my body?"

The avowal was so sudden, so absurd, so welcome, that for a moment Matthew was struck dumb. He glanced at the nearest people in line to see if anyone had overheard.

"I think I'd better stick with the notebook," he said.

She handed it over. Laying it flat on the table, Matthew asked, "How would you like this?"

"To Prakrti. Want me to spell it?"

But he was already writing: "To Prakrti. A Fresh Person."

This made the girl laugh. Then, as if making the most innocent request in the world, she said, "Can you put down your cell?"

Matthew didn't even dare to look up again. His face was burning. He was desperate for the moment to be over and thrilled by the encounter. He scrawled down his phone number. "Thank you for coming," he said, pushing the notebook away, and then turned to the next person in line.

The boy's name was Dev. Dev Kumar. He was twenty years old, worked in a store selling TVs and video equipment, and was taking night school classes toward a degree in computer science. All this Prakrti's mother told her on the plane back to the U.S.

The idea that she would marry this unknown person— or anyone for that matter, for a long, long time—was too preposterous for Prakrti to take seriously.

"Mom, hello? I'm only sixteen."

"I was seventeen when I got engaged to your father."

Yeah, and look how that turned out, Prakrti thought. But she said nothing. Discussing the idea would only dignify it, when what she wanted was to make it go away. Her mother was prone to wild imaginings. She was always dreaming of moving back to India after Prakrti's dad retired. She fantasized about Prakrti's getting a job there someday, in Bangalore or Mumbai, of her marrying an Indian boy and buying a house big enough to accommodate her parents. Dev Kumar was just the latest form this fantasy had taken.

Prakrti put on her headphones to block her mother out. She spent the rest of the flight writing her essay on *The Scarlet Letter.*

After they got back home, just as she hoped, the nightmare scenario went away. Her mother brought up Dev a few times, in a scripted, promotional way, but then let the subject drop. Her father, back at work, seemed to have forgotten the Kumars entirely. As for Prakrti, she re-immersed herself in schoolwork. She studied late every night, traveled with the debate team, and, on Saturday mornings, attended SAT prep sessions at her school.

One weekend, in December, she was in her bedroom, Facetiming with Kylie while they did their homework. Prakrti had her phone in bed next to her, Kylie's voice coming from the speaker.

"So, anyway," Kylie said, "he comes to my house and leaves all these flowers on the front porch."

"Ziad?"

"Yeah. He leaves them right there. Like grocery-store flowers. But a lot of them. And then my mom and dad and my little brother come home and find them. It was so embarrassing. *Hold* on. He just texted me."

While she waited for Kylie to read the text, Prakrti said, "You should break up with him. He's immature, he can't spell, and—I'm sorry but—he's large."

When her phone pinged a moment later, Prakrti thought Kylie had forwarded the new text from Ziad, so they could discuss it and decide what to write back. She opened the text without looking at the sender, and the screen of her phone filled with the face of Dev Kumar.

She knew it was him by his pained, overeager expression. Dev stood—or had been posed, most likely—in flattering light before the convoluted limbs of a banyan tree. He was skinny in a developing-world way, as though deprived of protein as a child. Her cousin Rajiv and his friends dressed the way boys at Prakrti's school did, maybe a bit better. They wore the same brands and had the same haircuts. By comparison, Dev was wearing a white shirt with absurdly large seventies-style lapels and ill-fitting gray pants. His smile was crooked and his black hair shiny with oil.

Normally Prakrti would have shared the photo with Kylie. Selfies of guys who were trying too hard, guys who sent chest pics or used filters, were normally guaranteed to send them into fits of laughter. But that night Prakrti clicked her phone shut and put it down. She didn't want to explain who Dev was. She was too embarrassed.

Neither, in the passing days, did she tell her Indian friends. A lot of them had parents whose own marriages had been arranged, and so were used to hearing the practice defended at home. Some parents advanced the superiority of arranged marriages by citing the low divorce rate in India. Mr. Mehta, Devi Mehta's dad, liked to bring up a "scientific" study in *Psychology Today*, which concluded that people in love marriages were more in love during the first *five* years of marriage whereas people in arranged marriages were more in love after *thirty* years of marriage. Love flowered from shared experiences was the message. It was a reward rather than a gift.

Parents *had* to say this, of course. To do otherwise would be to invalidate their own unions. But it was all an act. They knew things were different in America.

Except that sometimes they weren't. There was a group of girls at Prakrti's school who came from super-conservative families, girls who'd been born in India themselves, and partly raised there, and who, as a consequence, were totally submissive. Though these girls spoke perfect English in class, and wrote essays in a strange, beautiful, almost Victorian style, among themselves they preferred to speak Hindi, or Gujarati, or whatever. They never ate cafeteria food or used the vending machines but brought their own vegetarian lunches, packed in tiffins. These girls weren't allowed to attend school dances or to join after-school clubs that had boys as members. They came to school every day and quietly, dutifully did their work, and, after the last bell sounded, they trooped out to Kia sedans and Honda minivans to be returned to their quarantined existence. There was a rumor that these girls, protective of their hymens, wouldn't use Tampax. That inspired the nickname Prakrti and her friends had for them. The Hymens, they called them. Look, here come the Hymens.

"I don't know why I like him," Kylie said. "We used to have this Newfoundland, Bartleby. Ziad sort of reminds me of him."

"What?"

"Are you even listening to me?"

"Sorry," Prakrti said. "Yeah, no. Those dogs are gross. They drool."

She deleted the photo.

"So now you're giving out my number to random guys?" Prakrti said to her mother, the next day.

"Did you get the picture from Dev? His mother promised to make him send one."

"You say never to give my number to strangers and now *you're* giving it out?"

"Dev is hardly 'random.'"

"He is to me."

"Let me take a picture of you to send back. I promised Mrs. Kumar."

"No."

"Come on. Don't look so gloomy. Dev will think you have a terrible disposition. *Smile*, Prakrti. Do I have to force you to smile?"

Why don't you just sign my body?

At dinner, in a restaurant near campus, while making conversation with members of the lecture committee, Matthew kept hearing the girl's words in his head.

Did she mean what she said? Or was it just the kind of

dumb, provocative statement American college girls made nowadays? Equivalent to the way they danced, bumping and grinding, *twerking*, sending out messages that were unintentional. If Matthew were younger, if he were remotely the same age, maybe he'd know the answer.

The restaurant was nicer than he'd expected. A woody, farm-to-table place, with a warm interior. They'd been given a room off the bar, Matthew seated, importantly, at the center of the table.

The woman next to him, a philosophy professor in her thirties with frizzy hair, a broad face, and a pugnacious manner, said to Matthew, "Here's my cosmology question. If we accept an infinite multiverse, and the existence of every conceivable kind of universe, then there has to be a universe in which God exists and one in which He—I mean, She—doesn't. Along with every other kind of universe. So, which one are we living in?"

"Fortunately, one that has alcohol," Matthew said, raising his glass.

"Is there a universe where I have hair?" said a bald, bearded economist two seats away.

The conversation went on like that, quick, jovial. People peppered Matthew with questions. Whenever he opened his mouth to answer, the table fell silent. The questions had nothing to do with his talk, which had already faded from their minds, but were about other topics: space aliens, or the Higgs boson. The only other physicist there, possibly resentful of Matthew's relative success, didn't say a word. On the walk over to the restaurant, he had told Matthew, "Your blog is popular with my undergrads. The kids love it."

After the main course, while the dishes were being cleared away, the chair of the committee instructed the people sitting closest to Matthew to switch seats with those farther away. Everyone ordered pudding, but when the waiter came to him, Matthew asked for a whiskey. The drink had just arrived when his phone vibrated in his pocket.

The new person who sat down next to Matthew was a birdlike woman with pale skin, dressed in a pantsuit. "I'm not a professor," she said. "I'm Pete's wife." She pointed to her husband across the table.

Matthew took his phone from his pocket and held it discreetly below the table.

He didn't recognize the number. The message was simple: "hi."

Returning the phone to his pocket, he took a sip of whiskey. He leaned back and gazed around the restaurant. He'd reached the stage of the evening—of evenings like this on the road—when a rosiness came over things, a slow, flavorful, oozing light invading the restaurant almost like a liquid. The rosiness came from the glow of the bar with its rows of colorful bottles stacked on mirrored shelves, but also from the wall sconces and candlelight reflecting on the plate-glass windows etched in gold. The rosiness was part of the hum of the restaurant, the sounds of people talking and laughing, convivial, city sounds, but it was also part of Matthew himself, a rising sense of contentment at being who and where he was, free to get up to whatever mischief presented itself. On top of it all, this rosiness had to do with his knowledge of the single word—*hi*—that lay hidden in the cell phone tucked in his pocket snug against his thigh.

This rosiness wouldn't survive on its own. It needed Matthew's participation. Before excusing himself, he ordered another whiskey. Then he stood up, gaining his balance, and walked through the bar to the stairs that led down to the lavatory.

The men's room was empty. Music, which may have been playing upstairs in the loud restaurant, was pumping from high-fidelity speakers in the ceiling. It sounded surprisingly good in the tiled space, and Matthew moved to the beat as he entered a toilet stall and closed the door behind him. He took out his phone and began typing with one finger.

> I'm sorry. I don't recognize this number.
> Who is this?

The response was almost immediate.

> the fresh person :)

> Well, hello there.

> what are you doing?

> Getting drunk at a restaurant.

> sounds fun are you alone?

Matthew hesitated. Then he wrote:

> Desperately.

It was like skiing. Like the moment when, at the summit, you first lean downhill and gravity takes hold, sending you flying. For the next few minutes, as they texted back and forth, Matthew was only half aware of the person he was communicating with. The two images he had of the girl—one in the baggy sweatshirt, the other in the tight white top—were hard to reconcile. He couldn't remember exactly what she looked like anymore. The girl was specific enough yet vague enough to be any woman, or all women. Each text Matthew sent generated a thrilling reply, and as his tone escalated in flirtatiousness, the girl matched him. The excitement of hurling impetuous thoughts into the void was intoxicating.

Now ellipses appeared: the girl was typing something. Matthew stared at his screen, waiting. He could feel the girl at the other end of the invisible pathway connecting them, her head lowered, her black hair falling over her face as it had at the book table, while she worked the keys with her nimble thumbs.

And then her response appeared:

> you're married right?

Matthew hadn't seen that coming. It sobered him up at once. For a moment he saw himself for what he was, a middle-aged, married man and father, hiding in a bathroom stall, texting a girl less than half his age.

There was only one honorable response.

> I am indeed.

Ellipses appeared again. Then vanished. Did not reappear.

Matthew waited a few more minutes before exiting the stall. Seeing his reflection in the mirror, he grimaced and cried out, "Pathetic!"

But he didn't feel that way. Not really. On the whole, he felt rather proud of himself, as if he'd failed while attempting a spectacular play in a sporting contest.

He was climbing the stairs back to the restaurant when his phone went off again.

> I don't mind if you don't.

On the dresser in the master bedroom stood a wedding portrait. In garish color, it showed the boy and girl who would become Prakrti's parents standing solemnly beside each other, as though prodded into position by a goad. Atop her father's impossibly slender face sat a white turban. A diadem depended from her mother's smooth forehead, its gold chain matching the ring in her nose and shadowed by the veil of red lace that covered her hair. Both their necks were draped with heavy necklaces made of multiple strings of shining, dark red berries. Or maybe they were too hard to be berries. Maybe they were seeds.

On the day the photograph was taken, her parents had known each other for twenty-four hours.

Most of the time, Prakrti didn't think about her parents' wedding. It had happened long ago, in another country, under different rules. But every now and then, compelled by outrage as much as curiosity, she forced herself to imagine the events immediately following the taking of that photo. A dark, provisionary hotel room somewhere, and, standing in the middle of it, her seventeen-year-old mother. A naïve village girl who knew next to nothing about sex, or guys, or birth control, and yet who knew what was required of her in that particular moment. Understood that it was her duty to take off her clothes in front of a man no less a stranger than someone she passed on the street. To remove her wedding sari, her satin slippers, her hand-sewn underclothes, her gold bangles and necklaces, and to lie on her back and let him do what he wanted. To submit. To an accounting student who shared an apartment, in Newark, New Jersey, with six other bachelors, his breath still smelling of the American fast food he'd wolfed down before getting on the plane to fly to India.

Prakrti couldn't reconcile the scandal of this arrangement—it was almost prostitution—with the prim, autocratic mother she knew. Most probably, it hadn't happened like that at all, she decided. No, more likely nothing had gone on in the first weeks or months of her parents' marriage but only much later, once they'd gotten to know each other and any hint of compulsion or violation had disappeared. Prakrti would never know the truth. She was too scared to ask.

She went online to find other people in her situation. As usual with the Internet, it took only a few searches to locate message boards teeming with complaints, advice, rationalizations, cries for help, and expressions of comfort. Some women, usually educated and living in cities, treated the subject of arranged marriage with theatrical alarm, as though they were living out a zany episode of *The Mindy Project*. They depicted their parents as well-meaning people whose meddlesomeness, however infuriating, never kept them from being loveable. "So my mom keeps giving out my e-mail to people she meets. The other day I get this e-mail from some guy's dad and he starts asking all these personal questions, like how much do I weigh and do I smoke or take drugs and are there any health or gynecological issues he should know about, in order to see if I'm marriage material for his lame son who I wouldn't even hook up with if we were both at Burning Man on molly and I was feeling generous and/or horny." Other women seemed resigned to parental pressure and scheming. "I mean, seriously," one person wrote, "is it any worse than joining OkCupid? Or having some guy in a bar blow his boozy breath in your face all night?"

But there were heartbreaking posts, too, from girls closer to Prakrti's age. Girls who didn't write that well and who maybe went to bad schools or who hadn't lived in the States long. There was one post, from a girl whose username was "Brokenbylife," that Prakrti couldn't get out of her head. "Hi, I live in Arkansas. It's illegal here to get married at my age (I'm 15) unless you have parental consent. The problem is my dad wants me to marry this friend of his from India. I haven't even met him. I asked to see a photo but the one my dad showed me was of a guy way too young to be a friend of his (my dad's 56). So it's like I'm being catfished by my own father. Can anyone help me? Is there some kind of legal aid I can contact? What can you do if you're young and don't consent but are too scared to go against your parents because of past issues with verbal/physical abuse?"

After spending a few hours on the Internet reading stuff like that, Prakrti was frantic. It made everything *real*er. What she'd thought lunacy was everywhere being put into practice, fought against, or given in to.

From Dorset Matthew takes the train to London, and then another to Heathrow. Two hours later, he's in the air, heading to JFK. He's chosen a window seat so he won't be disturbed during the flight. Looking out the window, he sees the wing of the jet, the large, cylindrical, dirty-looking jet engine. He imagines opening the emergency door and walking out on the wing, balancing himself against the force of the wind, and for a moment it almost seems plausible.

In the four months he's been in England, he has kept in touch with his children mainly by text. They don't like e-mail. Too slow, they say. Skype, their preference, disorients Matthew. The streaming images of Jacob and Hazel that appear on his laptop render them simultaneously within reach and irreclaimable. Jacob's face looks fatter. He gets distracted and frequently looks away, possibly at another screen. Hazel pays her father undivided attention. Leaning forward, she holds a fistful of hair close to the camera to show off her new highlights, which she's dyed red, or purple, or blue. Often the screen freezes, however, pixelating his children's faces and making them seem constructed, illusory.

Matthew is unnerved, too, by his own image as it pops up in a window at the corner of the screen. There he is, their shadowy dad, in his hideout.

All his attempts at joviality sound false in his ears.

There's no winning: if his children seem traumatized by his absence, it's terrible; if they seem distant and self-reliant, it's just as bad. The familiar details of their bedrooms stab Matthew in the heart, the flocked wallpaper in Hazel's room, Jacob's hockey posters.

The children sense that their lives have become precarious. They have overheard Tracy speaking with Matthew on the phone, with her family and friends, with her lawyer. The children ask Matthew if he and their mother are getting divorced, and he tells them, honestly, that he doesn't know. He doesn't know if they will be a family again.

More than anything, what astounds him now is his stupidity. He'd thought his cheating only involved Tracy. Had believed that the trust he was breaking was with her alone; and that his deceit was mitigated, if not excused, by the travails of marriage, the resentments, the physical dissatisfactions. He'd careened out of control, with Jacob and Hazel in the backseat, and thought they couldn't be injured.

Occasionally, during Skype calls, Tracy blunders into the room. Realizing whom Jacob or Hazel is speaking to, she calls out a greeting to Matthew in a strained, forgiving voice. But she stays back, careful not to show her face. Or to see his.

"That was awkward," Hazel said, after one such episode.

It's difficult to know what the children think of his misbehavior. Wisely, they never bring up the case.

"You made one mistake," Jim told Matthew, in Dorset, a few weeks ago. Ruth was out for the night with her play-reading group, and the two men were smoking cigars on the terrace. "You made an error in judgment on a single night in a marriage of many hundreds of nights. Thousands."

"More like a few mistakes, truth be told."

Jim waved this away with the smoke from his cigar. "OK, so you're not a saint. But you were a good husband, compared to most. And, in this case, you were enticed."

Matthew wonders about that word. Enticed. Was it true? Or was that just how he'd portrayed the incident to Ruth, who'd taken his side, as a mother would, and then had given that impression to Jim. In any event, you couldn't be enticed by something you didn't already want. That was the real problem. His concupiscence. That chronic, inflammatory complaint.

There was a coffee shop near the university where Prakrti and Kylie liked to go. They sat in the back room, trying to blend in with the college students at the surrounding tables. If anyone ever spoke to them, especially a guy, they pretended to be first-year students. Kylie became a surfer girl named Meghan who was from California. Prakrti introduced herself as Jasmine and said she'd grown up in Queens. "White people can be so dumb, no offense," she said, the first time she'd gotten away with this. "They probably think all Indian girls are named after spices. Maybe I should be Ginger. Or Cilantro."

"Or Curry. 'Hi, my name's Curry. I'm hot.'"

They laughed and laughed.

In late January, as midterms approached, they started going to the coffee shop two or three times a week. One blustery Wednesday night, Prakrti got there before Kylie. She commandeered their favorite table and took out her computer.

Since the beginning of the year, colleges had been sending e-mails and letters encouraging Prakrti to apply. At first the solicitations had come from schools she wasn't considering due to their locations, religious affiliations, or lack of prestige. But, in November, Stanford had sent her an e-mail. A few weeks later, Harvard did.

It made Prakrti happy, or at least less anxious, to feel pursued.

She logged into her Gmail account. A group of girls in bright-colored rain boots came in from the wind outside, smoothing their hair and laughing. They took the table next to Prakrti's. One of them smiled and Prakrti smiled back.

There was one e-mail in her queue.

Dear Miss Banerjee,

   That is what my brother, Neel, suggests I write as a salutation, instead of "Dear Prakrti." Though he is younger than I, his English is better. He is helping me to correct any mistakes, so that I will not make a bad first impression. Maybe I should not tell you this. (Neel says that I should not.)

   My own feeling is that, if we are to be married someday, I must endeavor to be as honest with you as possible to show you my True Self, so that you will get to know me.

   I suppose I should ask you all sorts of questions, such as, What do you like to do in your leisure time? What movies are your favorite? What kind of music do you like? These are questions relating to our personal compatibility. I do not think they matter greatly.

   More important are questions of a cultural or religious nature. For instance, do you want to have a big family someday? Perhaps this is too big a question to ask so early in our correspondence. As for myself, I come from a very big family so I am used to a lot of commotion around the house. Sometimes I think it would be nice to have a smaller family, as is becoming more common.

   I believe my parents have told your parents about my aspiration to become a programmer for a major firm like Google or Facebook. My dream has always been to live in California. I know that Delaware is not close to there, but that it is close to Washington.

In my leisure time I enjoy watching cricket and reading manga. What do you like?

In closing, may I say that I thought you extremely nice-looking when I saw you at my great-uncle's house. I am sorry I could not say hello but my mother told me it was not customary to do so. The old ways are often curious but we have to trust in the wisdom of our parents, who have the experience of a longer life.

Thank you for the photograph you sent. I keep it close to my heart.

If the boy had sat down with the intention of revolting Prakrti with every word he wrote, if he were a Shakespeare of pure annoyingness, he couldn't have done better. Prakrti didn't know what she hated most. The mention of children, which assumed a physical intimacy she didn't want to imagine, was bad enough. But somehow it was the phrase "extremely nice-looking" that bothered her more.

She didn't know what to do. She considered writing back to tell Dev Kumar to stop bothering her, but she worried that this would get back to her mother.

Instead, Prakrti googled "age of majority U.S." From the results she learned that, when she turned eighteen, she would obtain the legal right to buy property, maintain her own bank account, and join the military. The phrase that encouraged her the most, however, was where it said that turning eighteen "brought the acquisition of control over one's person, decisions, and actions, and the correlative termination of the

legal authority of the parents over the child's person and af-
fairs generally."

Eighteen. A year and a half from now. By then Prakrti
would already be accepted to college. If her parents didn't
want her to go, or wanted her to go somewhere nearby, it
wouldn't matter. She would go on her own. She could apply
for financial aid. Or win a scholarship. Or take out loans,
if necessary. She could work part-time during college, ask
her parents for nothing, and owe them nothing in return.
How would her parents like that? What would they do
then? They'd be sorry they ever tried to arrange her marriage. They'd repent, and grovel before her. And then *maybe*—
when she was in graduate school, or living in Chicago—she'd
forgive them.

When Kylie was Meghan and Prakrti was Jasmine, they
were lazier, slightly dumber, but more daring. One time,
Kylie had gone up to a cute boy and said, "So I'm taking this
psych class? And we're supposed to give someone this personality test. It'll only take a few minutes." She called Prakrti
over, as Jasmine, and together they interviewed him, coming up with questions off the top of their heads. What was
the last dream you had? If you were an animal, what animal
would it be? The boy had dreadlocks and dimples, and after
a while, the inanity of their questions seemed to register on
him. "This is for a course? For real?" he said. The girls started
giggling. But Kylie insisted, "Yes! It's due tomorrow!" At
that point, the fiction they were creating doubled: they weren't
just high school girls pretending to be in college; they were
college girls pretending to be giving a psychological test in
order to talk to an extremely cute guy. In other words, they
were already inhabiting their future collegiate selves, the
people they might someday be.

Now all that felt far away. Prakrti looked at the girls in

the leggings and rain boots. At other tables kids were typing, or reading, or meeting with professors.

She had thought she belonged among them, not as Jasmine from Queens, but as herself.

She felt dizzy. Her vision dimmed. It was as if the floor of the coffee shop were giving way and a chasm opening between her and the other students. She grabbed hold of the edge of the table to steady herself, but the dropping sensation continued.

Soon she realized it wasn't a dropping so much as a retarding or encircling; a claiming. *She* was the one chosen. Closing her eyes, Prakrti pictured them coming toward her, as they did through the halls of her school. With their dark, downcast eyes, murmuring in foreign tongues that were her own, looking like her, and reaching out with their many hands to haul her in. The Hymens.

She didn't know how many minutes went by after that. She kept her eyes closed until the dizziness passed, and then got to her feet and made her way toward the front door.

Just inside the entrance was a bulletin board. It was covered with flyers and announcements, business cards, and tear sheets for tutoring or sublets. In the upper-right-hand corner, only partially visible, was a poster advertising a lecture. The topic meant nothing to her. What caught Prakrti's attention were the date of the event—next week—and the photograph of the speaker. A pink-faced man with sandy hair and a boyish, friendly face. A visiting professor from England. No one from around here.

When the girl came to his hotel room, Matthew had already made his decision.

He was planning to offer her a drink. Sit, talk, enjoy her

company, the nearness of someone so young and pretty, but nothing more. He was drunk enough to be content with just that. He felt no strong physical desire, only a rising sense of exhilarated apprehension, as though he were crashing an exclusive party.

Then the girl swept in and her powdery smell hit him with full force.

She didn't meet his eyes or say a word, merely unshouldered her backpack onto the floor and stood with her head down. She didn't even take off her coat.

Matthew asked if she wanted something to drink. She said no. Her nervousness, her possible reluctance to be there, had the effect of making him want to reassure or persuade her.

Stepping forward, he put his arms around the girl and buried his nose in her hair. She allowed this. After a while, Matthew lowered his head to kiss her. She responded minimally, without opening her mouth. He nuzzled her neck. When he returned to her mouth, she pulled away.

"Do you have a condom?" she said.

"No," Matthew said, surprised by her directness, "I don't. I'm afraid I'm not part of the condom generation."

"Can you go get one?"

All flirtatiousness had left her. She was all business now, her brow furrowed. Once again Matthew considered going no further.

Instead, he said, "I could do that. Where would I get one at this hour?"

"In the square. There's a kiosk. That's the only place open."

Later on, in England, during the months of recriminations and regrets, Matthew admitted to himself that he'd had time to reconsider. He'd left his hotel wearing only a jacket. The temperature outside had dropped. As he walked to the square, the cold cleared his head, but not enough, in the end, to keep him from entering the kiosk when he found it.

Once inside, he had another chance to reconsider. The condoms weren't on display but had to be requested from the clerk behind the counter. This turned out to be a middle-aged South Asian man, so that the crazy thought assailed Matthew that he was buying condoms from the girl's own father.

He paid with cash, not meeting the man's eyes, and hurried out.

The room was dark when he returned. He thought the girl had left. He was disappointed and relieved. But then her voice came from the bed. "Don't turn on the lights."

In darkness, Matthew undressed. Once in bed, finding the girl naked as well, he had no more reservations.

He fumblingly put on the condom. The girl spread her legs as he climbed on top of her, but he had hardly got anywhere before she stiffened, and sat up.

"Did it go in?"

Matthew thought she was worried about birth control. "It's on," he reassured her. "I've got a condom on."

The girl had placed a hand on his chest and become very still, as though listening to her body.

"I can't do this," she said, finally. "I changed my mind."

A minute later, without another word, she was gone.

Matthew awoke the next morning a half hour before his Q and A. Jumping out of bed, he took a shower, rinsed his mouth with hotel mouthwash, and dressed. Within fifteen minutes he was on his way back to campus.

He wasn't hungover so much as still a little drunk. As he walked beneath the leafless trees, his head felt light. There was a curious insubstantiality to things—the wet leaves on the pathways, the ragged clouds drifting across the sky—as though he were viewing them through a mesh screen.

Nothing had happened. Not really. He had so much less to be guilty about than might have been the case that it was almost as if he had done nothing at all.

Halfway through the morning session, his headache kicked in. By then Matthew was at the Physics Department. When he'd arrived, he was worried that the girl might be among the students gathered in the brightly lit classroom; but then he remembered that she couldn't come. He relaxed, and answered the students' questions on autopilot. He barely had to think.

By noon, with his honorarium check in his jacket pocket, Matthew was on his way back to New York.

Just past Edison, he'd nearly fallen asleep in his seat when a text came through to his phone.

> Thanks for signing my piece of paper. Maybe I can sell it someday. It was nice meeting you. Bye.

Matthew wrote back, "I'll send you a copy of my book to paste it in." Then, deciding this sounded too open-ended, he deleted it and replaced it with, "Nice to meet you, too. Good luck with your studies." After pressing SEND, he deleted the entire conversation.

She had waited too long to go to the police. That was the problem. That was why they didn't believe her.

The town prosecutor, with whom Prakrti had met once before, was a barrel-chested man with a kind, open face and wispy blond hair. He was gruff in his manners, and frequently used profanity, but he treated Prakrti with delicacy when it came to the details of the case.

"There's no question who's at fault here," the prosecutor said. "But I've got to bring charges against this reprobate, and his lawyer is going to try and impugn your testimony. So I have to go over with you the things he might say so that we're prepared. Do you understand? I'm not happy to be doing this, let me tell you."

He asked Prakrti to tell her story again, from the beginning. He asked if she'd been drinking on the night in question. He asked about the sexual acts in detail. What exactly had they done? What was permitted and what was not? Whose idea was it to buy the condoms? Had she been sexually active before? Did she have a boyfriend her parents didn't know about?

Prakrti answered as best she could, but she felt unprepared. The whole reason she'd slept with an older man was to avoid questions like this. Questions having to do with her willingness, her blood alcohol level, and whether she had acted provocatively. She'd heard enough stories, she'd streamed enough episodes of *Law & Order* on her phone, to know how these cases worked out for women. They didn't. The legal system favored the rapist, always.

She needed the sex itself to be a crime. Only then could she be its victim. Blameless. Blameless and yet—by definition—no longer a virgin. No longer a suitable Hindu bride.

This was how Prakrti had worked it out in her head.

An older man was preferable because, with an older man, it didn't matter if she'd sent flirtatious texts, or had come willingly to his hotel room. The age of consent in Delaware was seventeen. Prakrti had looked the statute up. Legally, she wasn't capable of consent. Therefore, there was no need to prove rape.

An older, married man wouldn't want to talk about what had happened, either. He'd want to keep it out of the papers. No one at school would ever know. No college admissions officer, googling her name, would find an electronic trail.

Finally, an older, married man would deserve what he had coming to him. She wouldn't feel so bad involving a guy like that as she would some clueless boy at school.

But then she'd met the man, the physicist from England, and followed through with her plan, and felt regretful afterward. He was nicer than she expected. He seemed sad more than anything. Maybe he *was* a creep—he definitely was— but she couldn't help liking him a little, and feeling sorry for tricking him.

For this reason, as the next months passed, Prakrti held off going to the police. She hoped she wouldn't have to put the last part of her plan into action, that something would alter the situation.

The school year ended. Prakrti got a summer job at an ice cream parlor in town. She had to wear a candy-striped apron and a white paper hat.

One day at the end of July, when Prakrti came home from work, her mother handed her a letter. An actual letter, written on paper, and sent in the mail. The stamps on the envelope showed the face of a smiling cricket star.

Dear Prakrti,
   I apologize for not writing you sooner. My studies at the university have been extremely onerous and it has been all I can do to keep up with them. I keep myself going with the thought that I am working hard to prepare a future for myself and my future family, which of course means you. I am beginning to see that it might not be so easy as I had hoped to get a position at Google or Facebook. I am now

thinking of perhaps working for a flash-trading company based in New Brunswick, where my uncle also works. I do not have a driver's license and I am beginning to worry that this may be a problem. Do you possess a license? Do you perhaps own your own car? I know our parents have been discussing the possibility of a car being provided, as part of the dowry. This would be most acceptable to me.

Prakrti read no further. When she got off work the next day, instead of going home, she walked to the police station behind the town hall. That was almost a month ago now. Since then, the police had been looking for the man, but there had been no arrest. Something was holding things up.

"The judge is going to want to know why you waited so long," the town prosecutor said to her.

"I don't understand," Prakrti replied. "I read the statute online. I'm seventeen now, but I was sixteen when it happened. By definition it's rape."

"That's right. But he's claiming there was no sex. No—penetration."

"Of course there was penetration," Prakrti said, frowning. "Check out our text messages. Or the video. You can see what was going on."

The reason she'd sent the man out to the kiosk was because she knew there was a security camera there. She'd intended to save the condom, too, to tie it in a knot to preserve the semen. But, in the complications of the moment, she had forgotten.

"The texts prove there was flirting," the prosecutor said. "They prove intention. So does the video of him buying the condoms. But we don't have any proof of what happened in the room."

Prakrti looked down at her hands. A fleck of green ice

cream had dried on the outside of her thumb. She scraped it off.

When the man had got on top of her, she'd been flummoxed by a wave of tenderness and protectiveness toward her own body. The man's breath smelled sharp and sweetish from alcohol. He was heavier than she expected. When Prakrti had entered the hotel room and seen the man standing in his socks, he'd looked old and hollow-cheeked. Now she had her eyes closed. She was worried it was going to hurt. She didn't care about losing her virginity but she wanted to give away as little of herself as possible. Only what would serve the legal distinction but nothing else, no outward approval and certainly no affection.

He was between her legs now, pressing. She felt a pinch.

And she pushed him away. Sat up.

Was the pinching she had felt not penetration? She would know if that had happened, wouldn't she?

"Obviously, if someone's buying condoms, he's doing it for a reason," she told the town prosecutor. "How can I prove that there was penetration?"

"It's harder because of the passage of time. But not impossible. How long did you have sex?"

"I don't know. A minute?"

"You had sex for one minute."

"Maybe less."

"Did he climax? I'm sorry. I have to ask. The defense will ask and we have to be prepared."

"I don't know. I've never been—this was my first time."

"And you're sure it was his penis? Not his finger?"

Prakrti thought back. "His hands were on my head. He was holding my head. Both hands."

"What would really help me is if we had a fresh-complaint witness," the prosecutor said. "Somebody you told right after

it happened, who could corroborate your story. Is there anybody you told?"

Prakrti hadn't told anyone. She didn't want anyone to
know.

"This asshole says there was no sex. So it would help
your case, a lot, if you had told somebody closer to the time
of the assault. Go home. Think about it. Try to remember if
there was anybody you might have talked to. Even texted or
e-mailed. I'll be in touch."

Matthew's flight over the ocean keeps pace with the sun. His
plane arrives in New York at roughly the same time of day,
give or take an hour or two, as it departed London. Emerging
from the terminal, he's assaulted by the sunlight. He feels that
the November day should be winding down, softening his
reentry, but instead the sun is at its zenith. The loading zone
is crowded with buses and taxis.

He gives the driver the address of his hotel. There is no
possibility of his returning home. Tracy has agreed to bring
the children to see him later this afternoon. When Matthew
invited her to stay for dinner, hoping to reunite them as a
family and to see where this might lead, Tracy was noncom-
mittal. But she didn't rule it out.

Just being back, with the Manhattan skyline in view, fills
Matthew with a sense of optimism. For months he's been
powerless, safe from arrest but in limbo, like an Assange or a
Polanski. Now he can act.

The news that Matthew was wanted for questioning arrived in August, while he was giving a series of lectures in
Europe. The Dover police had got a copy of his passport from
the hotel where he stayed, which he'd shown upon checking
in. From that they tracked him to his mother's address. After

finishing his lectures, he'd come to Dorset to visit Ruth and Jim, and the letter was waiting for him.

In the six months between his visit to the college and the arrival of the letter, Matthew had nearly forgotten about the girl. He'd regaled a few of his male friends with the story, describing the girl's bizarre come-on and her eventual change of heart. "What did you expect, you idiot?" one friend said. But he also asked, enviously, "Nineteen? What is that even *like*?"

In truth, Matthew can't remember. Thinking back to that night, the thing he remembers most clearly is the way the girl's stomach quivered when he heaved himself on top of her. It had felt as if a small animal, a gerbil or a hamster, were being crushed between them, and trying to wriggle free. A fearful or excited quivering, unique to her. All the rest has faded.

After Matthew received the letter from the police, another friend, a lawyer, advised him to hire "local counsel," meaning a lawyer from Dover, or Kent County, who would know the prosecutor and the judge there. "Try to get a woman, too, if you can," the friend said. "That could help if you end up going before a jury."

Matthew had hired a woman named Simone Del Rio. During their first phone call, after he'd given his version of events, she said, "This happened last January?"

"Yes."

"Why do you think she waited so long?"

"I have no idea. I told you. She's bonkers."

"The delay's good. That helps us. Let me talk to the prosecutor and see what I can find out."

The next day, she got back to him. "This will come as a surprise, but the alleged victim here, at the time of the encounter, was only sixteen."

"She couldn't be. She was a freshman at college. She said she was nineteen."

"I'm sure she did. Apparently she was lying about that, too. She's in high school. Turned seventeen last May."

"It doesn't matter," Matthew said, when he'd absorbed this news. "We didn't have sex."

"Look," Del Rio said. "They haven't even served you with a complaint. I told the prosecutor they have no right to ask you to appear for questioning when they haven't done that. I also argued that no grand jury would indict for this conduct in this situation. Frankly, if you never come back to the U.S., you won't have a problem."

"I can't. My wife's American. My children live there. I do too. At least, I did."

The rest of what Del Rio told him wasn't so reassuring. The girl had deleted their texts from her phone, just as Matthew had. But the police had obtained a warrant to recover the texts from the phone company. "These things don't go away," Del Rio said. "They're still on the server."

The time-stamped videotape from the kiosk was another problem.

"Without being able to question you, their investigation is pretty much at a standstill. If it stays that way, I may be able to make this go away."

"How long will that take?"

"No telling. But listen," Del Rio said. "I can't tell you to stay in Europe. You understand? I can't advise you to do that."

Matthew got the message. He stayed in England.

From that distance, he watched his life implode. Tracy sobbing into the phone, berating him, cursing him, then refusing to take his calls, and finally filing for a separation. In August, Jacob stopped speaking to him for three weeks. Hazel was the only one who continued to communicate with him the entire time, though she resented being the go-between. Now and then she sent him emojis of an angry red face. Or asked, "when r u coming home."

These texts had come to Matthew's UK mobile. While in England, he'd had his American phone turned off.

Now, in the taxi from the airport, he pulls his American phone from his bag and presses the power button. He's eager to tell his kids that he's back, and that he'll see them soon.

Two weeks passed before the town prosecutor called Prakrti in again. After school she got into the car beside her mother to drive to the town hall.

Prakrti didn't know what to tell the prosecutor. She hadn't expected to need witnesses to testify on her behalf. She hadn't anticipated—though she might have—that the man would be in Europe, safe from arrest and interrogation. Everything had conspired to stall the case and to stall her life as well.

Prakrti had considered asking Kylie to lie for her. But even if she swore Kylie to secrecy, Kylie would inevitably tell at least one person, who in turn would tell someone else, and before long the news would be all over school.

Telling Durva was impossible, too. She was a terrible liar. If she were questioned before a grand jury, she would fall apart. Besides, Prakrti didn't want Durva to know about what had happened. She had promised her parents not to say anything to her little sister.

As for her parents themselves, she wasn't sure exactly what they knew. Too embarrassed to tell them herself, she'd let the town prosecutor do that. When her parents emerged from their meeting with him, Prakrti was shocked to see that her father had been crying. Her mother was gentle with her, solicitous. She advanced propositions she would never have

come up with on her own and which must have come
from the prosecutor. She asked if Prakrti wanted "to see
someone." She said she understood, and emphasized that
Prakrti was a "victim," and that what had happened wasn't
her fault.

In the following weeks and months, a silence descended
on the matter. Under the guise of keeping things from
Durva, her parents didn't bring the subject up at home at
all. The word *rape* was never uttered. They did what was required, cooperated with the police, communicated with the
prosecutor, but that was it.

All this put Prakrti in a strange position. She was en-
raged at her parents for closing their eyes on an assault that,
after all, hadn't occurred.

She was no longer certain what had happened that night
at the hotel. She knew the man was guilty. But she was un-
sure if she had the law on her side.

But there was no turning back. She'd gone too far.

Over ten months had passed. Diwali was approaching
again, the date earlier this year because of the new moon. The
family had no plans to go to India.

In front of the town hall, the trees, which had been in
leaf when she first came in, were now bare, revealing the statue
of George Washington on a horse that stood at the end of
the colonnade. Her mother parked outside the police station
but made no move to get out of the car. Prakrti turned to her.
"Are you coming in?"

Her mother turned to look at her. Not with her newly
softened or evasive expression but the hard, strict, disap-
proving face that had always been hers. Her hands were
gripping the steering wheel so tightly her knuckles went
white.

"You got yourself into this predicament, you can get yourself out," her mother said. "You want to be in charge of your

life? Go on, then. I'm finished. It's hopeless. How can we find another husband for you now?"

It was the word *another* that Prakrti latched on to.

"Do they know? The Kumars?"

"Of course they know! Your father told them. He said it was his duty to do so. But I don't believe that. He never wanted to go along with the wedding. He was happy to undermine me, as usual."

Prakrti was silent, taking this in.

"I'm sure you're thrilled by this news," her mother said. "It's what you wanted, isn't it?"

It was, of course. But the emotion that surged through Prakrti was nothing as simple as happiness or relief. It felt more like remorse, for what she'd done to her parents, and to herself. She began to sob, turning her face to the car door.

Her mother made no move to comfort her. When she spoke again, her voice was full of bitter amusement. "So you loved the boy, after all? Is that it? You were just fooling your parents all this time?"

In his hand, the phone begins to vibrate wildly. Months of undelivered texts and voice mails, flooding in.

Matthew is looking at the haze over the East River, and the huge billboard ads for insurance companies and movies, when the texts flood in. Most are from Tracy or his children, but friends' names fly past, too, and colleagues'. Each text contains its first line. A review of the past four months flitting by, the appeals, the fury, the lamentations, the rebukes, the misery. He shoves his phone back into his bag.

Into the Midtown Tunnel his phone continues to buzz, the fallout, unfrozen, raining down on him.

•

"I'm not coming in," Prakrti said, in the doorway of the prosecutor's office. "I'm dropping the charges."

Her face was still wet with tears. Easily misunderstood.

"You don't have to do this," the prosecutor said. "We'll get this bastard. I promise."

Prakrti shook her head.

"Hear me out. I've been thinking about the case," the prosecutor pressed on. "Even without a fresh-complaint witness, there's a lot of leverage we have on this guy. His family is here in the States, which means he wants to come back."

Prakrti didn't appear to be listening. She was looking at the prosecutor with bright eyes as though she'd finally found what to say to make everything right. "I never told you, but I'm planning to go to law school after college. I've *always* wanted to be a lawyer. But now I know what *kind*. A public defender! Like you. You're the only ones who do any good."

The hotel, in the East Twenties, is one Matthew used to stay in years ago, when it had been popular with European publishers and journalists. Now it's been renovated beyond recognition. Techno thumps in the dungeonlike lobby and pursues him even into the elevators, where it becomes the soundtrack for lurid videos playing on embedded screens. Instead of providing a haven from the city streets, the hotel wants to bring them in, their restlessness and need.

In his room, Matthew showers and puts on a fresh shirt. An hour later, he's back in the lobby, amid the pounding music, waiting for Jacob and Hazel—and for Tracy—to arrive.

With a feeling of facing up to a dreaded task, he begins scrolling through his text messages, and deleting them, one by one. Some are from his sister, Priscilla, others from friends inviting him to parties months ago. There are payment reminders and lots of spam.

He opens a text that says:

> is this still you?

Directly after that, another, from the same number.

> ok well I guess it doesn't matter. this is the last time
> i'm ever going to text and you probably won't either.
> i just wanted to say i'm sorry. not for you so much but
> for your family. i know what I did was a little extreme.
> i overreacted. but at the time things were legit out of
> control and i felt i had no choice. anyway, i've got a
> plan for myself. it's called try to be a better person.
> you might be interested. bye bye. t. f. p.

For months Matthew has felt nothing but rage toward the girl. In his head, and out loud when alone, he has called her all kinds of names, using the worst, the most offensive, the most vitalizing language. These new messages don't rekindle his hatred, however. It isn't that he forgives her, either, or that he thinks she did him a favor. As he deletes the two texts, Matthew has the feeling that he is fingering a wound. Not compulsively, as he used to do, risking reopening or reinfection, but just to check if it's healing.

These things don't go away.

At the far end of the lobby, Jacob and Hazel appear. Following them, a few steps behind, is someone Matthew doesn't recognize. A young woman in a maroon fleece, jeans, and running shoes.

Tracy isn't coming. Now or ever. To convey this message, she has sent this babysitter in her place.

Jacob and Hazel haven't seen him yet. They appear cowed

by the sinister doormen and thumping music. They squint in the dim light.

Matthew stands up. His right hand, of its own accord, shoots straight into the air. He's smiling with an intensity he's forgotten himself capable of. Across the lobby, Jacob and Hazel turn and, recognizing their father, despite everything, come running toward him.

2017

Acknowledgments

Acknowledgments are due to the following editors: Peter Stitt, J. D. McClatchy, Bradford Morrow, Bill Buford, Cressida Leyshon, and Deborah Treisman.

Grateful acknowledgment is made to the publications in which the following stories, in earlier versions, first appeared:

"Air Mail," *The Yale Review*, October 1996.

"Baster," *The New Yorker*, June 17, 1996.

"Early Music," *The New Yorker*, October 10, 2005.

"Timeshare," *Conjunctions* 28, Spring 1997.

"Find the Bad Guy," *The New Yorker*, November 18, 2013.

"The Oracular Vulva," *The New Yorker*, June 21, 1999.

"Capricious Gardens," *The Gettysburg Review*, Winter 1989.

"Great Experiment," *The New Yorker*, March 31, 2008.